DEAD EVER AFTER

JACK STAINTON

ALSO BY JACK STAINTON

A Guest To Die For

You're Family Now

Mother

Last One To Lie

He Is Here

The Boss's Wife

1

───────

FOUR MONTHS FOLLOWING THE DEATHS OF
IMOGEN AND LIAM DALEY

WHO IS SHE?

My wife of over five years, a decade of shared existence, now a stranger who I may not know at all. The
woman who orchestrated the demise of the couple we
once held so dear, a couple now cremated and laid to rest
in the silent earth of a nondescript cemetery in West
London. Yet, Kat remained untouched by remorse, no
emotion, just an unbelievably positive outlook for what
they left behind. Together, we inherited their legacy, a
business forged from their passing. Our future at their
expense. Did I truly know the woman at my side?

But what about my guilt? A liar. An adulterer. A cold-
blooded murderer. Was I really blameless, or was I using
Kat as a shield to deflect my culpability? After all, I had
history, long before I met my wife.

. . .

Kat left me alone in the bedroom of our newly inherited holiday home. The house that once belonged to Liam and Imogen.

Unbeknown to my wife, since their sparsely attended joint funeral, I had visited their unobtrusive graves at the aforementioned nondescript West London cemetery on three separate occasions. But I never went for Liam. The headstone, which I paid for without Kat's knowledge, seemed inadequate to commemorate a combined period of over eight decades on this planet. Standing less than two-feet tall, it was a modest, unpretentious slab of white rock, depicting just their names and years from cradle to grave. Were their lives so undeserving? Imogen's certainly wasn't.

But they had no next of kin. All parents were deceased. They had no children, no siblings, and we were their only true friends. Ha! *True friends*. That's why only a handful of mourners witnessed the funeral – I didn't recognise anybody – and that's why we now controlled one hundred percent of their business, along with the house we were standing in. Imogen changed their will just days before they died, passing on all they owned to us, should anything untoward happen to them. Everything but their own house that was, which remained unoccupied, awaiting instruction from solicitors on what the hell to do with it next. The house opposite ours. The property where everything began on that fateful night I stayed over and slept with my boss's wife.

Shuddering, I closed the wardrobe doors and apathetically wandered downstairs to rejoin Kat and our son, Tom.

"So," Kat said, her back to me although alert and detecting my presence without even turning. She was preparing a healthy snack for Tom, who sat contented at the table overlooking the garden and the English Channel beyond. "What do you think of my idea?"

I studied her. Her happy-go-lucky demeanour, her ponytail bobbing up and down in unison with the task at hand, no doubt humming a cheery tune inside her head. I imagined her face, smiling, eyes glistening, full of joy.

Minutes earlier, we were standing in the bedroom discussing how I'd stabbed Liam Daley with Imogen's favourite pair of dressmaking scissors. We had spoken about drugging and gassing Pauline North and Bob Lane in fear they might know too much, and how I pushed Mark Harris into the river on the off-chance he discovered some imaginary misdemeanours in the way Liam and Imogen conducted their business. In short, we'd discussed murder. Killing innocent people. And Kat had known all along what was happening. She was just as culpable as me, even if I carried out the deeds. Would she have done exactly the same if I hadn't done it myself?

Who the hell were we?

"What idea?" I replied unenthusiastically, meandering over to the open bifold doors. I purposefully kept my back to her, not wanting to endure the exuberance written across her face.

"Taking on Kevin Doyle, of course."

As Kat strolled across the room behind me, my fists clenched in and out in rhythm with each step. How could she be so obtuse? Was recruiting Kevin as a fellow data analyst her top priority? My nerves were shredded, my angst heightened more than the occasions I'd killed. I counted to four, breathed out, counted again.

"Kat," I finally said, while subsequently bringing myself to turn and face her. My presumptions had been correct. She grinned from ear to ear, sliding a platter of sliced carrots, cucumber, and a carton of hummus across the glass table to Tom, her eyes not leaving mine. He looked at it as though she had given him a plate of poison.

"Yeah?" she asked.

I stalled, my mind momentarily drifting to Imogen. And far from the first time during the past four months, I deliberated where I would be if I'd chosen her instead.

"I said, yeah?" Kat repeated, her mouth straightening and her forehead creasing.

Did she know what I was thinking?

Deciding against discussing how the fuck she could be so dismissive now our secrets were out in the open, I placated her instead. It wasn't the craziest of suggestions, after all.

Kevin Doyle was twenty-five. The guy I set up to discard a USB stick on the train so his employer at the time, Wheelwright Solutions, would lose a major contract. Subsequently, if the plan came to fruition, that company would transfer all their business to Liam's firm. I'd used the poor soul for our gain. A multi-million-pound deal, which ironically never materialised. Another person caught up in our unethical deals to look after number one.

But perhaps it could be a way to reconcile with my inner self? An opportunity to give something back and relieve myself of a little guilt.

"Yeah," I repeated Kat's last word. "I'll contact him on Monday morning. See if he's available."

"I knew you would agree," she said, her smile returning like the flick of a light-switch. She stepped over and joined me at the doors, snuggling her head against my shoulder as we looked out over the English Channel below. Her arm interlocked mine. "It's going to be just fine, Adam."

But I didn't respond. Just followed Kat's stare, my mind awash with why I allowed her to live and Imogen to die.

Since that fateful day at the summerhouse, I'd grappled with the realisation that I was the one losing control. My life was hurtling down a path I never intended to travel, although it was somewhat inevitable given my background. Perhaps Kat and I were indeed meant to be together, our flaws perfectly intertwined to support and complement each other. The memories of our financial struggles during those dark times initially motivated me. I couldn't bear to see my wife endure that hardship again; it had nearly shattered us once, and I feared a repeat would spell the end of our relationship for good. Maybe even worse.

Then there was Tom and my fervent desire for him to have a childhood and upbringing so unlike my own, filled with promise and opportunity. I longed to give him the lavish gifts that Imogen had always showered upon him. It was agonising to watch when we visited the Daleys' house, witnessing them provide for Tom in ways I couldn't. Their wealth, their property – it served as a constant reminder that I wanted that for my family, whatever it took.

But what about Imogen? I'd allowed my feelings for her to grow so strong, yet I never resisted them as fiercely as I should have. I even convinced myself that she was responsible for all the misfortune, the killings, entertaining the idea that my actions could somehow shift blame onto her. So, when she pleaded for my help in her summer-house, I faced a critical decision.

The time has arrived, Adam. Time to make your choice.

And I chose family.

Only time would tell whether I'd made the correct decision.

2

____

SEVEN MONTHS FOLLOWING THE DEATHS OF
IMOGEN AND LIAM DALEY

IN EARLY SEPTEMBER, as the last remnants of summer stubbornly held on, Kevin Doyle arrived promptly to commence his first day with our company. Although he agreed to join us – albeit a few days after I made the initial phone call – his hesitation surprised me, as did the tone of his voice. Instead of the expected enthusiasm, his demeanour carried an air of uncertainty, punctuated by long pauses and hesitant responses. It wasn't the Kevin I remembered at all. And despite finally accepting the role, he requested a delay to his start date too, citing a pre-booked interrailing trip across Europe. However, although his delayed arrival felt somewhat inconvenient, as well as unappreciated, it ultimately fitted into our plans perfectly. Thanks to Kat's diligent efforts, new projects were already underway, with more on the horizon as winter approached. The prospect of additional work should have filled me with excitement, but unlike Kat, I couldn't muster anywhere near the same level of energy.

"Morning, Kevin," I said, desperate to make a good impression. It was the first time I'd seen him in the flesh since the day Samuel Finch, the managing director of Wheelwright Solutions, emphatically sacked him for leaving the USB stick lying around on an underground train. Kat convinced me there was no way he would know of my part in his misdeed, something I knew was true, yet I refused to accept this. "Besides," she added with a sickening grin. "It's not as though Imogen or Bob could tell him otherwise, is it?"

"Morning," he replied tepidly.

There it was again. Just as on the day I called him, he lacked the spark I'd always associated with Kevin Doyle.

At Wheelwright Solutions, he'd been keen, infuriatingly so. Forever asking questions, tapping into my knowledge surrounding the code and software we used, as well as having a mischievous side, which he soon established after a few nights out on the beer. Yet, that day, just as with the phone call, Kevin appeared subdued. He avoided eye contact, his speech was monotone, and his movements were lethargic. I resisted enquiring if he wanted the damn job at all.

"I thought you could sit here." I forced another smile, directing him to his desk with the palm of my hand inches behind his back without touching.

"Looks good," he replied, a little intonation finally in his voice.

For anybody interested in IT, the layout was indeed impressive. Dual monitors on adjustable arms were raised above a brand-new, top-of-the-range, seventeen-inch laptop. It was possibly more than we could afford, but I wanted to make an impression. My aim was to welcome him aboard and make him feel like an instantly valued member of the team.

Plus the guilt, Adam. Don't forget the guilt.

For the next hour, I showed Kevin around the system and the project he would initially tackle. It was small-scale, but he had to learn how we worked. From past experiences at Wheelwright Solutions, I knew he was a quick learner, and I had much larger plans as the months progressed. We were on the verge of landing a new client. Again, not multi-millions, but high six figures, none-theless. I wanted Kevin to run it alone, and I had complete faith in his ability to do so.

As five o'clock approached, I told him he was free to log off and leave.

"You've done well," I said, instantly regretting that I sounded a little patronising. Quickly, I recovered and added, "That's why I called you, Kevin. I knew you'd soon get up to speed with anything I gave you."

He had indeed done well. He always had at Wheel-wright, too. And as the day progressed, he emerged from his shell, bit by bit. He asked work-related questions, all good questions. His eagerness eventually rose to the surface, and a couple of times I caught him Googling appropriate terms relating to the software we used. The only thing which was lacking on his first day was Kevin's love of socialising. When we initially worked together, I introduced him to the world of alcohol and girls. Some-thing that surprised me at the time was to find a guy of twenty-five, still socially inept after living in the confounds of a capital city for his entire life. But once he got the taste, holy shit, there was no stopping him. So, I expected questions regarding where the best local bars were or whether we employed any good-looking girls. But nothing. No indication he was interested in such things any longer.

Until five o'clock, that was, after he shut down his laptop and collected his bag to leave. But even as he spoke, something didn't feel right. His absence of emotion was palpable, although it explained his lack of interest in the subjects I'd expected to be bombarded with.

"By the way," he said, as he departed, leaving me sitting alone at my desk. "I've got a girlfriend now."

And with that, he turned and left the office.

3

―――――

"Isn't that a good thing?" Kat enquired, laying the kitchen table to prepare for our evening meal. She didn't look up, but returned to the stove, before draining what looked conspicuously like fucking cabbage again.

Kat had been on a health drive since, well, since. The problem was that she forced me and Tom to take part too. She'd lost all the weight she'd gained during those infamous boozy nights across the street at the Daleys' house, but still seemed keen to lose more. I told her it wasn't necessary – and I meant it. I didn't want her to become too skinny. Not because it bothered me per se, but because I knew I would eventually get the blame for her shedding too much and her clothes no longer fitting. She blamed me for every bloody thing.

"Well, yeah," I replied, momentarily leaving the kitchen to stick my head around the living room door and tell Tom dinner was ready. He sat cross-legged on the carpet, his neck bent at an awkward angle to peer up at the television. "You're sitting too close to that TV," I said, ruffling his hair as he trudged past me. Tom's downbeat appearance suggested he already knew what we were about to eat.

"What do you mean, *well, yeah*?" Kat mimicked my final two words in a grumpy tone, her mouth downturned like a sad clown. It made Tom smile.

"It isn't so much that he has a girlfriend," I replied, ignoring her, before sitting down and dragging Tom's chair farther beneath the table. "It was the way he said it. Months ago, he would have been all over me to show off, but it was so matter-of-factly. Like it wasn't really any of my business."

Kat stepped over with two plates of food already dished up. Tom scrunched up his nose as soon as he set eyes on what we were about to endure. However, like me, he knew not to cross his mum.

"Perhaps it *isn't* any of your business," Kat replied as she finally joined us. She appeared as enthusiastic as Tom and me about the meal. Collecting the salt pot, she subsequently sprinkled far too much onto her food. Maybe that made it somehow palatable?

"That's not my point," I said, my voice exasperated in an attempt to drive home what I was getting at. It took very little for Kat to wind me up since what happened, and I often wondered if she did it on purpose. "It was the way he said it, or didn't tell me until he left, which took me by surprise."

During the meal, Kat made it perfectly clear she didn't want to discuss Kevin's private life any further, stressing again it was personal and none of my business. Instead, she asked how he settled in, was he still capable, and did I believe we'd made the correct decision. Perhaps she was right. So why did I allow his aloofness to bother me so much?

As I pushed my food around my plate, half thinking

of something to say and half thinking how on earth I could get away with leaving most of my meal untouched, Kat broke the silence. As soon as she uttered her opening words, I realised I would have preferred to continue with the tranquillity.

"Mum phoned today," she said, taking a gratifying break between mouthfuls. "She reminded me they haven't seen any of us since…"

Kat stalled and looked up at me. *Since she whacked Imogen with a garden spade and I stabbed Liam to death with his wife's scissors?* The subject was taboo. It had been that way ever since everything came out in the open three months previously. Neither of us specifically said we shouldn't talk about it, but there was an underlying understanding between us. A telepathic agreement that the topic was strictly off limits. As if not talking about it may mean it never actually happened. It suited me fine.

However, if I was honest with myself, I was finding it more and more difficult to talk to Kat about anything, or even be in her company. We were sleeping separately too. Blaming it on stress, I told her I needed time to return to some kind of normality. Inside, I often wondered if that day would ever arrive. What the hell was *normal,* anyway?

I glanced at Tom. He, too, was pushing his food around his plate, lost in a world of his own. Kat and I both knew, again without discussing it, that he needed protecting as well. It could never come to light what his parents had done, especially me. I'd shudder when I allowed such thoughts to enter my head, mostly in the dead of night when the demons were at their worst. Of course, one day, he could easily discover Kat killed Imogen in self-defence. It wasn't a secret; it was on police files, or a quick Google search would give him all the information he desired. But in Kat's case, it was just that.

Self-defence. His mum hadn't committed murder or any other such hideous crime, not in the eyes of the law at least. Maybe we would need to tell him one day before he found out from somebody else. But that day was still far off. His sixth birthday was in three weeks' time and I prayed he discovered nothing for years to come, if ever.

"Yes," I said, momentarily averting my gaze from Tom and back to my plate of food. "It's been months since you saw them. Tom too."

Kat cleared her throat, and I knew exactly what was coming. I collected half a forkful of cabbage and mashed carrots and forced it into my mouth, at least delaying having to reply.

"You haven't seen them in almost two years, Adam. It would be nice if all three of us visited them for the weekend."

I couldn't be sure, but I believe Tom smirked, even though there was no way he would understand the subtlety of my rolling eyes. I chewed on the tasteless food for so long, it genuinely seemed to transform into some kind of flavour. Yes, that was it. Vomit.

"When were you thinking?" I eventually asked, swallowing hard.

Kat stood and collected the plates, although the contents of all three appeared to have actually grown in size since we started. She didn't answer until she turned her back and scraped the remains into the bin underneath the sink.

"I've already arranged it. The first weekend in October. I said we would travel up Saturday morning and stay overnight."

. . .

Four hours later, both Kat and Tom were safely tucked up in bed. She did ask if I would join her, but I feigned another headache and said I'd only keep her awake if I was moving around all night. It wasn't far from the truth, but not the real reason. Even though seven months had passed, my memories of Imogen were still vivid. I could never forget the times we had been alone; they were forever inscribed in my thoughts. And I liked to think of her, during those extended periods of restlessness. Just me and her. Where we might now be. Long holidays together in the sun; endless days on the beach, followed by infinite nights in bed. Sometimes, without even realising, I'd catch myself crying, tears soaking my pillowcase, and with a desire to scream out in the still of darkness.

I wasn't in a good place, and I truly doubted if I ever would be again.

4

EVER SINCE THE day my dad died – two years after Mum – my whole life changed. I was just thirteen, thrust into a world of grief and uncertainty. Aunt Cynthia, my mother's sister, became my reluctant guardian. She was a stern woman with a no-nonsense demeanour. From the moment she took charge of my upbringing, life turned into a regimented routine of rules and unrealistic expectations.

Aunt Cynthia believed in discipline above all else. She imposed strict curfews and enforced rigid study schedules, leaving little room for any other activities. There were no late nights with mates, no weekends spent exploring the world beyond our doorstep. Instead, I spent countless hours alone in my room, surrounded by the suffocating silence of my own thoughts.

I had no real friends during those years. Aunt Cynthia discouraged socialising with other children, believing it to be a distraction from my studies. And so, I became a loner, finding solace in the companionship of books and my imagination. I immersed myself in fictional worlds, escaping the harsh realities of my existence whenever I could.

But despite the solitude, I grew accustomed to my own company. I learned to rely on myself, to find strength in loneliness and resilience *in adversity. And, as the next five years passed, I became adept at navigating the complexities of Aunt Cynthia's expectations, bending to her will while secretly nursing a rebellious streak buried within.*

As soon as I reached my eighteenth birthday, I was away. I chalked down the years, the months, the days, like a prisoner in a cell. I imagined all kinds of bad things happening to my aunt, despite knowing deep down she had only done her best. She never wanted children, so what more could I expect from her?

But, by the time I left home, I'd grown to despise her. Her voice – shrill and unforgiving – was engrained in my mind as I spent hour after hour wallowing in my own sad company in the confines of my tiny bedroom. Every word, every admonishment, felt like a weight dragging me down, suffocating me.

I resented her for the childhood she had stolen from me, for the years spent locked away in solitude while other children laughed and played outside. I resented her for the dreams she had crushed, the aspirations she had dismissed as frivolous distractions. And most of all, I resented her for the loneliness she had inflicted upon me, for the void in my heart that no amount of success or accomplishment would ever fill.

But as much as I despised her, I also feared her. Her presence loomed over me, a constant reminder of the power she held over my life. Even after I left home and ventured out into the world on my own, her influence lingered, shaping my decisions and colouring my perceptions in ways I could never fully escape.

And yet, in spite of it all, a part of me still yearned for her approval, for some semblance of acknowledgement that I had turned out alright despite her best efforts to the contrary. I knew she had only ever wanted what she believed was most suitable for me, even if her methods had been flawed and her intentions misguided.

But as the next couple of years passed, and I forged my own path in life, I came to realise that her approval was something I no longer needed. I had survived her tyranny, emerging stronger and more resilient than I ever thought possible.

Aunt Cynthia died when I was twenty-two − four years after leaving her home, her prison. I barely saw her during that time, and our phone calls became less and less frequent. By the end of the first year, our communication dwindled to exchanging birthday and Christmas cards, with only a single phone call on Christmas morning. I would picture her mantlepiece above the fireplace she never lit. A lone, cheap card, sitting alone amongst the worthless tat of ornaments not even worthy of a fairground prize. Or maybe she just discarded it in the bin the day it arrived? I would never know, because I only ever visited her once more.

She was a sad old spinster who I believed should never have been born.

5

Towards the end of Kevin's second week with the company, I departed for work sooner than usual to pick up Tom from his friend's house. Kat had arranged for me to take him and his pal to school in exchange for his parents hosting a sleepover. Despite only starting their second year four days earlier, the boys had formed a friendship towards the end of year one and spent some time together over the summer holidays. Tom had pleaded with his mum to allow him to stay over, even though it was a Thursday with school the next morning.

"His mum is lovely," Kat said to me, although I wasn't particularly interested in her persuasive attempts. As far as I was concerned, Tom could have stayed all weekend. "And I know she'll make sure they get to bed early, even if they don't sleep as well as usual."

After passing my local tube station, I followed Google Maps for a further ten minutes and arrived at the address that Kat had scribbled down on a piece of paper. The row of houses mirrored those on our own street: white-painted, two or three storeys high, with an array of sleek cars parked along the roadside, signalling the affluence of the residents. It was a scene straight out of a glossy magazine, a picture-perfect facade of wealth and privilege that seemed to mock my own humble upbringing.

Kat would have been thrilled to witness Tom playing with his new friend and effortlessly mingling with children from such prosperous families. To her, it was a sign of our ascent into a higher social sphere, a world of prestige and sophistication that she had always coveted. But for me, the sight of those ostentatious displays of prosperity only fuelled my growing sense of resentment. I was becoming more and more uncomfortable with the trappings of wealth. It was a life full of pretence, where appearances mattered more than substance, and I found myself increasingly disillusioned by it all.

Perhaps it was my own modest upbringing that coloured my perception, a reminder of the struggles and sacrifices that had shaped my early years. I had worked hard to build a life for myself and my family, but now, surrounded by the grandeur of our affluent neighbours, I couldn't help but feel like an outsider, a fish out of water in a world that prized opulence above all else.

As I made my way towards the front door, I actually feared who might greet me. The prospect of making small talk with people from such a background filled me with dread. I fidgeted with the collar of my shirt as I rang the doorbell.

"Tom!" I heard somebody shout from the other side. "It's your father."

Father? I'm his bloody dad.

"Coming, Mrs Bennett," he called in return, obviously comfortable in the company of his friend's mum given how much time they had spent together over the summer.

When the door finally opened, I was pleasantly surprised by who greeted me and I momentarily forgot all my concerns about money and those less fortunate than me. Mrs Bennett stood a fraction over five feet tall with blonde hair cut in the shape of what I think is called a bob. But instead of curling under at the bottom, it spread outwards, resembling the outline of a bell. I was never really attracted to blondes, always preferring darker shades, auburns and browns. But Mrs Bennett caught me off guard. Her eyes, a subtle shade of blue, sparkled with warmth, and as she extended her hand to greet me, a smile played at the corners of her lips, revealing her teeth, the front two overlapping slightly which only seemed to add to her attractiveness.

"You must be Tom's dad," she said, our hands still locked.

"Yes. I'm Adam."

She finally let go and her expression altered somewhat. Was it a look of pity, a realisation of who stood before her and all that I'd been through? Or was it something else? A look of concern that this person might be dangerous, a threat to her child?

"Come in," she said, taking a small step backwards. "By the way, my name is Lauren."

6

I SMILED, nodded, and accepted the invitation into her hallway. Tom's shoes were laid out ready, and I heard his distinctive giggle from somewhere above. It was quickly followed by another laugh, his friend, and then a loud bang as something, or somebody dropped to the floor.

"What's going on up there?" Lauren called, peering up the stairs as if she might possess the ability to see through floors.

"Sorry," came the reply, but it wasn't Tom's voice. I kicked myself for not asking Kat what his friend's name was.

Lauren looked at me, smiled, and rolled her eyes, as if to say *boys will be boys*. "Max and Tom get on so well together," she said, again showing her teeth. I momentarily became transfixed by them, their imperfection somehow making her perfect. "They're like two peas in a pod."

She walked off, leaving me unsure whether to follow or to stand and wait. I watched her slim body, her tight jeans, and her hair bobbing up and down with each step.

Bloody look away, you fool.

Lauren turned abruptly, catching me staring after her. I instantly felt my cheeks burn, but she had the decency to not make me feel more awkward. In fact, she smiled again, almost as if to approve of me ogling her. "Time for a quick coffee?" she asked.

With a glance up the stairs, I scampered after her.

"Excuse the mess," Lauren said, picking up on my subtle surprise as she led me into the kitchen.

Her voice was warm and welcoming, but there was a hint of self-consciousness in her tone, like the need to apologise for the state of the room. And indeed, as I glanced around, I couldn't help but feel a little surprised at the sight that greeted me.

The kitchen was a stark contrast to the pristine, showroom-worthy space I expected to find. Instead, it was a scene of controlled chaos, with pots and pans stacked haphazardly on the worktops, and a sink piled high with dirty dishes. The air was thick with a scent of spices and herbs, the distinct aroma of cooking food, and I couldn't help but feel a sense of homely warmth that was oddly comforting. A far cry from the meals I'd had to encounter in recent months.

"It's absolutely fine," I replied, genuinely touched by her hospitality and warm welcome. "It feels like home."

And indeed it did. Something stirred deep within me. At that moment, surrounded by the reassuring chaos of the kitchen, I felt a sense of belonging that I hadn't experienced in a long time. It was a feeling that I had missed, a reminder of the simple joys of domesticity that I had all but forgotten.

As Lauren glanced over at me, that already familiar smile playing at the corners of her lips, I knew that she had picked up on my surprise. But instead of being offended or embarrassed, she seemed to take it in her stride, as if she were perfectly at ease with the idea of someone seeing her kitchen in anything less than perfect condition.

"Black or white?" she asked, collecting two clean mugs from a cupboard above her head.

"White please. No sugar."

She turned, the smile still etched across her face, before clicking the kettle on. No fancy machine, just coffee direct from the jar and milk straight from the bottle. Despite my preconception from the street outside, this was the exact way I was raised during my early years, and it made me feel so at ease. Or was it Lauren herself and not the situation at all?

I tried to take in my surroundings. Was there a Mr Bennett? Of course there was. She was beautiful, friendly, affluent. If Mr Bennett had done a runner, he needed his head examining. But as she passed me my coffee, I noticed the distinct lack of a ring on her wedding finger. I blushed again as her eyes followed mine.

"We're having a break," she said, as if discussing her favourite drink. "Sean, my husband, has..." she paused, and unexpectedly seemed momentarily at a loss for words. "He has got himself into company. How should I put it? Company who don't exactly abide by the law. He still has Max on a Tuesday and Fridays." Lauren lowered her head, avoiding eye contact for the first time since I arrived.

"Hey," I replied, desperate to help her. "It's none of my business. You don't have to explain."

But I could tell she wanted to explain, to release an obvious pent-up frustration, and to share her woes. I quickly changed the subject.

"Thanks again for having Tom," I said, a genuine

expression of gratitude; it had given me the opportunity to meet her.

"He's no problem." Lauren recovered, the smile returning. "As I said, he and Max get on so well."

Right on cue, they appeared in the doorway, mischievous grins spread across their faces. Max was a similar height and build to Tom, but the difference in hairstyles was amazing. Max's curls grew out into a full, voluminous mane that seemed to have a life of its own. Unlike Tom's neatly cropped style, Max's resembled a bird's nest, with unruly tangles and strands poking out in all directions. And judging by his broad smile, his hairstyle looked to be a perfect accompaniment to his vibrant personality.

"Come on, Daddy," Tom said, nudging his friend for attention. "We'll be late for school."

Taking a huge gulp of hot coffee, I reluctantly stood and nodded my regards to Lauren. She appeared to pause for a split second, looking at me as if trying to read my mind or understand who I was.

"What do you say to Mrs Bennett?" I asked as Tom sat down in the hallway to put his shoes on.

"Thank you, Mrs Bennett," he responded like a pre-recorded tape machine.

"My pleasure, darling," she replied, patting him delicately on the shoulder. "And both of you have a good day at school."

Max shouted, "I will!" and both boys dashed out of the front door with a boundless energy I couldn't recall ever having. I turned back to Lauren.

"Thanks again," I said, wishing I didn't have to leave.

She reached out and placed her hand on my arm, and that all-too-familiar bolt of electricity shot through me, leaving me momentarily breathless.

"Call round anytime," she said. "It can be lonely on your own."

7
______

A WEEK LATER, I decided I needed to get out of the office and take an extended lunch break. If the boss of his own company couldn't allow himself such treats, then what was the point in putting myself through the stresses of such a role? So, after grabbing a sandwich and a cold drink, I set off through Regent's Park and allowed my mind to drift.

Ever since I met Lauren, I found myself thinking about her more and more. It wasn't just her looks and her overfamiliarity in my presence that gripped me; it was the way she opened up about her husband so quickly. She didn't know me, so why did she divulge Sean had got in with the wrong company when it was clearly none of my concern? Although I knew the answer, it left me deliberating who I wanted to meet the most, Lauren again, or her husband.

During that week, I cursed myself over and over for not asking for her phone number.

.   .   .

The park was a welcome respite from the confines of the office, with its lush greenery and winding pathways, offering a sense of tranquillity that I desperately yearned for. As I walked, my thoughts moved on from Lauren and turned to Imogen instead. It had been a while since I visited her grave, and the guilt gnawed at me like a persistent ache.

I couldn't help but wonder what she would say if she could see me. Would she be appreciative of the fact that I had taken over the business and tried to resurrect its failing fortunes, or would she be disappointed that I had thrown myself in head-first without a thought for her? Not that I'd actually thrown myself at it; quite the opposite. But why would she be angry? She and Liam – the latter, albeit reluctantly – signed the company over to us in their last will and testament, should anything ever happen to them. No, I'm sure she would be proud, but I also knew she would wish it was her beside me instead of Kat, who revelled in the money which Imogen had fought so hard to build up herself.

As I made my way through the park, more personal memories of Imogen flooded my mind. Her laughter, her smile, the warmth of her embrace – all imprinted into my memory with a clarity that bordered on obsession. Visiting her grave felt like penance, a way to atone for the sins of my past and seek forgiveness for the pain I had caused. I really did need to revisit the cemetery soon.

Paying no attention to where I wandered, I shortly found myself on the far side of the park, with Primrose Hill to my left. The road swept alongside and I continued until I came across a cute-looking bookstore, its blue canopy vivid against the grey skyline above.

Once inside, my fingers trailed along the spines in the crime section, although none stood out, possibly because I no longer had any idea about books or popular authors. I hadn't read a book since leaving Aunt Cynthia's house, perhaps in rebellion for all those hours she forced me to study. Lost in thought, I realised I was only killing time, attempting to distract myself from returning to work.

After a while, I inadvertently stepped sideways and paused before a section of children's books. A 'New Titles' sign stood prominently at the top of the shelves, and as I chose a particularly vibrant title, a familiar voice appeared to echo throughout the entire bookstore. I turned, and there, standing in the aisle, was someone I instantly recognised, and it only took seconds to put a name to the face. Luke Wilson – an old colleague from my first job as a junior software developer. A rush of conflicting emotions washed over me as I struggled to comprehend seeing him again after all those years.

"Adam Chapman, is that really you?" Luke's face lit up with a wide grin as he approached, his voice filled with genuine surprise. Despite the time that had passed, he looked much the same, his amiable smile and infectious energy as vibrant as I always remembered.

I managed a strained grin, trying to hide the turmoil within me. The last thing I wanted was to have to make small talk with him. I'd always been unsure of how we'd parted all those years ago and if there were any under-lying tensions between us. "Hey, Luke. Yeah, it's been a long time."

His eyes sparkled with excitement as he clasped my palm in a firm handshake. He appeared genuinely delighted to see me, already dispelling any fears I had. "Man, it's so good to see you!" He looked at the book in my hand.

"For my son," I said sheepishly, holding the copy aloft. "It's his birthday tomorrow."

"Ah, right," he replied. "So, what have you been up to all these years?"

Does he not know?

Oh, you know, just murdered a few people. Nothing out of the ordinary.

But as we exchanged pleasantries, I couldn't shake the feeling that something was off. Was the meeting more than just an accident? Perhaps Luke's presence was intentional? Despite the unease gnawing at me, I tried to push the thought aside as he and I reminisced about old times.

Luke joined the software house the same day as me. We were two of four new recruits, all junior programmers embarking upon our chosen career paths in the days when Information Technology promised riches that many other professions couldn't touch. But, as with most apprentice-type roles, the other two candidates lasted six and nine months respectively, the work boring and the people even more so. I didn't take it personally. I was pleased that they left, and I wished Luke Wilson had done the same.

He was good. He learned quickly and was often assigned the more complex code to write. Towards the end of our second year, I heard on the grapevine that the company was looking to promote him, with over twelve months remaining of our three-year programme. It made me angry, envious of his proposed acceleration in the world of IT, years ahead of me. However, the company did not follow through with the promotion, and at the end of the three-year traineeship, Luke, like myself, received a minimal pay raise and an offer for a development role that was far below his expertise. He subsequently left, and I soon followed him out of the door to explore new opportunities. I hadn't seen him since, not until that chance meeting in a London bookstore.

"What you doing now?" he asked, his enquiry taking on a more serious tone. "You work around here, do you?"

"Yeah. On the other side of the park. I own a data analyst company."

He looked genuinely surprised. "Ooh, look at you," he replied.

"What about you?" I asked, not appreciating his mockery, even if it was intended as a joke.

"Still a programmer," he replied, a little downcast, as if suddenly realising I may have outdone him after all. Luke was always so much better than me, something he would obviously know, so my news had potentially struck a nerve. "In fact," he added, reaching inside his jacket. "If you're looking for anybody, I'm ready for a new challenge. I've changed jobs recently, but I'm not enjoying the new role. It's beneath me and I need stimulation."

Taking the business card from him, I slipped it into my trouser pocket but refused to dwell on his offer. "If we do, I'll be sure to be in touch."

After we said our goodbyes, I allowed myself a last glance over my shoulder and I noticed Luke still observing me. And once more, the sensation washed over me that our encounter was not merely coincidental.

8

THE NEXT DAY, I greeted Priya Singh at our office. She represented the Equity Alliance Group, a consortium of building societies headquartered in Brighton on the south coast. They had decided to renew their analytics outsourcing contract, but unlike other new clients, Kat hadn't contacted them. Neither Liam nor Imogen had been in touch during their ownership of the company. The request for the proposal came as a surprise, as they were now putting the agreement out to tender.

With no real face-to-face experience of dealing with clients, alongside a spiralling lack of interest in the business, it felt surreal escorting Miss Singh to my office. I was a software engineer, a programmer. I didn't know how to communicate with customers for potential new business, let alone someone as poised and self-assured as Priya Singh.

She nodded in Kevin's direction as she passed his desk and I noticed her do the same with one or two others in the open-plan area. Kevin smiled in return, his gaze flickering between her and me. He seemed to take pleasure in my nervousness, the way I was stumbling over my words when I asked whether she would like a drink. However, his face faltered when she said she would love a coffee and I instructed him to make it.

As we settled into the meeting, I still couldn't shake the nervous flutter in my stomach, the gnawing fear that I would say something foolish. Priya studied me with a keen gaze, her dark eyes assessing me with a level of scrutiny that made me squirm in my seat. It was as if she could see right through me, realising I had no experience of dealing with clients. Or was it something else? Did she know who I was? As I fumbled with the papers on my desk, struggling to find the appropriate words to begin the conversation, I couldn't help but feel a sense of inadequacy wash over me. Maybe this new role wasn't for me. I was slowly comprehending I was completely out of my depth.

After the formalities, Priya explained she had heard good things about us, and said we stood a decent chance of landing their business for at least three years. She was petite in stature but made up for it with her authoritative style. I soon realised she would accept no fools, although she appeared to have a soft side too, enquiring about Tom after she noticed his photograph on my desk. Priya also asked about Kat, already knowing we were a husband-and-wife team. Again, that nagging doubt re-entered my head. Was it due diligence, or did she have knowledge regarding our situation for other reasons? She said it was a shame that Kat wasn't there, only adding to my unease, as though she needed to scrutinise both of us.

We lunched at a small Italian restaurant close to the office. Sitting opposite her, and maybe because of the calming effect of a glass of wine, I noticed for the first time how pretty Priya was. Her jet-black hair shone below the subtle downlights, and her eyes were an amazing dark brown. When she smiled, I observed how perfectly aligned and white her teeth were. My mind momentarily drifted to Lauren. After I enquired about her marital status, she replied in a gruff voice, contrary to her previous demeanour. Had I offended her by asking? Nonetheless, she confirmed she was married and had three children, all in their teens. On the brink of saying she didn't look old enough, I quit before I did any further damage.

After additional questions and a quick tour of the office, Priya Singh left around three o'clock that afternoon. She declared that she would present a full report to her boss the following week, and we should hear within days of that. It sounded so positive. She even said she couldn't wait to meet again as we exited my cubicle for the last time. Kevin looked up from his monitor and smiled. I wondered how much he'd heard of the meeting, and I felt a twinge of apprehension creeping over me. The thought of Kevin dissecting every word and gesture from our private conversation made my stomach churn with unease. What if I had said something wrong? But it wasn't only that. His mannerisms still bothered me. He'd only been with us for two weeks, but on the odd occasion when he did converse, he came across as cocky, as though he'd been in the job for years instead of days.

"She's pretty," he said casually as I passed his desk on my return. At least he was grinning, with that look of mischief I recognised from our early encounters when I first met him.

"And old enough to be your mother," I quipped.

"But not too old for you," he replied, rather too abruptly.

9

———————

IGNORING KEVIN'S CHILDISH RETORT, I informed him I had to leave for the day, and as usual, in my absence, Kathy from accounts would activate the burglar alarm as she left. I said he was free to finish work any time after four if he had reached a satisfactory juncture to recommence on Monday morning. It was one of my traits. I was one of those people who needed a cut-off point; somewhere I could reconvene the next working day without spending time refreshing where I was up to. It used to really annoy me whenever George or Bob just slammed their laptop lid shut at the mere mention of finishing for the day.

Although I needed to get back for Tom's birthday party, I craved my own company for a while, not only to revel in self-appreciation for what I'd achieved with Priya Singh, but also because I was mentally exhausted. I promised myself a stroll before taking the tube ride home. However, as soon as I ventured outside the office block, something felt instinctively wrong, and my short-lived optimism took an unexpected nosedive.

I noticed a white BMW parked opposite. I'm unsure why it caught my attention, apart from it being a no-waiting street, as there were often vehicles hanging around there. Delivery vans, taxis, and people being dropped off in a central location. Nonetheless, there was something ominous about the car, and a chill ran down my spine, some kind of primal instinct warning me of danger.

I had to cross the street to get to the park and quickly tried to dispel my initial sense of unease as being a result of my overactive mind. Everything had me on tenter-hooks and ever since the incidents of seven months previous, I'd become completely paranoid, seeing threats lurking around every corner. The slightest noise made my heart race, and I feared all passing strangers were watching me with suspicious eyes. As I approached the car, I couldn't shake the feeling that someone, or some-thing, was observing me from behind the impenetrable barrier of the car's windows reflecting against the shim-mering sun.

My heart quickened, desperately struggling to pinpoint why the vehicle bothered me so much. A flicker of movement from inside jolted me, barely distinguish-able, but no doubt somebody was occupying the driver's seat as I stepped past. Or was it merely a trick of the light or my imagination running in overdrive yet again? Either way, I turned full circle and crossed the road before pressing the key code to re-enter our building. It wasn't until I reached the far side, and shut the door behind me, that I allowed my breathing to relax.

As I took the stairs, I regulated my steps, realising I had to appear at ease for those still working. I could feel the eyes of one or two people as I strolled across the building, and Kevin looked at me in amazement as I hurried past him.

"You okay?" he asked, his head turning in unison with my hastened pace. Was that a smirk on his face? I nodded my response.

"I forgot something, that's all," I called over my shoulder.

Once inside my office cubicle, I closed the door behind me and walked directly to the window which over-looked the street below. However, as soon as I parted the blinds, I saw the vehicle was gone, leaving only an empty space and nothing to suggest it was ever there at all.

People crossed the road, a taxi drove by, and a mother pushed her pram towards the park entrance. Just normal, everyday activity on the streets of London. But I was convinced the car had been there and equally assured that whoever was inside was looking at me.

Tom's birthday party was in its final stages by the time I arrived home. Following the incident with the vanishing car, I allowed myself some time alone in the park and subsequently lost track of it. Kat wasn't happy, so I kept the news of the probable upcoming new business with Priya Singh to myself. Why should she share in all my good news if she couldn't even be bothered to greet me with an enthu-siastic smile and an 'I'm pleased you're home' welcome?

Grabbing myself a beer, I strolled towards the living room door from where most of the noise emanated. I was aware that some children and parents had gathered in the garden too, but thought I'd heard Tom's voice from inside. True enough, he sat in a circle on the carpet with three of his mates, including Max, to his immediate right. They were talking and giggling and trying to out-shout each other with remarkable ease. It was lovely to see. Friends. Children playing together, full of innocence and without a care in the world.

Minutes later, a couple of his guests began to drift out of the front door, a parent or two in tow. Kat asked Tom to stand in the hallway and thank each of them individually for coming over and for the presents they had given him. I took my position outside to ensure they all made it safely to their vehicles and nobody ran into the street.

Another car pulled up outside, and I immediately recognised Lauren as she stepped out before subtly waving at me. I felt my heart flutter and quickly glanced over my shoulder to confirm Kat wasn't watching.

Max's footsteps broke my trance as he rushed by me and towards his mum, calling over his shoulder, his hair bouncing wildly with every step.

"See you at school on Monday, Tom," Max shouted.

"Yeah, see you, Max," Tom called back. "Thanks for coming."

Lauren beamed at her son with pride as he clambered into the passenger seat before she looked up and beckoned me over. With another nervous look around, I stepped over to join her and she discreetly pushed a piece of paper into my palm, holding my hand just long enough for that jolt of electricity to surge through my entire body again.

After she drove away, I unfurled the scrunched-up note, already knowing it contained her phone number.

10

After all the guests had departed, I finally shared the news with Kat about the possibility of landing the Brighton consortium contract. She was ecstatic, planting a long kiss on my lips – the first in what felt like an age. I would have distanced myself if I didn't still have lingering thoughts of Lauren in my mind.

Kat grabbed me another beer and told me to spend some time with Tom while she tidied away. I reluctantly offered to help, but she was so thrilled with both how popular her son was and the news I brought home, she was determined to do it herself.

Tom showed me his presents, his excitement finally wavering as fatigue set in. He was determined to cling to every last moment of his birthday, resisting sleep as long as possible. The beer helped me relax, and I soon forgot about the white car and my ongoing delusions of being followed everywhere I went. I even convinced myself that Kevin was just a strange kid and provided he was good at his job, that was all that mattered.

However, as Tom made his way through the ridiculously large pile of gifts, one caught my attention.

"What's that?" I asked, leaning forward with my elbows on my knees.

"A car," he replied nonchalantly, and I detected a hint of disappointment in his tone. He set it aside with no further comment and returned to sifting through his other new presents.

But the toy car held my interest, so I reached past him to grab it. Tom still showed no enthusiasm, only offering a momentary glance at my curiosity.

I instantly recognised the make of the vehicle, still in its plastic casing. The colour was a perfect match too, sending a wave of unease through me. Inside was a model of a Ford Escort, meticulously detailed, with tiny fog lights suspended from the front grille. It was the replica of the first car I owned, around fifteen years previously.

But it wasn't the accuracy of the model that unnerved me. It was the memories it stirred – the precise same model and colour of the car, reminding me of a pivotal moment from my past. It felt as though the present wasn't for Tom at all.

"Who got you this, champ?" I asked, trying my best to remain upbeat and just enquiring through curiosity.

Tom shrugged his shoulders. "Can't remember," he replied. "I got so many."

"Yeah, I can see that," I said, standing and leaving him in his own little world.

"It's a pure coincidence," Kat said after I found her in the kitchen and showed her the present. I purposefully left it inside its plastic case, as if removing it may cast some kind of spell upon me.

"Coincidence?" I retorted, holding the toy aloft in the

event that she hadn't truly comprehended what I meant. "It's the same model as the first car I owned. Down to the colour, too." I spun it around to check the number plates, fearing that whoever bought it had gone to even further lengths to unhinge me. "Do you know who it's from?"

Kat shrugged her shoulders, her finger poised over the vacuum cleaner button, desperate to finish her chores. "He got so many, and was ripping the paper off them without bothering to read the labels."

Under normal circumstances, her reply would have made me smile as I pictured Tom doing exactly what she described.

"Where's all the paper and tags?"

She looked at me as if I were mad. "Why does it matter so much? It's a toy car, given to your son as a sixth birthday present. How on earth would any of his friends know it's the same car as the one you once owned?"

Kat obviously had a point, but the coincidence continued to unnerve me. What if it wasn't from one of his mates, but from an adult instead? But that still made no sense. Apart from his friends, who would even know it was his birthday? And not only that, who could possibly be aware what my first car was?

"Yes, but you must agree, Kat, it is a bit of a—"

My wife looked exasperated. She placed one hand on her hip, sighing heavily as she leant on the vacuum.

"A bit of a coincidence? Yes, it's exactly that. Anything else is all in your imagination. It's a child's toy, no more, no less."

She switched the vacuum on to inform me the conversation was over. Of course, I couldn't tell her of the added significance of what happened in the car, and I begrudgingly left her to her chores.

But instead of returning the toy to Tom's pile of presents, I scooted upstairs and hid it in the bottom of my sock drawer. Something told me I didn't want Tom to play with it, like it held mystical powers or would act like some kind of voodoo doll. Thankfully, when I returned downstairs, he didn't even ask where it was.

11

—————

Anticipation weighed on me as we drove along the winding road, which ultimately led to Kat's parents' house. It had been over two years since I last saw Edwina and William, and the memory of their general disapproval of my being married to their daughter still lingered fresh in my mind. Now, with Kat driving, and Tom sat in the back, I braced myself for the inevitable tension, boredom and lack of common ground.

"Everything okay?" Kat asked, breaking the arduous silence.

Yeah, I can't stand your parents, and the prospect of spending thirty-six hours in their company is my idea of hell.

"I never told you, did I?" I said, trying to deflect from what was really on my mind. "I met an old colleague in a bookstore a couple of weeks ago." My revelation was greeted with silence. "It just felt a bit weird, that's all."

Kat momentarily allowed her eyes to leave the road ahead and glance sideways at me. She drove like a ninety year old, her hands at ten-to-two on the steering wheel, forever looking in the mirror and slowing down whenever we met a vehicle coming in the opposite direction. At one point, we entered a village with two prominent thirty miles per hour speed limit signs, and I resisted sarcastically suggesting she put her foot down so we could reach the permitted speed.

"Weird?" she asked. "In what way?"

Although I immediately regretted bringing it up, the confines of the car left me with little choice but to elaborate.

"I don't know," I replied, genuinely. "Just seemed strange to see him after all this time, coincidently bumping into him at a bookstore on the outskirts of a London park."

Kat ignored my oversensitivity. "What's his name? What did he say?"

I stared at the empty road ahead.

"His name is Luke Wilson. I worked with him before I met you. We just reminisced about the three years we had sat alongside each other. To tell you the truth, I can't remember a lot of what he said."

Kat allowed herself a second glance, and I considered it as reckless as I'd ever seen her drive.

"So, how is that weird?"

Deciding not to divulge any further details, I instead shrugged my shoulders. After another half a mile or so of sticking meticulously to the speed limit, Kat spoke again. She wasn't letting it go.

"What does he do now, this Luke Wilson?"

With an exaggerated sigh, I said he was still in IT, although I didn't mention he may be interested in a job.

"Uh-huh," Kat finally said, and like the toy car a week prior, I presumed she had lost all interest in my story.

. . .

The row of quaint cottages emerged from the trees, bathed in the early-October sunshine. Kat eventually parked the car following a series of forward and reverse manoeuvres, and as I stepped out, the sight of the property for real only seemed to amplify my unease. Delaying the inevitable, I helped Tom out of the back seat, despite him being more than capable of getting out himself. With a deep breath, I steeled myself for the inescapable, and advanced towards the front door, Kat leading the way, seemingly oblivious to how I felt.

A smell of home baking greeted us as we entered. Edwina and William stood in the small living room, which was far too cluttered, complete with a mahogany sideboard, matching folding table, and a couple of two-seater sofas, both facing William's pride and joy: a fifty-two-inch television. His favourite channel played silently in the background. Bloody horse racing. Glancing back at our hosts, I couldn't help but notice their faces, full of scepticism.

"Adam." William stepped forward, his voice tinged with a hint of formality that didn't quite mask his disapproval at seeing me. "It's been far too long."

I forced a smile, extending my hand in greeting. "It's good to see you again, William."

Edwina's gaze lingered on me for a moment too long, her eyes carrying a glimmer of suspicion that put me further ill at ease. "Yes, good to see you, too," she murmured, her tone cool and distant.

The tension in the room was palpable as we exchanged pleasantries. Just like with my reacquaintance with Kevin and my coincidental meeting with Luke, I couldn't shake the feeling that Kat's parents were holding something back. But they obviously knew parts of what happened, what we'd been through, so why did I feel so guilty in their presence?

An hour later, as we gathered around the dinner table, the conversation flowed awkwardly, punctuated by long silences and forced laughter.

"So, Adam, how's the newly acquired business?" William asked, breaking another uneasy silence.

I hesitated, my mind racing for an appropriate response. Surely Kat would have told them during one of their weekly phone calls? It would be paramount in their minds. Their only child now involved in running a medium-sized IT company in Central London? They couldn't have saved the question just for me?

Catching Kat's eyes, I squinted, silently asking why me. But she just smiled, proud the conversation was taking place at all.

"It's erm… busy," I finally replied, choosing my words carefully. "Lots of projects on the go. You know how it is."

William arched an eyebrow, his scepticism evident. "Kat mentioned you've taken on a new analyst. I'm presuming he'll be a great help?"

Swallowing hard, I detected the taste of guilt on my tongue. "Yes, that's right. Kevin is a good worker," I replied, my voice breaking like a teenager's.

As the meal progressed, I couldn't shake the feeling that Kat's parents were probing for something. I caught Edwina's gaze lingering on me more than once, her eyes filled with a mixture of curiosity and suspicion.

"And how do you enjoy running your own business?" she finally asked. "Is it worth all the effort you've been through?"

It wasn't just their cryptic questions that troubled me – it was the gnawing fear that they knew, somehow, what had actually happened, and how exactly we acquired the company.

Later that evening, we retired to bed soon after Tom. His behaviour was bothering me, too. Since his birthday a week earlier, he'd somewhat shrunk into his shell, a shell I'd never even noticed existed. As Kat led him upstairs, I promised myself to speak to him, ask what was troubling him.

"Why were your parents grilling me so much?" I asked Kat as I unbuttoned my shirt, finally inside the sanctuary of the freezing cold spare room. "Have you told them anything?"

Kat stopped whatever she was doing and waved her arm frantically to gain my already committed attention. "Keep your voice down," she instructed, gesticulating with the same arm. "Of course they don't know anything. Only what everybody knows from the news. They were just being polite."

Was she right and I'd misinterpreted the entire situation? Not for the first time, Kat read my mind. She was like my bloody shrink.

"You've got to calm down, Adam," she said, her mouth fixed in a tight line like a ventriloquist desperate not to move their lips. "You thought that... what was his name at the bookstore...?"

"Luke Wilson," I filled in the annoying blank.

"Yes, Luke bloody Wilson had somehow followed you. Now you think my mum and dad have got it in for you when they were only enquiring about our new business." She paused for breath. "For fuck's sake, you're a paranoid wreck."

Half not wanting to cause a scene, and half not

having a clue how to respond – she was right, I was a bloody paranoid wreck – I left her alone and headed for the bathroom. But I got the fright of my life when I opened the bedroom door, and there, standing directly outside on the landing, was William.

12

———————

THE FOLLOWING day was more bearable, perhaps because our departure was finally in sight. We took Tom to the local park before settling down for a pub lunch in Edwina and William's village. It wasn't a place they frequented – William admitted he couldn't remember the last time they had been there – but I found the neutral ground relaxing and liberating. Inside their home, I felt stifled, as if the walls were closing in on me and I had to stretch out my arms to keep everyone at bay. Away from their property, there was no chance of Edwina or William sneaking around or appearing out of nowhere.

The previous evening, Kat dismissed her dad standing outside our bedroom door as pure coincidence. He was just passing by on his way from the bathroom when I stepped out. There was no way to prove his actual intent or if he was indeed eavesdropping on our conversation. So, with no other option, I accepted the chance meeting, and climbed into bed beside Kat, expecting another restless night.

The next morning, there were no further probing

questions about work or hints of past events, just restrained chatter about mundane issues. I wondered if Kat had said something before I finally joined them for breakfast. Initially, I appreciated the lack of tension, having barely slept in anticipation of walking on eggshells. But as the conversation grew more strained over lunch, I considered Kat might have been right all along. Maybe they were just being polite, unable to think of anything else to talk about. I hadn't helped break down barriers either, not once volunteering a topic of my own.

However, it wasn't the conversation alone that troubled me. It was the doubting looks, the uneasy silences – not purely because of lack of mutual interest, but more aligned to not wanting to say something they shouldn't. I often caught Edwina looking at me, and her eyes would flick away before returning only seconds later. What was she searching for? Secrets? Guilt? An admission?

After settling the bill, we strolled back to their home, but thankfully only to pack the car in the excitement of leaving. Realising it was the keenest I'd been all weekend, I purposefully slowed my stride in between collecting bags and toys from the house and loading up the boot. Finally, I double-checked that Tom's seatbelt was properly fastened before saying my goodbyes. Kat finished hugging her mum whilst I shook William's hand firmly. I didn't like the way he held mine, far longer than necessary. Edwina's embrace was far less formal, and she obviously wanted to hold me as much as I wished to reciprocate.

I'd already told Kat I would drive home. The prospect of a three-hour journey hugging the slow lane of the motorway had me imagining pulling my hair out. I got in and started the engine whilst Kat lingered outside, still chatting to her parents.

"Keen to get off?" William called from the far side

through the open window. He laughed at his little joke, quickly followed by Edwina and then Kat. At first, it was just a few snickers, barely noticeable over the background noise of the engine. But then it was escalating, as the three of them stood side-by-side, mocking me. The laughter grew louder and more raucous with each passing moment, drowning out any semblance of reason or decency. My attempt at laughter joined the cacophony, but it was hollow and forced. Their faces twisted into grotesque caricatures, their eyes alight with glee. The sound of their guffawing filled the air, suffocating and oppressive, until I was immersed in it. I wanted to scream, to make it stop, but the laughter swallowed up any words that escaped my lips.

"What's wrong, Daddy?"

Tom's words halted the noise like the flick of a switch. The three adults remained on the far side of the car, but were in conversation and not even looking at me. All but Edwina, that was. She nodded as her husband and daughter spoke, but only had eyes for me.

"Daddy?"

I turned to my son in the rear. He appeared concerned, an expression of fright etched across his face.

"Nothing, champ. Nothing," I replied, allowing myself another quick glance at Edwina. But she no longer stared at me, and was instead giving her daughter one last hug. Tom shrugged his shoulders before waving to his grandparents out of the window. Kat finally joined us, closed her door, and fastened her seatbelt.

"You okay?" she asked. "You look like you've seen a ghost."

"Eh?" I replied, frantically trying to get the car into gear. It eventually engaged with a crunch, and I added far too many revs to the accelerator. We bounced off like a kangaroo.

With her parents retreating into their cottage in my rear-view mirror, I finally allowed myself to breathe. My palms were sweating as they gripped the steering wheel and my shirt felt cool and uncomfortable against my back. I detected Kat's eyes still on me, but she knew better than to take the piss out of my driving. Eventually, we departed the village, joined a busier road, and I began to relax.

"I thought today was nice," Kat said, breaking the silence. I glanced to my left. She was looking ahead, her mouth straight, showing no indication of anything on her mind.

"Er, yes," I replied awkwardly. The laughing episode still played heavily on my conscience, and I wondered how much was reality and how much was in my irrational mind. "The pub was nice."

Although silence descended, experience told me there was more to come, and right on cue, Kat spoke again.

"Mum and Dad are coming down to London next month. They recognise they've put it off for too long, and despite their health issues, they really want to see our house, and they can't wait to see where we work."

I bet they do.

"I thought you could show them around the office?" she continued. "I know Dad's especially keen."

13

———

At the start of Kevin's second month with the company, I arrived at work before him for only the third time since he started. One of the girls from accounts was always the first in the office, soon followed by Kevin. His enthusiasm and my lack thereof meant he was usually already at his desk when I turned up. But on this particular occasion, I beat everyone in and settled down for what should have been a productive day. However, the will to even boot up my laptop evaded me.

I had told Kat that Priya Singh had promised to call me early, but really, I needed to get away from her. Inviting her parents behind my back was uncalled for, and she knew it. She also knew that if she had asked, I would have said no, but that wasn't the point. As we'd left their house, I'd watched them in the rear-view mirror and silently prayed I would never encounter them again. But only minutes into our journey, Kat sprang her surprise announcement on me, and for the rest of the drive home, I sat in near silence, contemplating how I could make my wish a reality.

"Oh, morning," Kevin said, popping his head around my office door. "Didn't expect you to be in."

He continued unpacking his bag and attached his laptop to the external monitors. I stood from my desk and walked slowly across my cubicle, casually leaning against the doorframe.

"Why wouldn't you expect me in?" I asked, as unconcerned as I could muster. He immediately stopped what he was doing and turned to face me. Kevin looked genuinely surprised at my reply.

"Hey, sorry," he said, although I couldn't determine his tone. "Just you said you were going up to the Midlands for the weekend. I thought you might be late back or something, especially if you were having a good time."

Good time? I'd sooner chop my fucking hands off with a blunt saw.

"No, we travelled in the afternoon. We needed to get Tom home so he could prepare for school."

Kevin returned to his original task, and turned his monitors on before sitting down and wheeling his seat underneath his desk.

"Ah, okay," he replied cheerily, before turning to face me. "Couldn't wait to get away from the in-laws, eh?"

He chuckled to himself, returning his gaze to the screens, typed in his login credentials, and hit 'Enter' with an exaggerated flick of his forefinger. I wanted to tell him to go steady with our equipment and remind him how bloody much it cost. But I knew I had become ruffled. It felt as though the tables were turned and he employed me, as if I should somehow be grateful to him for the opportunity to work there.

"How did you know I was visiting my in-laws?" I asked. He spun around again and his eyebrows shot upward as if gripped by surprise.

"You said last week. Don't you remember?"

"Ah, right," I replied, angry with myself for increasingly forgetting every damn thing that was going on. "Yeah, I guess I couldn't wait to get away." I laughed pathetically, but noticed Kevin remained silent. Instead, his mouth downturned exaggeratedly, and he nodded his head. It was as though he was thinking, *I thought you might say that.*

Leaving him, I returned to my desk, still flustered. But it wasn't Kevin not joining in with my attempted in-law humour, which bothered me. I genuinely couldn't recall telling him that's who I was visiting over the weekend.

After finally booting up my laptop, I replied to a few emails, and tried to get my head in the right space to do a half-decent day's work. There was plenty to do and I couldn't allow things to slip. But my enthusiasm for the role of director was waning rapidly, and I longed for the days of working for someone else again. Nine to five, do an honest day of toil, but then pack away and not think about it again until the following morning. It didn't help that every single evening Kat grilled me about how things were going, or about a new client she had contacted. She was loving it, a lifelong dream now a reality.

"Adam?"

Kevin popped his head around the door.

"Yeah?"

"I noticed that wine bar just along the road."

He had my attention, and I glanced up from my screen. "The Sunset? What about it?"

But I knew exactly what he was referring to. I'd taken him there to meet Liam and Imogen. They wanted to ensure I'd chosen the correct person to plant the USB stick on. He instantly met their approval, especially after Imogen's flirtatious moves had taken his testosterone to a level it had never previously reached. It appeared to spark something within Kevin. An experience he'd never encountered before. The combination of alcohol and girls had transported him to an entirely new world.

"It's the one where I met your previous bosses, isn't it?"

"Uh-huh," I replied, desperately trying to disguise any concern.

"Weren't you there that day when they got killed?"

Bollocks. It wasn't what he knew – the entire episode made the national news – but the way he spoke. A definite undercurrent. Probing.

"Yes, Kevin, I was." Again, I tried to stay neutral. "It's not something I really want to talk about, though."

He smiled.

"Yeah. I thought you'd say that."

14

THE WEEK SEEMED to crawl by at a snail's pace, each day dragging on as if time itself had stood still. With every passing hour, the weight of the world pressed down on my shoulders, my troubles looming over me like storm clouds gathering on the horizon. Instead of working, I stared at the tiny clock in the corner of my screen, feeling trapped in a never-ending cycle of despair.

My heart sank with a sense of dread as I woke each morning. The once familiar routine of life was becoming a monotonous slog, every task a Herculean effort. Yet amidst the gloom, I clung desperately to a glimmer of hope. Despite the absence of a happy outcome, I found a flicker of determination burning within me, and each day, I resolved to soldier on, holding onto the promise that soon, the clouds would part and the sun would shine down upon me again. And on Thursday of that week, I finally had something to celebrate.

Priya Singh called a few minutes after ten o'clock. I'd just fetched coffees from the café along the street. I should have made Kevin do it, but a combination of not wanting him to feel used and relishing the fresh air and time away from the stifling sensation of the enclosed office suited me fine.

"Adam," she said before I'd had a chance to ask about her wellbeing. "I have some good news."

She explained that the Equity Alliance Group would love to entrust us with their data analytics. It meant millions of rows of data to be realigned with their new business model. They had recently invested in two additional smaller building societies and wished to bring all their respective client databases in line with their own. It was too much for their small tech team, but would mean several months' work for us as well as maintaining the data for at least a further three years. It was our largest piece of business since Kat and I acquired the company, but instead of wanting to call Kat, I pined to share the news with Imogen. She would be so proud.

With a renewed spring in my step, I asked the staff to gather around a small square table in the centre of the open-plan office. Smiles and imaginary backslapping greeted my announcement. Although I knew I should have run it by Kat first, I got carried away with the euphoria of the moment and promised everybody a raise. The grins became even more elongated, and the chatter didn't subside until lunchtime approached.

Upon returning home after a distracted afternoon at my desk, I faced Kat's displeasure when I revealed I had offered the staff a bonus to celebrate their hard work in securing the business from Priya Singh. Whilst thrilled with the contract, she maintained I had no authority to promise additional payments without consulting her beforehand. I couldn't handle it. I couldn't do right from wrong. However, I listened as Kat poured out her frustrations and reiterated the need to get the business back on track after Liam and Imogen had left it in such a mess. After a while, it became white noise, a blur of words tripping over themselves, mixed with the occasional expletive which snapped me back to the present. But my mind wandered, and after a while, I found myself at the kitchen window, staring into our rear garden. With no conscious decision, I waited for Kat to finish, and as soon as she did, I let myself out of the rear door.

"Where the hell are you going?" she called after me. Ignoring her tone of amazement, I strode purposefully to the end of the path. Upon reaching my destination, I began scouring the ground with a fervour akin to someone on a quest, meticulously scanning every inch as if determined to unearth some hidden treasure. What was I trying to achieve? The item I was searching for would be obvious to the naked eye from afar, yet there I was, all but getting down on all fours to forage.

Once satisfied it wasn't in proximity, I stood on tiptoe and stretched my neck to peer over the fence, far enough to inspect the ground immediately behind. Puzzled, I searched the space around my feet again, my eyes darting back and forth.

"Adam!" Kat called, momentarily distracting me. "What *are* you looking for?"

I looked up as if it were her who was crazy.

"Where's that planter? The oblong one?"

Kat folded her arms and rolled her eyes in frustration. The fingers on her free hand drummed lightly against her bicep.

"What fucking planter?" she asked, riddled with exasperation. "What the hell are you talking about now?"

I looked at Kat and then back at the ground behind

me. My head flicked between the two as I pointed to where the object should be.

"The terracotta one. It's oblong. Four feet long. How can…" I broke off, my eyes transfixed on the grass. Had there ever been a planter there?

"Come inside," she said, her voice calmer and a look of genuine concern on her face. Once I reached her, Kat interlaced her arm with mine and led me back indoors, resembling a carer with an elderly patient who had ventured outside the grounds of their care home.

She sat me down at the table and fixed me a whisky.

"Here, sip this."

The heat burned my throat, and the drink had an immediate and desired calming effect.

"Forget the bonuses," she said, her tone soft. "You only did what you thought was best." I peered up at her to gauge if she was being sincere. "And it's probably a good thing in retrospect. Keep the troops happy, and all that," she added with a smile.

Nodding my appreciation, I swallowed the remaining Scotch and held out the glass in hope of a refill. Kat gladly obliged and returned moments later.

"Adam," she said, pulling out a chair next to me. "Do you think you should see somebody?"

15

Following dinner – more vegetables piled high and something called a vegan patty to "add substance" – I informed Kat I was going to take a long bath, followed by a lie-down. The whisky had eased my mental state, and I quickly added the incident in the garden to the growing list of taboo subjects. *Out of sight, out of mind.* Tom was quiet during the meal again, his thoughts definitely elsewhere and his usual sparkle conspicuously absent. I still hadn't found time to speak to him, but maybe I was scared to uncover the real reason behind his sombre moods. Now and then, I glanced at Kat, hoping she would notice too, but like with everything else, I knew her mind was awash with business plans and what the Equity Alliance Group contract would mean for us, or more importantly, to her.

"Do you think it will go beyond the initial three-year deal?" she asked between mouthfuls. She appeared as if she was finally becoming acclimated to the muck she insisted on serving each meal.

It's not as though you are offering to jump into the kitchen to help, Adam.

"Let's just take it one step at a—"

"Yeah, I know," she interrupted, reaching out and placing her hand on my forearm. Her touch felt foreign, like an unexpected intrusion into my personal space. "But if they're acquiring two more building societies, then surely it could go on and on?"

I did my best to raise a smile, to share in her enthusiasm, but my heart just wasn't in it. Looking down at her hand, she apologised and swiftly retracted it.

"Sorry," she said, yet the grin refused to leave her mouth. "But there's something else we urgently need to consider, Adam."

What, the owners of a white BMW stalking me? Or maybe your parents grilling me? What about our son getting given a toy car, a replica of the one I used to own? And don't forget the missing planter.

All in your fucked up mind, mate.

"What's that, darling?" I asked, adding the last word somewhat facetiously. Had she already forgotten her suggestion I seek help, or was that just to placate me during my most recent episode of lunacy?

"There's no way young Kevin can handle a contract like that on his own."

I hadn't even considered it.

"Well, I still work there, if you haven't overlooked it?"

Tom smiled for the first time during the meal, picking up on my sarcastic tone. I winked at him, but he immediately retreated into his shell, piling a heap of the hideous food onto his fork before allowing it to drop back to his plate.

"Yes," Kat replied, although not looking anywhere near enthusiastic about my statement. Did she know I was slacking? "But you're getting more and more bogged down with the paperwork and stuff. Look how much preparation you had to do before Priya Singh came to see you."

While she had a point, I decided it was best not to tell Kat I'd done barely any prep work at all. The contract just fell into place with little input from me. For the first time, I considered how strange that was and the minimal role I actually played in the business.

"Shall I contact the agency, then?" I asked, dreading the prospect of having to sieve through CVs before interviewing prospective candidates.

"What about that guy you bumped into at the bookstore?" Kat suggested, albeit a little too quickly. She was orchestrating the entire fucking conversation. And as soon as she said it, I regretted ever telling her about bumping into him. I'd just wanted to offload the news, gauge Kat's opinion on him turning up after all those years.

"Who, Luke Wilson?"

"Yeah, why not? You said he's really good."

I stopped eating and looked at her.

"Did I say that?"

Fortunately for Kat, she had finished her meal and stood quickly before collecting her plate and stepping over to the dishwasher. With her back to me, it was impossible to read her expression, but I was certain I hadn't mentioned Luke's proficiency in our previous conversation.

"Of course you did," she eventually replied, now composed and returning to the table to collect my and Tom's half-eaten plates of food. "And if he's really good, why should we waste time bothering with agencies and interviews?"

Scraping my chair back – I suddenly felt claustrophobic and trapped – I gestured to Tom that he was free to leave the table. He sauntered off into the living room without saying a word. Once at the fridge, I collected two cold beers and held them aloft until Kat nodded she would like one too.

"I doubt he's available," I said, after popping the tops and passing a bottle to Kat. "I'm certain he'll be settled down somewhere else." Kat continued to look at me as if to say, 'is that all you've got?' "And he won't come cheap. I'm sure he'll still be pretty proficient."

Kat took a swig of her beer. "Exactly," she said, wiping her mouth with the back of her hand. Both her actions and words were disgusting me in equal measure. "That's why we need to reach out to him. Kevin is okay, but he's young."

It was impossible to argue with anything she was saying, although I was desperately trying to think of something. And almost as if she could read my mind, Kat stepped over and held my free hand with hers.

"Just imagine, darling," she said convincingly. "Luke can take Kevin under his wing, handle most of this new contract, and ease all the pressure you've been feeling since… well, since you know what?"

The plan did indeed sound flawless, and I already knew Luke was interested in joining us. But therein lay the problem. It felt as if the entire thing was fitting into place, as if meticulously scripted in preparation for that day.

16

––––––

M⒴ suspicions intensified when Kat asked if I had any means of contacting Luke. Of course I had. He'd given me his business card during that chance meeting at the bookstore. I'd discarded it in my desk drawer at work, thinking I'd never need it again. Did Kat know? For a moment, I considered telling her I might have mislaid it, thrown it in the bin, or it could have gone in the washing machine in the pocket of my trousers. But in the end, I dismissed my doubts. If Luke had other intentions, surely he would have disclosed them during our initial encounter? There was no way he could know I would want him to join our company a few weeks later. So, on the following Monday morning, while chiding myself for overthinking, I dialled his number. As expected, he was just as eager as he had been a month prior, and he happened to be available for an informal chat that very day.

I decided the café next to the office block would be the best meeting place – I didn't want Kevin overhearing any discussions between us, partly because of sensitive issues such as salary, but more so, because I did want Luke to take Kevin under his wing. Because of Kevin's somewhat unreadable behaviour since he joined us, I was unsure how he would react to such news, not that he would have any say in the matter.

You're the boss, Adam.

"Luke," I said. "Let me get these." He was standing near the front of the queue when I stepped inside. His eyebrows lifted and his mouth curved in a half-smile, a familiarity that was already grating on my nerves.

"Adam!" he exclaimed, his tone overly friendly.

"Can I help you, sir?" The girl behind the counter leant forward to get Luke's attention, glancing at the queue already forming behind me.

"Ah, sorry," he said, reading the girl's name badge before grinning broadly. "Large cappuccino, please, Laura," he added before turning to me. "What are you having, Adam?"

"Oh, thanks. Large Americano, please."

Luke nodded over my shoulder. "There's a table free over there. Grab it before someone else does."

As I followed his instruction, I felt my authority slipping away within moments of our meeting. Again, I reminded myself who the boss was, but Luke's confident manner and ease of taking charge left me feeling vulnerable. He'd always exuded a self-assuredness that I struggled to match, his laid-back attitude belied by a sense of command that made it clear he was used to being in control. Despite my attempts to assert myself, I couldn't shake the sensation that I would play second fiddle in his presence.

Reluctantly, I sat at the table and spun a salt pot between my fingers whilst waiting for Luke to join me. An elderly lady on the table opposite was observing me and smiled when our eyes briefly met. I immediately averted my gaze in fear I might think she too, was looking out for me. I almost laughed when I considered she could be my hidden assailant in the white BMW.

"So," Luke said, pulling his chair in opposite me. His cappuccino was enticing, served in a large cream mug with chocolate sprinkled on top in the shape of some sort of leaf. "This is exciting. Are your offices around here somewhere?"

"Yeah, just along the street, but I thought this would be a more relaxed place to meet."

He looked genuinely pleased. "Good thinking," he replied. "Easier to discuss things on neutral ground."

Luke Wilson was six feet tall with shortish brown hair, greying at the temples. His blue eyes glistened, hinting at a depth of experience and wisdom beyond his age. His chiselled jawline added an air of strength to his otherwise unassuming appearance. But it was his temperament which had stayed with me over the years. Forever upbeat, his infectious enthusiasm for anything he spoke about would brighten any room. Yet, beneath his exterior confidence, lay a resilience and a determination to succeed in whatever he did. I thought of the three years we sat alongside each other in our first programming roles.

"Yes, well," I stammered. "As I explained on the phone, we've landed a new client. Equity Alliance—"

"Group," he interrupted with a cheeky grin. "You said on the call earlier."

"Did I?" I asked, surprised if I'd given away the name of a customer before gauging whether Luke would be interested in joining us. "That's not like—".

"Yeah. The building society group from Brighton." He leant forward. "I hope you don't mind, mate, but I looked them up on my way over here. They are onto big things. Did you know they are in the process of buying out two more societies?"

What the hell was he playing at? Trying to impress me or trying to take control.

"Yes, Luke," I dismissed him rather firmly. "Of course I know that. It was paramount in my discussions with Priya—"

He held up his hand to stop me, the smile still fixed on his face like he'd taped the corners of his mouth back. "Singh," he completed my sentence. "Priya Singh. Yeah, she's quite the high-flyer. Have you seen her LinkedIn profile?"

Desperately trying to hold myself together, I took a slurp of my coffee and immediately thought of Kat and how annoying she would have found the noise.

"Somebody's been doing their homework," I replied. Of course, I hadn't looked up Priya bloody Singh on LinkedIn. But I also knew I should have done. Like I should have read about the Equity Alliance Group online and their ambitious plans for the future.

"Hey, sorry, buddy…"

Buddy? The way Liam always addressed me.

"…I thought I was doing right. I presumed that's why you told me the name of the company."

I can't even remember telling you the name of the company.

"Yeah, yeah." I tried to recover. "It's great to see you taking such an interest. Kat will be very impressed."

Luke's eyes narrowed. "Kat? Are you married then?" he asked.

I didn't like the one-sided exchange, but I had little choice but to comply. "Yes, I am," I replied, sensing a pang of discomfort at the direction of Luke's enquiries. "A girl called Katrina. I met her in a pub. Soon after we parted ways in fact. We co-own the company."

Despite my efforts to steer the conversation to safer ground, Luke's probing questions left me feeling uneasy, as if he were peeling back layers of my personal life. He took a slurp of his coffee, the froth sticking to his top lip, which he subsequently licked off. Everything he did and said was increasing my displeasure.

"Katrina, eh? I remember you had quite the thing for Sandra when we worked together."

Oh shit. Why was he even going there? I hadn't given Sandra Law a moment's thought in years, well, until the toy car turned up in Tom's pile of presents. But why should I have done? And more importantly, why would he? That was one of the reasons I'd been so reluctant to call him.

"Yes…" I stalled. "I haven't seen her for years. I left that company only weeks after you. Got another role in the City."

"Right," he said, nodding whilst annoyingly tapping on his phone. Was he even listening to me? "Here," he said, spinning his mobile around. "That's Sandra's number. You know, if you ever want to reach out. We're still in regular contact."

Retrieving my phone, I added Sandra to my contacts just to pacify him. I had no intention of calling her or "reaching out", as he annoyingly put it. However, I couldn't get rid of the nagging question of why Luke would have her number.

He took another swig of his drink, prompting me to do the same. I wanted the meeting to end, get to work, and forget all about Luke Wilson and Sandra bloody Law. I wish I'd lost his business card after all.

"You know what?" he continued, his eyes now boring into mine. I fidgeted in my seat, my palms slippery as I pushed down on the red leather. "You did right to get out of there. There was something about that place. My career stagnated as a result of working for them, a major opportunity denied."

I just glared at him, unable to formulate any words.

"Then again," his face beamed once more. "One door closing always means another one opens, doesn't it, mate?"

I nodded.

"So, tell me all about this exciting opportunity you have lined up for me."

17

"We must invite him over," Kat exclaimed shortly after I arrived home that evening. I'd called her as soon as my *interview* with Luke concluded and he duly accepted the role. He didn't want to negotiate on the salary or discuss things such as pensions or working hours. Instead, he agreed to the position without hesitation, as though our meeting was just a formality.

"What for?" I asked, sitting at the table whilst anticipating what delights we would eat that evening. "We haven't invited anybody else round from the company."

The idea of spending time with Luke Wilson in our house made my skin crawl. His confidence would destroy me, especially given my current state of mind, and I knew Kat would love his infectious charm: such a contrast to the lacklustre, miserable husband she usually had to contend with. She stopped whatever she was doing.

"Because he's going to be an integral part of the business, Adam. The girls in accounts are replaceable, and receptionists are available at the drop of a hat, but talented programmers are extremely difficult to find.

You…" – she waited until she had my undivided attention – "… of all people should know that."

The way she dismissed the girls in accounts and receptionists as disposable objects made me feel sick. She had completely forgotten her roots, where we once were, broke and desperate.

An image of Imogen lying motionless outside her summerhouse after Kat struck her with the garden spade flashed through my mind. She had hit her with intent, determined to see the back of her, and it wasn't because of our brief affair, it was because she wanted her company. The business would be her payback, the months of pain resulting in years of gain. Who or what had my wife become?

"Okay," I accepted, the prospect of a full-blown argument was the last thing I needed. "I'll ask him if he wants to come over."

Kat stepped over and planted a kiss on my forehead. "Thank you, darling," she said. "I believe it's for the best. We really need to keep him sweet."

Falling into silence, I turned my knife and fork over and over, completely lost in thought. And one person occupied them. Luke Wilson.

Leaving home felt like a stepping-stone into a world of uncertainty. Aunt Cynthia's strict rules and stifling presence had shaped me into a reserved and introverted individual. By the age of twenty-four, two years after her funeral and a couple of dead-end jobs later, I navigated the complexities of adulthood with trepidation, unsure what the future would hold for a man with no social qualities.

But finally, there was hope on the horizon. Securing a junior programmer role at a local software company provided a ray of opti-

mism amidst the chaos of my newfound independence. It was the perfect job for a misfit, a loner like me. But whilst I was content in my own company, hiding behind a computer screen and headphones constantly stuck in my ears, Luke exuded confidence and competence in equal measure. His proficiency in programming soon surpassed mine, even though I was more than capable of handling intricate code myself. Nevertheless, in spite of my best efforts to mask it, I couldn't help but feel a twinge of envy whenever he effortlessly tackled complex challenges.

Despite our initial differences, as time passed, Luke and I forged an unlikely friendship. Sitting next to each other, and the shared responsibilities of the work, often thrust us into collaboration on demanding projects. While our working relationship started out as purely professional, gradually we found common ground beyond the confines of our coding tasks.

I also had my first ever romance during my first year with the company, my first proper girlfriend. But that only lasted six months. However, from an early stage of working for that company, one individual had stood out – the receptionist, Sandra Law. Her warm smile and genuine kindness towards me offered a ray of light. A hope that not all people were the same, in it for themselves. And as time drifted by, I found myself drawn to her, seeking solace in her company whenever the opportunity arose.

Sandra was one of those unassuming types who didn't draw attention to herself in a crowded room. Petite in both stature and behaviour, she stood just over five feet tall, with an air of shyness which only added to her appeal. Her shoulder-length brown hair framed her delicate features, often falling in loose waves around her face. With almond-shaped hazel eyes and a gentle smile that rarely left her lips, Sandra exuded a subtle charm that captivated only those who took the time to notice her. She had a gracefulness about her movements, a quiet elegance that spoke volumes without her having to say a word.

However, my burgeoning friendship with Sandra was not devoid of its complications. It soon became apparent that Luke harboured a similar interest in her, his outward confidence masking a hint of possessiveness whenever she was around. Though he never voiced his feelings outright, I never could shake the sense of tension between us every time we were in Sandra's presence.

Once I picked up the courage to ask Sandra on a date – something she gladly accepted, to my ultimate surprise – I found myself with a renewed lease of life. I would throw myself into my work with determination. Luke's proficiency served as a source of inspiration, driving me to hone my skills and prove myself worthy of my place in the company. He rarely mentioned my courtship with Sandra, and I wondered if I had misread his own intentions towards her after all.

As the weeks turned into months, I slowly emerged from the cocoon of my insecurities. With each passing day, I grew more confident in my abilities, forging connections with my colleagues and embracing the challenges that lay ahead.

Yet, despite my best efforts, one thing remained constant – Luke Wilson was better at the job than me. And although his hinted at promotion never materialised, I longed for the day when I didn't have to live within his shadow.

18

ONE MONTH LATER, and two weeks after Luke Wilson's arrival at our company, he was already making waves. It was as if a gust of fresh air had swept through the office, revitalising the staid atmosphere with a newfound energy and enthusiasm. Just as I feared, Luke's infectious charisma and natural charm seemed to win over everyone he encountered, and it wasn't long before he became the focal point of every conversation and gathering.

From the moment he stepped through the doors, he exuded a confidence and warmth that drew people to him like moths to a flame. His easy-going nature and quick wit made him an instant hit with everybody.

Luke had a knack for finding common ground with everyone he met, effortlessly striking up conversations and forging friendships. Whether it was sharing a joke with the girls in accounts or discussing how we should approach software development during our impromptu meetings, Luke had a knack of making everybody feel valued and appreciated. Especially Kevin, who had been so standoffish since joining the company a couple of months earlier, and whose confidence tangibly grew in Luke's presence. Gone were the tense exchanges and awkward silences that we'd endured each morning. Instead, Kevin appeared genuinely enthusiastic, eagerly collaborating with Luke on various projects and tasks. He offered to fetch the ten o'clock coffees, something he'd never volunteered to do for me personally, and stayed late instead of clocking off at five o'clock on the dot. It was the Kevin Doyle I thought we had hired, but it had taken the introduction of Luke to finally show what he was capable of.

And as Luke's popularity continued to soar, I couldn't help but feel the same inevitable envy creeping in. Despite my years of experience and now being owner of the company, I struggled to command the same level of respect that Luke effortlessly achieved. It was as if he had already eclipsed me, becoming the golden boy of the office while I languished in his shadow. Not that my personality ever reached the echelons of a *golden boy*. *Miserable bastard* was the more apt label of the boss.

It was a bitter pill to swallow, watching someone else receive the praise and recognition that I always thought I would get as the owner. Even when Liam was the proprietor, it was my expertise with the software development that made the business the money. My proficiency paid the wages, but nobody took notice of me, nobody cared. Just like the days of wallowing alone in my room at Aunt Cynthia's house, I was a stranger, an unseen face. After two weeks, I realised that Luke's presence wasn't an inspiration to me, but rather a painful reminder of my history. No matter how hard I'd tried over the years to formulate my own success, I couldn't seem to escape the gnawing feeling of failure that lurked beneath the surface. However, he worked for us now and I had to make an effort. It would be too grim if I allowed him to get under my skin. Maybe Kat's suggestion of inviting him round for dinner might help forge a better relationship between the pair of us. After all, Luke had done nothing to suggest he didn't like me being present at work. Quite the contrary. He'd asked me twice if I fancied a beer in the Sunset – something I regretted turning down with lame excuses. He also asked me a myriad of questions about the upcoming building society contract and when we could expect to start work on it in earnest. No, Luke was keen, and he appeared to want to involve me in all he would work on. So why did I cringe every morning I saw him? Silently wince whenever I heard Kevin break into raptures of laughter outside my office cubicle? Go bright red every time I tried to intervene in one of his conversations with the girls in accounts when it immediately went quiet and the conversation dwindled to an *as you were*?

As I heard both Luke and Kevin packing away on the Thursday evening towards the end of his second week, I waited until Kevin said his goodbyes and watched from my window until he disappeared from view. Trying to act as relaxed as possible, I stood in my doorway and cleared my throat until I gained Luke's attention.

"Hey, Adam," he said, maintaining his bright demeanour despite it being after five o'clock when anyone normal would be exhausted and ready to go home. "How goes it?"

I fucking hated the way he flipped words around to make his phrases appear cool.

"Yeah, all good thanks." It took all my acting abilities to look and sound as though what I was about to ask was the top of my list of desires. "Would you be interested in coming round for dinner one night next week? I think it would be great if you met Kat, too. She doesn't like to come into the office, but I know she'd love to meet our new superstar programmer."

If somebody had said that to me, I would have cowered, blushed and most probably giggled like a school-child to hide my embarrassment. Not Luke fucking Wilson.

"Well, yeah," he exclaimed, spinning in his chair and leaping to his feet. Did he have to stand up, giving the sensation that he was now towering over me and again holding the upper hand? "That would be amazing, buddy. And tell your good wife I'm already looking forward to it."

"Yeah, yeah," I said, retreating into my cubicle as if my confidence was physically draining from me and leaving a puddle of ineptitude on the floor behind me. "I'll let her know."

"Cheers, pal." He followed me and stood in my door-way. I wanted to tell him to fuck off, tell him the conversation was over. But I didn't.

"I'll get a couple of dates off Kat and let you know our address."

Luke nodded and turned to leave. I waited until he sat back in his chair and thought that was the end of the matter. But Luke had one more surprise up his sleeve.

"Thanks again, buddy," he called out. "And don't worry about the address. I already know where you live."

19

___

"THINK ABOUT IT." Kat's voice carried a hint of annoyance. "Anyone living in London would be familiar with the street, or at least the district. That's how he must know where we live."

Was she right? Was that how Luke knew?

"But he said he knows our exact address," I protested. During the entire journey home on the tube, I had replayed the conversation in my head, yet Kat dismissed my concerns as though I were a fool for not working things out for myself.

"Did he actually say that?" she enquired. "The *exact* address or just where we live?"

I tried to recall Luke's words. "Well," I hesitated, already doubting my memory. "Not the *exact* address."

Kat sighed heavily. "Adam, we were on the news. Imogen and Liam's house was plastered across the front pages of the newspapers. They mentioned the street. The district. Anyone who's lived in the city would have a rough idea, and if Luke knows the area, he'd definitely have recognised it."

Her way of articulating things left me perpetually questioning my own thoughts. "And where does Luke live?" Kat pressed. "Do you remember?"

I shook my head. He would have given his personal details in order to put him on our payroll, but with everything else, I had taken no notice.

"For all we know," she continued, "he could live around the corner. He'd know the street, and it wouldn't take much to figure out we're the couple across from where it all happened."

We barely spoke for the remainder of the evening, only for Kat to confirm a couple of dates when it would be convenient for Luke to come for dinner. She went to bed soon after Tom, leaving me alone downstairs with my thoughts.

Pouring myself a generous glass of wine, I returned to the living room and plonked myself down in my favourite armchair. Kat bought it for me three months prior as a *reading chair*, believing I might find some solace in books. However, I hadn't read a single word since, but I found the seat extremely comfortable, high-backed with supporting winged sides. It also meant I didn't have to sit next to her.

So I sat there, in silence, in the dark, sipping red wine, like some kind of crazed fool, desperately searching for answers. If it had been a rocking chair, the scene would have been complete.

Many theories came and went. I contemplated whether I should just up and leave? Although still a novice, Kat was revelling in her new role within the organisation. And now we'd found the ideal replacement for me, could Luke, alongside his protégé Kevin, handle the software side of the business? But not only that, owning the company meant nothing to me, apart from financially, ever since…

Cursing myself for thinking of the word *since* yet again, I stood and paced the room. Inadvertently, I found myself standing by the curtains. Unsure why, I glimpsed through the parting, across the road, to Imogen's house.

You know why.

It looked eerie, its darkened upstairs windows akin to two eyes peering down, as if expecting me. The blinds were at half-mast. Opening or closing? Perhaps blinking from the glow emanating from the orange street lamps. The trees blew gently in the cool November breeze, casting dancing shadows against the pure white brickwork of the crescent-shaped row of houses beyond. I could just make out Imogen's once perfectly trimmed boxwoods in the oblong terracotta pots, occupying both Juliet balconies on the upper two levels. Much to what would have been Imogen's deep dismay, they were now hideously over-grown, wilting and dead to the world.

Terracotta pots?

I'd forgotten all about the missing one from our garden. The one that never existed.

My eyes drifted back to the pots opposite. Strands of unkempt branches hung nonchalantly over the edges. It reminded me of Imogen on the day I found her in the summerhouse. The day she discovered Liam.

Her beautiful face, so full of horror. Three or four strands of hair lay limp from her forehead, partially obscuring her eyes. Her light blue sweatshirt saturated in crimson fluid. And in her right hand, raised ever so slightly above her head, she held a pair of scissors. Her favourite pair of dressmakers' scissors. I stood, powerlessly, as a single droplet of blood clung desperately to the tip of the serrated blade.

Perhaps I should get the keys from their solicitor? Maybe go inside, tidy around, remove the dead boxwoods from their planters? Imogen would be so proud if I made an effort.

The sound of stirring from somewhere above snapped me from my reverie. My daydreaming was becoming a habit – a bad habit. My work was suffering, only saved by my capability to recover and make up for lost time. But for how long? What if I made another mistake, just as I did with the Eve Finance contract, ultimately denying any of us that huge bonus? If it ever existed, of course.

As soon as I averted my gaze from between the curtains, something caught my eye. A light. Not a conventional bulb, but more of a flashlight. A torch, maybe?

Allowing the curtains to close on themselves, I stuck my finger through the gap to make the tiniest of openings. Closing one eye tightly shut, I peered through, squinting, trying to focus on the house opposite. There! Another flash. Like somebody walking and turning, the beam making occasional twists in my direction, a fleeting dance of light momentarily illuminating the darkness.

Shit.

There was somebody in Imogen's house.

20

___

Straining harder still, I desperately tried to determine whether it was my eyes playing tricks or whether the light was indeed real. Another flash confirmed I wasn't imagining it. It was downstairs, but didn't appear to be rooted to one room. I pictured the layout, similar to our own, yet larger. The hallway was to the right and the living room to the left. The light was definitely coming from the right, but why would somebody be walking around an empty hall?

The kitchen, stupid.

The hallway led through to a vast kitchen beyond. If the door was open, the beam could easily travel the distance through to the front of the property. But the house was locked. Soon after the events of that day, I noticed a guy in a grey suit let himself in on a couple of occasions. I presumed it was an estate agent, but Kat had since determined that the estate was in the hands of a solicitor and wouldn't yet be available for sale. So, if it was nobody authorised to be in there, how the hell had they got indoors?

But was I sure they were inside? I thought again, placing the windows at the rear of the property, and again I cursed myself for being so foolish. Whoever it was could be in the rear garden. Should I check?

Stepping back from the curtains, I realised I still held the glass of wine in my hand. Taking a huge gulp, I placed it on the coffee table and left the room to sneak upstairs. Maybe the front window of the guest bedroom, *my* bedroom, might offer a better view?

The floorboards along the landing, which to my knowledge had never made a single sound before, creaked underfoot. Standing perfectly still, I heard Kat turn and murmur something undecipherable on the other side of her closed door. I inched forward once more, finally making the spare room and closing the door with a click behind me.

At first, I saw nothing, again making me believe I'd been imagining things. But then the beam of the torch materialised at the side of the house. The path we often took when joining our neighbours for another infamous boozy barbecue in their rear garden. But as soon as the light bounced off the wall, it went out, quickly followed by somebody appearing at the corner.

Clad entirely in black, they had their hood drawn up, concealing any chance of identification. Their dark shoes added to the effect, giving them the appearance of a human shadow. They rapidly scanned the street, making sure it was deserted. They needn't have worried. It was always quiet at that time of night, apart from the occasional dog walker.

The figure darted to the end of the footpath and once again paused, searching left and right for any passers-by. Finally content, they pulled their hood further forward, hunched their back, and turned left. Toward the tube station.

But then they stopped, and with a quick turn of the head, stared directly at the window I stood in.

Jumping backwards, I caught my heel underneath the corner of the bed. Stifling a curse, I hopped on my good foot, the other dangling inches from the floor. *Holy fuck*, I screamed under my breath.

Several minutes later, I found myself sitting in my favourite reading chair once more. Fortunately, I hadn't drawn blood from my heel, only a layer of skin scraped back in an elongated white graze. I cradled my wine glass, now empty, like a mug of hot chocolate on a freezing cold day.

Had they spotted me? But I'd been careful, only allowing the tiniest of cracks between the curtains. So they couldn't have truly *seen* me, but were obviously aware of somebody watching.

And then the inevitable question. Who was it? An opportunist thief? I was certain they hadn't actually entered the house as the torch light only ever caught the front of the property via the hallway. I couldn't imagine a burglar concentrating all their efforts on an empty kitchen and not venturing any farther. And that meant they had been restricted to the garden. Maybe looking for a way in and eventually giving up?

But what if it wasn't an opportunist thief? What if it was somebody who genuinely knew whose house it was and what happened there?

My heartbeat quickened as I recalled them stopping in their tracks and looking directly up at my window.

Despite my earlier consideration, maybe they hadn't been aware of anybody watching them, but instead, were well acquainted with the owner of the house?

Meaning one thing, Adam.

They know where you live.

21

———————

FOLLOWING YET another sporadic night's sleep, I showered and reluctantly made my way downstairs. Having no intention of telling Kat about the would-be intruder, I also convinced myself that whoever it was might be aware who's property it is, but they couldn't possibly know anything different about what happened. How could they? Everything was an open and shut case. The police confirmed the very same.

One. George Platt was serving time for the manslaughter of Mark Harris. Eyewitnesses saw them arguing on the common next to the river. One saw an altercation, and George strike out at Mark. Nobody actually observed the fatal blow, or George dragging the body into the river, but the evidence was so stacked against him that even his lawyer told him to accept charges of manslaughter. I don't believe George ever realised whether his blow had played a fundamental part in Mark's demise, which is most probably why he didn't push things further. He allegedly did appeal, but it soon fell on deaf ears. I'd got very lucky.

Two. Pauline North and Bob Lane had been destitute, and the latter only had himself to blame. He'd given his two children, a consequence of his failed marriage, every last penny he earned. He set them up for life, from savings accounts to deposits on houses. In return, he saw very little of them, but remained content that he'd served his purpose as a decent parent.

Bob and Pauline used to meet frequently, discussing their futures, as well as other things, but the police would never know what they actually talked about. Again, eyewitnesses, mostly neighbours, testified to their regular gatherings. And they had huge financial problems – again, I'd got lucky – and had been out of work for months. With age against them in an unforgiving society, they hadn't secured a solitary job interview since Liam made them both redundant. And they had an axe to grind with their former employer. Erecting posters near where Mark Harris met his fate, they didn't help themselves at all and their ultimate meddling cost them very dear.

Of course, I relayed most of this information to the police. Said they even pestered me to help. It's why I was there on the day they died, after they summoned me for yet another meeting. That's why I happened to *discover* their bodies.

The police soon satisfied themselves that Pauline and Bob took sleep induced drugs before turning on all the gas rings on the cooker, waiting for the inevitable conclusion. In short, they couldn't continue any longer.

And three. Liam and Imogen Daley. Liam had several affairs. Prolonged stays in hotels whilst "searching for new business opportunities". Imogen found out, with a little help from Kat, and finally snapped, allegedly stabbing her husband to death with her favourite pair of dressmakers' scissors. And because of her frenzied state of mind, we relayed to the police that Imogen tried to attack Kat and me too, resulting in her own death thanks to the swift action of my wife. The garden spade was placed perfectly for Kat to retrieve and hit Imogen with such force that she crumpled on the spot before us. As with everybody else, the authorities took pity on our situation, and often offered calls of psychiatric help if either of us so desired. I frequently contemplated accepting their proposal. Not because I needed it – *who are you kidding?* – but just to keep up the pretence that we could have played no part whatsoever in all that unfolded around us.

So, that was my conclusion in the dead of the night. How could the Daleys would-be intruder know anything different from the facts obtained by the authorities?

"You look like shit," Kat said as I entered the kitchen. She had such a way with words, I thought, despite realising her observation was probably spot on.

"Didn't sleep much," I replied, heading for the coffee machine. "Morning, champ," I said as I passed Tom, ruffling his hair.

"Don't," he shouted through a mouthful of cereal, before patting his hair back down.

It stopped me in my tracks. Tom had never once complained about me messing up his hair. More often than not, he would respond with a giggle or an exaggerated light-hearted "humph". I looked from Tom to Kat, who, too, had turned from the kitchen sink to face her son. However, after a moment's deliberation, she shrugged her shoulders, half-smiled, and resumed her task. I was far too exhausted to probe him further.

"Can you pick Tom up from school today?" Kat

asked, her forever cheerful behaviour returning in a heart-beat. When I didn't reply, she continued, "I'm going into the city this afternoon. Remember?"

The coffee machine whirred into action, allowing me a brief respite whilst trying to recall what she was talking about. I realised I needed to make more of an effort and start listening to my wife, if only to remove those awkward silences. When the machine finished, and I still didn't reply, Kat tutted aloud and reminded me what she had allegedly told me two days before.

"The new client," she said, yet it remained meaning-less to me. "I contacted them last month and they've agreed to see me. It's not as big as the Equity contract, but it's still fresh business."

Once she said it, my face must have taken on a faint expression of remembrance. Kat smiled, obviously hoping I would join in with the premature celebration that she had a meeting lined up. Again, I didn't reply.

"Why can't you show some bloody interest?" she asked, throwing the tea towel onto the worktop before marching over to collect Tom's bowl. He was smiling, his eyes fixed on me, knowing I was in trouble.

"I do remember," I lied, slurping my coffee just to annoy her. Her facial expression contorted in distaste. "I've just got a lot on at the—"

"You've got a lot on?" she interrupted, placing her hands on her hips. "And I haven't?"

I opened my mouth to intervene, not that I had much to say. However, I couldn't stand the prospect of a full-on mouthful from my wife. I'd barely slept. I'd witnessed someone walking around Imogen's rear garden in the still of the night. And then they had the fucking audacity to peer up at my bedroom window as I stared down at them. Kat continued regardless.

"You need to pull yourself together. Moping around. Uninterested in the business. Jesus, do you realise why we went through all of that?" Although she paused for breath, she proceeded without allowing me an opportunity to reply. "For this chance in life, for us. And now we have it, you don't give a shit."

Tom laughed out loud at the sound of the naughty word. I wanted to tell him to never repeat it, but he glared at me as if just as infuriated as his mum. It felt as if they were colluding with one another. Everybody against Adam Chapman.

"Of course I care," I said, not even convincing myself. "You're doing really well in drumming up new clients. I'm happy, I really am."

"Well, you've a bloody funny way of showing it," she replied, banging the dishwasher door shut before storming out of the kitchen. "Just remember to pick your son up from school," she shouted as she ascended the stairs. "If it's not too much trouble."

22

I LEFT for work an hour after Kat took Tom to school. She said she would continue with her journey into the city after dropping him off, work on our company accounts for a short period of time in a café, and then go to meet the prospective new client.

Once outdoors, I paused, and looked across the street at Imogen's house. To be fair, I could never stop myself from having a quick glance. All those memories, those happy times, as well as the bad. However, that particular morning was different. The trespasser still played heavily on my mind despite attempting to persuade myself there was nothing to concern myself with. Glancing swiftly up and down the nearly deserted street, I hurriedly crossed over and slipped out of sight to the rear of the property.

The first thing that struck me was the state of the garden. Always so well-manicured by Imogen's own fair hands, it now resembled a jungle. Grass overgrown, flowerbeds choked with weeds, even the pavement was invaded by thistles. A wave of sadness washed over me at the sight of her hard work falling into ruin within a matter of months. But then, something else caught my eye.

The lawn bore a zigzagged line, not a well-worn path, but freshly made, cutting through the two-foot-high blades of grass, leading directly to the summerhouse. Tracking its origin just feet away, I cautiously followed what must be the intruder's trail, arriving at the place I never wished to revisit: where Liam and Imogen had fallen.

But why was the hooded figure so interested? It reinforced my uneasy suspicion that they knew something. Why else prioritise the summerhouse over the vacant property itself? I forced myself to consider the options: perhaps they couldn't find an entry into the house and believed something valuable might be in the garden building instead? Was it too much of a coincidence?

Shielding my eyes, I leant forward and peered through the glass door. I recoiled as soon as I spotted the space where Liam fell, the pool of crimson blood still vivid in my mind. Swiftly trying to push such images aside, I instead focused on what might be worth searching for. However, as expected, nothing stood out. There was the bench where Imogen used to sit and sew, making curtains or dresses, or whatever else she could fashion from her fabrics. The sewing machine remained, alongside plastic containers filled with pins, needles, and goodness knows what else. Beside the bench stood a clothes rail, its dozen or so coat hangers looking lost and lonely with nothing to support, their purpose unfulfilled. Boxes littered the floor, containing materials, cushions, and all sorts of paraphernalia Imogen used for her favourite hobby. Apart from that, there was nothing. Though the sewing machine might fetch a good price, there was absolutely no other item a burglar would find enticing, and if they were anything like me, they wouldn't have a clue about the machine's value on the black market. Certainly not worth the risk of breaking in and attracting a neighbour's attention as you carted it down the street.

Reluctantly, and a little downcast, although secretly pleased I'd discovered nothing untoward, I retraced my footsteps. Halfway back, my phone vibrated in my pocket, making me jump like a nervous cat. Retrieving it, I glanced up at the house next door, but already knew they couldn't see into Imogen's garden from their rear windows. The height of the conifer hedge separating the two properties saw to that.

"Hello," I said quietly, hastening my pace to get to the relative sanctuary of the back of the house.

"Mr Chapman? Is that you?"

The female voice sounded authoritative.

"Yes. This is Adam Chapman. Who is this, please?"

I spoke quickly and my speech had a slight tremor.

"It's Miss Reeves. Tom's teacher."

Oh fuck, no.

"What's happened? Is he okay? Is he hurt? What's—"

"Mr Chapman," she cut me off. I was already halfway around Imogen's house, retreating into the realms of the real world. "He's absolutely fine."

"Then what is it?" I demanded, my worry quickly turning to anger.

"Can you come in, please?" she replied as if she'd asked the same question a million times before. "Tom has been involved in an, how shall I put it? In an altercation."

23

"WHY DIDN'T you call my wife?" I asked, standing as Miss Reeves approached me.

I'd been sitting impatiently for ten minutes while the receptionist arranged for somebody to fetch Tom's teacher. She made me complete a form as I waited.

"Nice to see you, Mr Chapman," she replied, a little too facetiously for my liking. "I tried your wife two or three times before calling you. She didn't pick up. I hope you don't mind?" Again, I didn't like her insinuation that I might not have time for my child. But why hadn't Kat picked up? What did she say? She was going to work in a café before meeting her client. Perhaps she had it on silent?

"No, no," I replied, scampering after the teacher as she resolutely made her way along an elongated corridor. I noticed children's paintings adorning each wall, plus a couple of cork noticeboards with flyers attached. "I just thought my wife would have answered."

Miss Reeves stopped in her tracks and turned to face

me. Her posture was relaxed and her expression approachable. "Mr Chapman—"

"Adam, please," I cut her off. I hated formality.

"Adam," she continued, as if I hadn't even spoken. "I hope you don't mind me asking, but is everything okay at home?"

She knew. Of course she knew. Everybody associated with me, however distant, would know what happened. The couple who witnessed death. The wife who defended both herself and her husband from the crazed scissor murderer.

"Yeah, yeah," I stalled, my face reddening. "Well, it's been traumatic, as you can imagine, but it's—"

She held up her palm, at least showing enough empathy to stop me from becoming even further flustered. I soon realised that Miss Reeves, presumably in her late twenties, had a mature head on her shoulders way beyond her years.

"I can only imagine," she replied before turning and marching off once more. Yet again, I scurried after her like one of her badly behaved pupils.

"Wait in there, please," she said, pushing a door open and holding it ajar until I did as I was told. "I'll fetch Tom."

"Hey." A stocky guy rose from his seat to greet me. "You must be Tom's dad?" He offered me his hand. "I'm Sean. Max's dad. I've heard our kids get on like a house on fire."

The tube ride back to work was a blur, as was the short walk to the office. I noticed the Sunset Wine Bar to my right, the place Liam and I had frequented far too often. The venue where we'd met Sharon and Beth, a couple of single and feisty East London girls. The same Sharon who I pushed down a flight of steps at the underground station. With an all too frequent repetition, I shuddered at the memory and the ease with which I'd inflicted pain upon people.

My mind drifted back to Miss Reeves and the meeting with Tom, as well as Max and his dad. Yet it was the latter who occupied my thoughts the most.

The boy's teacher had returned with the children moments later, only allowing Sean and me time for quick introductions. I studied a tattoo on his neck. What was it? A bird of some kind. A swallow, a swift? He had more faded tattoos on the back of both hands, and he scratched nervously at them throughout the meeting. Now and then, Sean caught me watching him, yet I couldn't determine the look he gave in return. What had Lauren said, he'd got in with the wrong company? He looked as hard as nails, a far cry from his beautiful wife and son, whose hair still mesmerised me.

Tom looked sheepish, avoiding any eye contact, his posture slouched and his hands fidgeting with the buttons on his blazer.

Miss Reeves asked the four of us to sit opposite her. The chairs were orange, plastic, and far too low. I sagged before pulling myself upright. My knees were at chest height and I felt incredibly uncomfortable. It didn't help when Miss Reeves pulled up a similar chair and appeared totally at ease once she sat. Tom's feet swung back and forth, annoyingly catching the floor every now and then.

"Should I tell your parents, or do you want to, Tom?" his teacher enquired in a relaxed manner. Tom glanced at her before his eyes flicked sideways to me. He blinked heavily and shook his head. "Max?" she then asked, focusing her attention on him. I noticed Max didn't dare look at his father.

"Okay," Miss Reeves took over, altering her posture to face me. "At playtime this morning, Tom and Max got into a fight with another boy in the playground."

I looked at him, my eyes wide. Again, he stared at the ground and swung his legs alternately, as if he was riding an imaginary bicycle.

"Please, Tom," she continued, pausing until he looked up. "Tell your dad why you got into a fight."

We remained silent, patiently waiting for him to speak, realising the prolonged silence would eventually break him. His eyes didn't move, but his legs still kicked.

"He told me my mum and dad were murderers and they would be going to prison."

My face coloured for the second time in the past fifteen minutes. How the hell should I respond to such a statement? Sean's smirk escaping from his mouth didn't help my cause. Miss Reeves glared at me for a response.

"Why would he say that?" I finally asked, directing my question at Tom. He shrugged his shoulders dramatically.

"Okay, Tom, Max," their teacher took control again. "You can go back to class now."

Before she even completed the sentence, they were on their feet and heading for the door.

"See you later, champ," I called after him, not knowing what else to say.

"And why am I here?" Sean spoke for the first time since the meeting began. He appeared irritated, and I could see his point. Dragged to school, from wherever or whatever he'd been doing, only for his son not to contribute at all.

"Because Max was extremely aggressive, Mr Croft. We have zero tolerance to such behaviour in this school. Max might only be six years old, but he was very feisty during the fight, shall we say? It took two teachers to pull him away."

Sean shuffled in his seat, his legs outstretched and his arms folded. He had the look of a proud father, a glint of 'that's my boy' in his eyes. He was clearly unaffected by the entire situation; no shame, no humiliation at his son's behaviour.

Miss Reeves ignored his obvious indifference and moved on to explain that children could be the cruellest of human beings. Their innocence knew no bounds, and what may feel like an extremely hurtful statement to some was just a joke to others.

"I've spoken to the other boy concerned," she continued. "And I'm more than happy there won't be any recurring incidents."

Finally, we were allowed to leave, like obedient children, and she said she hoped we would talk to our boys in our own time too. We both nodded, but even in the brief time I'd known him, I knew Sean wouldn't say a word to Max. I also knew I wouldn't repeat a word of it to Tom, either.

Once we were safely outside the confines of the school car park, Sean turned to face me. His stance was confident, his movements deliberate, like a predator sizing up its prey. His clothes were dark and nondescript, but there was an air of danger about him that made it clear he was not to be trifled with. From the tattoos peeking out from under his sleeves to the faint scar across his cheek, every aspect of Sean's appearance spoke of a life lived on the edge, a man who had seen and done things most people could only imagine. "Let me give you my phone number," he said in a thick East End accent. "I know you've been through a lot, mate, and my boy thinks the world of yours." I felt intimidated in his presence, unable to respond in case my voice was high-pitched or I couldn't formulate a sentence worthy of him. "If you ever need anything…" he cleared his throat, "…then just call me."

24

Not only had I decided not to mention the impromptu meeting with Tom's teacher to him ever again, but I also kept it from Kat, too. There was no chance Tom would bring up the incident, and I'd tell him later to keep it as our little secret. Why worry his mum unnecessarily?

He told me my mum and dad were murderers and they would be going to prison.

Miss Reeves promised there would be no repeat from the other boy, and Tom appeared to realise his mistake in lashing out. Or so I hoped.

However, despite his teacher explaining how cruel kids could be, why would a six-year-old say such a thing to his counterpart? And more concerning, that child could never make something up like that himself. So, he heard it from somewhere, or somebody else. His parents? Should I find out the name of the boy and visit them, ask why they would put such ideas into their son's mind, or would that just inflame the situation further? I chuckled to myself as I imagined asking Sean to call round and sort them out on my behalf.

It was lunchtime when I finally arrived at the office, and following the memories stirred as I passed the Sunset, I suddenly craved alcohol. Once Kevin left to grab himself a sandwich, I asked Luke if he fancied a couple of beers after work. He almost bit my arm off at the opportunity.

The wine bar had barely changed at all, and as we stepped inside, it only seemed like yesterday since I last visited. All kinds of emotions washed over me. The good times, the crazy times, and the downright sinister times. The Sunset could tell an awful lot of stories regarding my past. Maybe where they should have remained, I considered, scanning the room, searching for available seats.

"Grab that one," I said, pointing. A familiar table was unoccupied, one me and Liam had frequented on many an occasion. I desperately tried to push the image to one side.

Luke waved off my offer with a casual gesture. "I'll get these," he volunteered. His eyes sparkled, and I couldn't recall knowing anyone else who was always so bloody happy.

"You sure?" I asked, already regretting the spontaneous invitation for him to join me. The prospect of making small talk suddenly felt like a Herculean task. He nodded eagerly.

"Thanks," I said. "I'll have the same as you."

"Good man," he replied, slapping me on the back. His enthusiasm was draining me, like a leech sucking the last bit of energy from my veins.

"I'll get a bottle of wine, save having to keep going to the bar."

Once he returned, we exchanged pleasantries, and the conversation flowed sporadically as we reminisced about old times and how he was settling into work. We talked for over an hour, the alcohol finally helping me to relax, and to begin with, it was good to unwind with no mention of the immediate past. However, after Luke shared the remaining contents of the bottle between our glasses, he took a long sip and looked me directly in the eye.

"So, Adam," he began, his tone still casual but his eyes keen. "I couldn't help but notice your name in the news a few months ago. Quite the scandal involving Liam and Imogen Daley."

My heart skipped a beat at the mention of their names, my throat tightening with apprehension. "Yeah. It's been a difficult time," I admitted, my voice strained as I searched for the right words. "But I'd rather not talk about it if that's okay." I recalled Kevin asking something similar.

Luke placed his glass on a coaster. He looked as though he was settling down for the long haul. I suddenly felt trapped, a considerable distance from the exit and the safety of the streets.

"That's fair enough, mate," he replied. "Must have been quite the ordeal?"

Although I thought I'd made it abundantly clear I didn't want to discuss it, the way Luke left his question open-ended, and that he remained perfectly silent, left me with no choice but to reply. The amount of alcohol we'd consumed in a relatively short space of time didn't help.

"It was, yes. It's not every day you see a dead body."

"I thought there were two bodies?" he replied quickly, his forehead creased as if concentrating hard.

Where's he going with this?

"Yes, there were. Body. Bodies. It's still the same thing."

He had a sip of his wine before placing the glass in the exact centre of his beer mat. I took the opportunity to take a huge gulp of my own.

"But Liam's body was already there when you arrived, wasn't it?"

It felt like a bloody interrogation.

"Yes. Yes, Liam was there when I found him."

I had another lengthy drink. There was less than a mouthful remaining. Luke glanced at my glass, and I'm sure a wry smile passed over his lips.

"How long had he been dead?"

"Hey," I replied, half smiling, attempting to lighten the mood. "I said I didn't want to talk about it. It's difficult for me."

He showed the palms of his hands in recognition. "Yeah, I'm sorry, but the story kind of fascinated me when I read about it. I think it did a lot of people. And when I saw your name, hey, that's when it really piqued my interest."

I nodded. I realised it would have had the same effect on anybody who knew me. Incredibly, Luke took my silence as a cue to continue.

"So, his wife killed him and then she tried to attack you? What made her go so bloody crazy, mate?"

Unbelievably, I felt my cheeks redden. He sat back, again raising the palms of his hands. "Wow," he exclaimed. "Were you having a thing with her?"

I stood too quickly, an instant feeling of vertigo hitting me hard. Grabbing the side of the table, I desperately tried to retrieve the situation.

"Of course not," I said, my voice sounding feeble

inside my head. "Now, are we going to have a second bottle or not?"

Unable to think of anything else to say, I immediately regretted it when his eyes opened wide and he looked like a child on Christmas morning.

At the bar, I asked for a pint of tap water and downed it before asking for a refill. I glanced across the room at Luke, who contentedly glanced around the bar, taking in everything and everybody around him. He seemed genuine, harmless.

Although unsure of my intentions, the lack of alternatives left me with little choice. I needed to find a way to unburden myself, to share the heavy weight of my struggles with someone who might understand. It could have been a gamble to put my trust in him, but who else did I have to turn to? He appeared legitimate, upbeat, and someone to listen. And although I didn't like his questioning of what happened all those months before, he only showed such an interest because he recognised my name in the middle of it all. His old working pal.

What did I have to lose?

25

PLACING the fresh bottle of wine between us, I waited for Luke to pour it out. My hands were perspiring and trembling slightly, and I knew Luke's keen eye would soon pick up upon my sudden nervous disposition. He spoke as he replenished our glasses.

"Hey," he said with a warm smile. "You look like you've got the weight of the world on your shoulders."

There it was again. Genuine concern on his face. Did he really have my best interests at heart? Inhaling deeply, I settled into the chair before taking a long drink.

"Luke. Do you mind if I tell you something?"

His expression softened further as he leant forward. "Sure, mate," he said. "You know what? I've suspected something has been on your mind ever since the day we bumped into each other in that bookstore."

I looked him in the eye, searching for any telltale sign of how much he might know, but he gave nothing away.

"I've been struggling…" I paused. "I guess with depression. To tell you the truth, it's something I first had to deal with years ago, when I was a kid."

Luke nodded. Had I told him about being bought up by my aunt when we originally worked together? It was such a while back, but I was sure it was a subject I'd barely broached with anybody since leaving home at eighteen. I may have confessed to Sandra, and Kat knew the basics: the loss of my parents and the strictness of my subsequent upbringing.

"Go on," he said, sitting upright on his stool.

"Well, I lost my mum and dad when I was young. My Aunt Cynthia raised me, much to her disdain, and I struggled to put myself out there. I became a recluse, you know, until around the time I met you when we worked together."

Having recalled Luke's enthusiasm at mentioning her before, the last thing I wanted was to bring Sandra Law into the conversation, but it was no coincidence that the day I met her was the beginning of the end of my sorrowful existence. "Meeting Sandra served as a temporary reprieve. We were good for a while." Luke nodded slowly, as if deep in thought. I recalled him giving me her number, and that doubt kicked in once more why he would have it in the first place. "But even that eventually turned sour, and I soon slipped back into my dark ways."

"Uh-huh," he interjected like a bloody psychiatrist, nodding for me to continue.

"And recently," I attempted to laugh. "Well, for obvious reasons, those hideous apprehensions have resurfaced."

Luke listened intently as I divulged more than I originally intended, his gaze unwavering, prompting me to talk. When I eventually fell silent, my breathing rapid, Luke reached across the table and placed a reassuring hand on my forearm.

"I'm so sorry, Adam," he said softly. "I had no idea you were going through all of this."

I shook my head, tears pricking at the corners of my eyes as I struggled to contain my emotions. For so long, I had felt isolated and abandoned, convinced that no one could possibly understand all I had been through. But now, sitting opposite Luke, I realised I might not be alone after all. But what he said next totally flummoxed me.

"I've been there too, pal," he admitted, his voice barely above a whisper. "Ever since my time towards the end of that company we worked for."

"Really?"

Luke laughed at my surprise. "Yeah, really. They were dark times, mate. I didn't know where I would go next. I'd just bought my first flat, something I could scarcely afford, and then I found myself scratching around in junior roles that were paying less than the wage we both started on."

I felt a surge of guilt at Luke's revelation, my mind reeling at the thought of him, with his unwavering confidence, suffering from similar struggles to me. It was a sobering reminder that appearances could be deceptive and that everyone had their own battles to fight. Little did he know I played a significant part in his downward spiral.

"I tried a couple of different things, anything to earn a bit more money. And although I ultimately fell back into software development, I at least found there was more to life than tapping away at a keyboard all day long." He paused whilst he took a drink. "Eventually, those dark times passed, as I'm sure they will for you." He nodded his head. "Given time, I'm sure you can put all of this behind you."

As we left the Sunset Wine Bar that evening, a strange

sense of peace washed over me, the weight of my burdens lifted, if only for a moment. Maybe with Luke by my side, there would be a way out of it after all?

Despite my headache, I awoke the next morning with a renewed vigour in my step. Kat smiled as I joined her and Tom in the living room, a fresh coffee in my hand.

"You were in a good mood when you arrived home last night," she said, half-watching some cartoon on TV with Tom. "And you only had positive words to say about Luke."

"He's a good listener," I replied, trying to recall if I said too much.

"Well, that's wonderful," Kat said, standing. She pecked me on the cheek as she made her way to the kitchen, an empty mug in her hand. I turned to Tom.

"Fancy going to the park, champ?" I asked, desperate to spend time with my son.

"Great idea," Kat called over her shoulder. "I need to go to the shops, anyway."

Fortunately, Tom leapt to his feet and ran off to find his shoes and ball.

. . .

The park lay approximately a quarter of a mile away from our house. Tom clutched his beloved blue Chelsea FC football, despite my warnings that he would inevitably drop it along the way. The smirk on his face upon our safe arrival reminded me so much of his mother.

After some time kicking the ball around, Tom insisted on going on the swings. Secretly, I dreaded him using them, fearing he would fall backwards every time he shouted "higher". However, his squeals of delight made it all worthwhile.

The swings were arranged in a line of four, with a large climbing frame nearby and a small copse of trees beyond. After missing a few pushes, Tom complained I wasn't even trying. "Sorry," I shouted as he swung back towards me, giving him a harder push to make up for lost momentum. He squealed again, completely oblivious to any worries I had about him falling.

"Come on, mate, let's go on the roundabout," I said, grabbing the swing's chains and bringing him to an abrupt halt. The roundabout was near the trees. Luckily, Tom agreed, and he dashed off, leaving me trailing in his wake.

"Come on, Daddy!" he shouted. "I can't push it on my own."

Once I was sure Tom had a firm grip on the handle, I gently pushed the roundabout into motion, watching his excited face.

"Faster! Faster!"

After spinning him to a speed he seemed content with, I let go, took a step back, and watched as he whizzed past me in rapid succession. I attempted a trick with his football, but lost control and it rolled close to the roundabout. As Tom spun by, he swung out his leg and made a perfect connection with it, giggling profusely. "Goal!" he screamed. The football sailed into the trees.

"Good shot," I said, feeling quite proud of my son. "Hold tight. I'll get it."

Unable to suppress a grin, I trotted over to the small copse, assuming the ball to be on the periphery. However, as I reached the edge, a sudden movement inside made me recoil. I heard the distinct sound of twigs snapping underfoot and what sounded like rushing feet amongst the leaves. Slowing down, my enthusiasm for Tom's flawless contact with the ball dwindled by the second.

Stepping into the trees, my eyes darted right and left, searching frantically for the ball, desperate to retrieve it and get back into the open. Twisting my head, I realised Tom was no longer within my sight. Kat would kill me if she knew I had left him unattended.

The football was nowhere to be seen. He had kicked it hard, but surely it wouldn't have rolled far once inside the small wood? The trees were dense, and the ground was thick with undergrowth. A flash of movement caught my eye.

"Who's there?" I shouted. Footsteps hurried away, disappearing into the distance. My heart raced as my newfound zest for life threatened to disperse much faster than it had arrived, the benefits of my full disclosure with Luke disappearing by the second. As I spotted what I presumed was a glimpse of a figure, I heard Tom scream from behind.

Fuck.

Scampering back out into the clearing, I saw my son lying sprawled on the surface surrounding the round-about. A young woman was crouched down by his side. She had a small child with her. I ran as fast as I could.

"Hi," I said, barely able to speak as I gasped for air. "I'm his dad."

The woman stood and backed off a step or two. She glared at me as if to say, 'and you should be thoroughly ashamed of yourself'. However, my attention was fully on Tom.

"Hey, champ. You okay?" I said, dropping to my knees.

Fortunately, he sat up with the widest of grins. The relief hit me so hard, I momentarily felt faint.

"Did you see me, Daddy? I went flying." He stretched his arms out wide to emphasise his point.

Picking him up, I dusted down his jogging bottoms and sweatshirt and examined him; there were no cuts or bruises on his exposed skin. I feared adrenaline hadn't yet allowed the pain to hit home.

The woman walked off, dragging her child in her wake, mumbling something under her breath about my inept parenting skills. I considered asking if she'd seen anybody in the trees, but thought it might either freak her out or make her doubly doubt my ability to look after my son.

"Where's my football?" Tom asked once I finished cleaning him up.

"Oh, it's in the trees. Come on, race you there."

Letting him win by a matter of inches, we made it to the edge of the copse within seconds. Tom giggled and cheered after beating me in yet another running race. I was just so relieved he appeared to be okay.

Grasping his hand, we ventured inside. He tripped regularly, the branches and roots hidden underneath the canvas of deep leaves a constant hazard.

"Where is it, Daddy? I didn't kick it this far, did I?"

Gripping his hand a little tighter, we ventured farther

into the gloom. I hadn't gone in so far before, and I doubted the ball could have made it so far in.

Stopping, I spun around, trying to gather my bearings. Rotating back again, it didn't make any sense. The football was bright blue. It should have been as conspicuous as a light bulb in a dim room.

Eventually, much to Tom's annoyance, we gave up. At least there was no repeat of footsteps or flashes of somebody close by, and as we reluctantly left, I became less convinced I had seen or heard anything after all. Besides, who would steal a child's football?

Tom fought back tears all the way home, infuriating me further. I begged him not to cry, especially in front of his mum. I couldn't handle the blame. But as we turned the final corner, Tom stopped grumbling and stood perfectly still. I almost bumped into him.

"What's that, Daddy?" he asked, slowly stretching out his arm and pointing towards our house.

My eyes followed, tracing the line of his finger, my brain trying to compute what I was actually seeing.

"No idea, champ," I replied. I began walking again, quickly completing the short distance, Tom scampering after me. At the end of our pathway, we both stood transfixed, staring at the property.

Red paint was smeared on our light blue front door. A thick viscous blob adorned the top where it made its impact, while a network of streaks radiated downwards, resembling tendrils of some ominous substance.

"Daddy?" Tom said in a high-pitched and unnerving voice, whilst annoyingly pulling sharply on my arm.

"Yes?" I replied, still mesmerised by the sight afore me.

"Is that blood?"

27

———

MY HEART THREATENED to burst from my chest as I approached the front door, my steps quickening with each beat. As Tom suggested, the sight of the vivid red paint smeared across did indeed resemble blood, sending a shiver down my spine. Who would do this? And why?

Fumbling for my keys, my hands shook nervously as I struggled to unlock the door. The sound of a car approaching from behind stopped me in my tracks, but a sense of relief hit me hard once I spotted Kat. She peered over from the driving seat, her eyes wide, taking in what lay behind me. She pulled into the driveway with a squeal of tyres, somewhat reckless given her usual timid driving antics, and rushed down the pathway to join us.

Quickly, I pushed the door open and told Tom to go inside and find something to play with.

"What is it, Daddy?" he asked once more, walking backwards along the hallway.

"Just somebody being silly, mate," I replied, doing my utmost to fix a smile to reassure him there was nothing to worry about. "Put the TV on. Boot up your PlayStation if you want. We'll be inside in a minute."

Tom strolled off, the drama already overtaken by the prospect of watching a movie or playing a game. Kat joined me, her expression filled with concern as she took in both the door and the sight of my pale complexion. "What the hell has happened?" she asked, her voice barely above a whisper.

Words failed me. All I could do was stare at the door. "It looks just like blood," Kat said, leaning closer to inspect the damage before asking the same question whirring through my mind. "Who did it?"

Minutes later, after checking Tom was okay, we waited in the kitchen. To fill time, we made coffee, neither of us speaking, simply lost in our thoughts. After examining the door – the paint was still wet, but I'd already presumed that – Kat instructed me to call the police. I argued it wasn't necessary. The prospect of opening old wounds and giving new statements played heavily on my mind. "What if they ask about before?" I asked. But she dismissed my fears and said we had no choice but to report it.

As we tried to process what happened, the doorbell rang, its sound piercing the silence of the house. I exchanged a wary glance with Kat before making my way along the hallway, my heart again pounding in my chest.

Two police officers stood on the doorstep, their expressions grim. They were still inspecting the damage when one peered up at me. "Mr Chapman?" he said, his voice serious.

I nodded, my throat dry. "Yes, that's me."

They introduced themselves as Officer Anderson and Officer Rodriguez, explaining that they were responding to our report of vandalism at the address. After confirming it was I who made the call, I allowed them to further inspect the defacement, before inviting them inside, my mind racing with what questions would inevitably follow. I recalled the last time we had the police in our house, the day of the killings.

As they stepped into the kitchen, Officer Anderson's gaze took in his surroundings before finally introducing himself to Kat. She offered them both coffee, which they promptly declined. "Do you have any inkling who might have done this?" Officer Anderson asked, his tone probing.

I shook my head. "No, I have no idea. We haven't had any problems like this since, well, since what happened across the street."

The officers exchanged a knowing glance before Officer Anderson turned his attention back to me. "We'll need to take a statement from you and your wife, as well as search your property," he said, his tone businesslike. "Do you know if someone tried to break in?"

The thought hadn't even crossed my mind. I looked at Kat. She shrugged her shoulders in return.

"I haven't checked," I replied on our behalf.

"I'll go," Kat responded, a little too quickly, and she left us alone before anybody could respond.

Over the next ten minutes, I recounted the events leading up to the discovery of the paint-daubed door, providing the officers with as much information as I could. I didn't mention the missing football and my possible sighting in the copse but as I purposefully left out that part of the story, I wondered if the two could be connected. And then the intruder from two nights previous. They had to be connected, but I couldn't face another vigorous cross-examination. Officer Anderson took notes as I spoke, his expression unreadable.

As the interview drew to a close, Officer Rodriguez cleared his throat, his gaze lingering on me. "We are obviously aware of the house across the street," he said, his voice carefully neutral. My heart skipped a beat. "And what happened there. Do you think this has anything to do with that?"

28

———————

KAT REJOINED US MOMENTS LATER, confirming there were no signs of an attempted break-in. I noticed her shifting her weight from one foot to the other and silently wished she would stand still. I told her about the officers knowing what happened across the road, and Kat foolishly confirmed it was where Liam and Imogen were killed.

Officer Anderson's eyes narrowed, his expression becoming more intense. "Yes." He exchanged a glance with his partner. "We are well aware of the details. But, as I said, do you think this has anything to do with that?"

"I can't imagine why," Kat replied, her tone growing in confidence. "That was months ago, and as far as we're concerned, everything was resolved and put to rest."

"Yes," the officer complied. "It does appear as though the whole sorry case was settled at the time."

I didn't like what he was implying and the use of the word *appear*, suggesting doubt in his mind. I glanced at Kat and realised she was probably thinking the same. Officer Anderson took further notes, and I desperately wanted to know what he was writing.

"And you've lived here since then?" he asked neither of us in particular. "I'm surprised you haven't felt the urge to move away. It must be difficult living in such close proximity to what you both went through?"

I nodded, feeling a knot form in my stomach. "Yes, we considered moving on, but as my wife just explained, everything was resolved. Our son is settled in the area and it's perfect for us to get to work," I replied.

The officers exchanged a further glance before Officer Anderson spoke again. "We'll have to look into this incident," he said, putting his notebook away, indicating that the conversation was coming to a conclusion. "And if you can think of anybody who would do such a thing, please do not hesitate to call."

Once they were gone, I turned to Kat. "We need to talk," I said, exhaustion hitting me hard.

Kat stared at me as she took in my sombre expression. "What is it?" she asked, her emotions completely under control, as if the drama was all over.

I took a deep breath, steeling myself for what I was about to share. "I think someone is targeting us... me," I admitted.

Kat's eyes rolled, as if to say, 'Not again'. "Who?"

I recounted the events of the day so far, from the disappearance of Tom's football in the park to the painted door. As I spoke, a sense of unease settled over me. My voice faltered as realised I sounded irrational. The prospect of somebody hanging around to steal a ball seemed absurd in my head, let alone once I said it out loud.

"If Tom kicked the ball that hard, it could have gone anywhere. Did you look everywhere?"

Ignoring her counterclaims, I asked about the door.

"Forget the ball then." I nodded along our hallway. "Even you can't dismiss that."

"It's a prankster, Adam. I'm sure of it. And I'm convinced the police thought the same. I doubt we'll hear from them again."

I considered telling her of the intruder at the house opposite, or the white BMW parked outside the office, but knew she would ignore those too. And even as I played the events through my mind, I realised how incredulous they sounded. Besides, Kat was determined to move on. She had already suggested that I seek professional help to overcome my anxieties and she was entirely focused on building the business instead. However, the sight of the paint had unnerved me.

"But what kind of prankster does that? It's as though they've deliberately made it look like blood. Even Tom—"

"Shh," she interrupted, taking my hands in hers. "It's red paint, not blood. Come on, darling," she continued, "we were all over the news months ago and this is just a kid who wants to get off on what happened. Just someone attempting to scare us."

I allowed her to finish. The way she put it kind of made sense, and her calming energy seeped through me. Her steady grip and reassuring tone chipped away at my anxiety. I took a deep breath, feeling the tension in my shoulders ease slightly. Maybe she was right. Maybe it was just a harmless prank.

"We'll figure it out together," she whispered, holding me close. "You had a great evening with Luke last night. We really need to move on before you become totally consumed by it all."

Perhaps Kat had a point, but deep down, I knew my troubles were far from over. The night before had indeed given me hope, but the day's events had knocked me right back to square one.

As we clung to each other in the dimly lit room, a shadow of fear loomed over me like a spectre and I couldn't shake the feeling that somewhere, somehow, I was being watched. And I feared that whoever was behind the painted door was only just getting started.

29

———————

THANKFULLY, the following week unfolded without incident, offering a welcome respite from the unsettling events of the recent past. Engrossed in the routine of work, I desperately tried to find solace in mundane tasks that would hopefully divert my thoughts. My chat with Luke had certainly helped buoy my mood, but then the sight of the bloody paint smeared over our front door threatened to overwhelm me yet again.

As I left our house on the last morning of that week, Kat called out to me from the kitchen.

"Don't forget Mum and Dad arrive today."

Holy fuck.

It had completely slipped my mind.

Why on earth were *they* coming? They hadn't bothered before and we'd lived in the property for over two years, forever citing ill health and having to navigate the London Underground system as an eternal excuse, which suited me just fine. But what had Kat said as we drove home weeks before? "They really want to see our house, and they can't wait to see where we work…"

Surely they wouldn't visit the office? If they were adamant, maybe Kat could take them on a tour on Saturday or Sunday when nobody else was present. The last thing I wanted was my in-laws strolling around, interrupting the team during working hours. But as the day progressed, and we reached mid-afternoon, I thought my worst fears were behind me. Who was I kidding?

With the clock ticking slowly towards three thirty, my tranquillity was shattered by my dreaded guest – William.

I glanced up from my desk to see him standing in the doorway, a genial smile on his face. "Adam, my boy! Time for a visitor?" he exclaimed, his voice booming with enthusiasm.

My boy? Who the hell was he trying to impress? I recollected the last time I saw him and that hideous laughing experience when I believed he and Edwina had fallen into fits of giggles at my expense. At least it appeared as though my mother-in-law hadn't accompanied him. Even so, my heart sank at the sight of him, my mind reeling with questions. What was he really doing there?

Before I could muster a response, William strode into the office, his eyes scanning the room with curiosity. "Quite the operation you've got here," he remarked as I scooted after him, his tone tinged with admiration.

I exchanged a nervous glance with both Luke and Kevin, before plastering on a smile. They seemed as bemused as me, although Kevin appeared to be taking pleasure in my discomfort.

"Thanks, William. What brings you here?" I asked, my voice strained. "I remember you saying you wanted to see where we worked, but didn't think you would come during working hours."

William chuckled, his eyes twinkling with mischief. I

could feel my blood boiling and my hatred towards the man intensifying. "Just thought I'd drop by for a visit. Edwina and Kat are at home, so don't worry, you've only got me to show around," he replied with a sarcastic grin, before strolling off, his head flicking from side to side.

Scampering after him, I smiled awkwardly at the girls in accounts. They grinned uncomfortably as he approached.

"Best let them get on with their work, William," I said, gesturing for him to follow me to a quieter area and away from personnel.

"It's quite the arrangement," he remarked aloud, then shifted his gaze towards me. "I've always had faith in my Katrina's abilities," he continued, his expression radiating with pride. Deliberately sidestepping any acknowledgement of my contribution, he seemed intent on magnifying Kat's accomplishments while diminishing mine. I could feel my face redden as the girls watched on.

"Yes, well," I replied, my mouth dry. "It's all about the data analytics, and I'm responsible for all of—"

"She's truly exceptional, isn't she?" he interrupted. I wanted to fucking kill him. My hands perspired as they clenched into fists. "Always had that spark of brilliance. It's no surprise that she's the driving force behind your success. I've always said she's destined for greatness." He turned to face me. "As for the rest of us, well, we're just lucky to be along for the ride."

As William continued with his self-appointed tour of my office, I was called away to take an urgent phone call. I passed Kevin, who couldn't control the smirk on his face, and a knot of apprehension tightened in my stomach as I made my way to the rear of the building where I could speak in private. Standing with my back to everyone, I was relieved, at least momentarily, to put some distance between me and William.

The call I took was brief but unsettling, leaving me with more questions than answers. I remained hidden away, my mind racing, before hearing William's distinct voice across the open-plan expanse.

Stepping quietly forward, I spotted him with Luke and Kevin. They were deeply engaged in conversation.

Cautiously, I sidestepped to my right and crept along the empty perimeter of the office space. We'd never used that area, even when Liam owned the business. It had dim lighting and our predecessors could have easily utilised it as a storage facility. Although a decent place for me to hide, the three of them were so engrossed in conversation, I doubted they would spot me, anyway. They bent their heads together over Luke's computer screen.

I stood back, deeper in the shadows, watching from afar. Their voices were hushed, their expressions serious as they leant in closer, their words obscured by the distance between us. I strained my ears, trying to catch snippets of their conversation, but it was no use. They stood too far away, and their conversation vanished into the air. Finally, I stepped over, clearing my throat and holding my phone aloft.

"Customers," I tutted, whilst doing my best to look at ease.

With a final glance at each other, William moved away and I noticed Luke swiftly click his mouse before the home screen reappeared on his monitor.

What were they looking at?

William soon made his excuses and said his goodbyes. I spotted one more glance and a knowing nod between him and Luke.

As the afternoon wore on, I couldn't shake the feeling that something was amiss, that there was more to their conversation than met the eye. With Luke engrossed in his work, I approached cautiously, unsure of how to broach the subject. "Hey, Luke. Can I ask you something?" I said, my voice tentative.

Luke looked up, his expression guarded. "Sure, Adam. What's wrong?" he replied, his tone giving nothing away.

I hesitated, searching for the right words. "I couldn't help but notice you and William talking earlier. What was that all about?"

Luke's demeanour remained impassive. "Oh, he was just interested in what kind of project I'm working on. Nothing important," he responded.

I nodded, trying to hide my disappointment as I realised it was futile to probe further. "Okay, thanks," I said, averting my eyes before moving away, yet still glancing back in time to catch Luke wink at Kevin.

30

THAT EVENING, when William and I were alone in the living room, I broached the subject again, unable to shake the feeling of secrets at my expense. "So, what did you find so interesting at Luke's desk earlier?" I asked.

William's gaze altered slightly with what I presumed was guilt. I'd caught him off guard. "Oh, it was nothing," he replied. "Merely some work-related stuff."

I frowned, my frustrations deepening. "But you seemed pretty engrossed in whatever you were looking at."

William shrugged, his eyes now avoiding mine. "It was just a passing interest, that's all. You have no reason to worry," he reiterated. "His code looked complicated, so I was just asking him."

"Oh," I quickly replied, barely letting him finish. "Luke said you were interested in the project he was working on, not how complicated the code looked."

Kat and Edwina joined us at the moment I considered I had William on the ropes. I could see he was struggling as he fidgeted and the palms of his hands ran up and down the arms of his chair.

"You both okay?" Edwina enquired, slowly easing herself down into my favourite armchair and ruining my chance of any further probing of her husband. Instead, I watched as she grimaced and I knew her hips were causing her pain.

Normally, I would have felt some sympathy and maybe offered to prop her upright with the help of a cushion or two. But after William's pathetic attempt to conceal the truth, and the sight of Edwina making herself so at home, I caught myself smiling at her discomfort and only wished William would suffer a similar fate.

That side of me was rising rapidly to the surface, and I knew I had to somehow restrain it. And so, with every ounce of willpower I could muster, I fought to keep myself in check. But it was becoming a constant struggle, a delicate balancing act. Nonetheless, I knew it was necessary that I curtail those emotions before they consumed me once again.

The next day, I managed to escape a family trip to the park, instead suggesting I wanted to remove the unsettling sight from our front door. Officer Rodriguez said the paint looked water based, and a good amount of warm water and soap, as well as some serious elbow grease, should eventually shift it. Kat, Tom and William, who suddenly carried an energy defying his years, headed off, whilst Edwina again sat in my chair ready to immerse herself in a new romance novel. Her hips were still causing her too much pain to venture far from the house.

"Can I get you anything?" I asked. It took all my

strength to express myself politely, and I silently prayed she would decline.

"A nice cup of tea would be lovely," she replied, a genuine look of gratitude on her face.

When I returned to the living room, a drink in hand, Edwina was watching me, her expression unreadable. After placing the cup and saucer on the small table next to her, she gestured for me to remain.

"Adam, can I talk to you for a moment?" she asked.

My heart skipped a beat, a sense of dread settling over me. What the hell could she possibly want to discuss with me? And why did she sound so serious?

"Of course. What's on your mind?" I replied, trying to keep my voice steady.

Edwina took a deep breath, her gaze not once leaving mine. "I hope you don't mind me asking," she said. Her words were carefully measured, as if practised a thousand times inside her head.

"Go ahead," I responded, dreading what might come next.

"Can I ask the last time you and my Katrina were intimate? You know, in the bedroom?"

What the actual…

"I'm sorry," I said, my eyes widened with incredulity. "What kind of question is that?"

But Edwina's expression didn't change. Instead, she picked up her book and flipped it to the back as if to read the blurb on the cover, although she soon made it clear she had no intention of doing so.

"A woman has needs," she continued. "And my Katrina is no different." She stopped looking at the novel and turned her attention back to me. "You need to keep her happy, Adam."

"With all due respect, that has absolutely nothing to

do with you." My face burned with anger. "You need to keep your opinions to—"

She held her arm aloft, cutting me off mid-sentence. "That's all I wanted to say. Now," she smiled, as if we'd been discussing the weather. "I'd like to read my book in peace."

As I stepped away, bewildered by the conversation I'd just been part of, I considered what Kat's parents could truly want from me? The fact that we never agreed in the past was always on my mind, but their sudden fascination with my every move was making our already strained relationship even more uncomfortable and worrisome. It was as if they were taunting me, trying to provoke a reaction. But why?

First, when we'd visited their home over a month earlier, they'd grilled me about work. Later the same night, William *happened* to be passing our bedroom door as I spoke to Kat regarding their behaviour. And then, the day they arrived at ours, William turned up unannounced at the office and I caught him in deep conversation with Luke and Kevin. Finally, Edwina took it upon herself to grill me about my intimate relations with her daughter. What kind of mother-in-law asks such impertinent questions?

As I rubbed the warm, soapy sponge up and down the front door, I imagined a world without my enemies. Would that make life easier?

William and Edwina were old, fragile, and easy targets. If only I could get them on their own. I contemplated how easy it had been to bring Pauline's and Bob's sorry existence to a conclusion, a brief smile forming across my mouth.

"Daddy!" Tom screamed from the end of our foot-path, jolting me back to the present. Kat was just behind him, out of breath and trying to keep up. Then I noticed William bringing up the rear, a good twenty metres down the road. But as I concentrated my efforts onto Tom again, I soon recognised what the excitement was all about.

"Where did you get that?" I asked, looking at Kat for some kind of explanation. She shrugged her shoulders.

"Grandad found it," he said, bouncing his blue Chelsea football up and down on the path.

"What do you mean, Grandad found it?" Again I looked at Kat. "Did he buy him a new one?"

"No!" Tom snapped on her behalf. "I just said. Grandad *found* it."

Right on cue, William joined us. His breathing was laboured, and I secretly hoped he might collapse in front of me. A little something to bring some joy to my existence.

"That's true," he said between long drawn-out breaths. "It was in the copse, wasn't it, son?"

Son? Don't you dare call my child, son.

Tom persisted in bouncing the football on the path, the rhythmic thud echoing relentlessly in my ears. I glared at him to stop, but he continued regardless.

"What do you mean, in the copse?" I asked William, desperately trying to keep my growing fervour under control. How could it have been in the copse? I searched the area thoroughly, didn't I?

"Well," William persisted, his voice animated and that annoying grin returning to his face. "Tom pointed to the spot where he thought you'd lost it, so I took a stroll into the trees. It wasn't that far inside." He stepped past me, his breathing still heavy, not helped by the fact that he couldn't get his words out fast enough. Still, Tom played with the football, and with each bounce, my irritation grew further, a mounting frustration like a pressure cooker about to explode. I flinched as William patted me on the shoulder. "Are you sure you checked properly, old boy?"

He strolled inside the house, leaving me alone with Kat and Tom. I glared at her for some kind of explanation, but again she shrugged her shoulders as if agreeing with her dad.

And that left Tom. Concentration was etched across his face.

"Tom!" I screamed. He finally looked up at me. "Stop bouncing that fucking football!" I shouted before storming off around the rear of our house.

31

AFTER WAKING ON SUNDAY MORNING, I left the house before anybody else stirred, attributing my early Saturday night to tiredness from the effort of removing the paint from the door. I'd scarcely crossed paths with Edwina and William after my outburst, not daring to discuss the former's preoccupation with her daughter's bedroom activities and avoiding the latter revelling in his arrogant triumph over discovering Tom's football. I knew Kat would be furious with me, but her lack of compassion was becoming just as irritating as the actions of those who were determined to make my life hell.

Closing the front door behind me, I took a moment to inspect my handiwork in daylight. I'd stayed outside until dark, removing the red paint until my arms ached, but at least it saved me from having to converse with my in-laws. Kat did bring Tom to see me before bed and I hugged him tightly and apologised for swearing. He nodded sympathetically, but even he had a look in his eye which suggested a lack of trust. What was I doing? The others I could cope without in my life, but the idea of becoming isolated from my son consumed me with dread.

As I trudged through the relatively deserted Sunday morning streets towards the underground, I couldn't shake the rising anxiety that gnawed at my insides. It had been a restless night, filled with tossing and turning, haunted by my past and the uncertainty of the future. Soon, my mind returned to the unsettling conversation I'd had with Edwina the previous day.

Had her comments got to me? I couldn't deny that they had struck a nerve. Part of me was angry; angry that she would dare to discuss such a private matter in such a casual manner, as if it were any of her business, but beneath the anger lay a seed of doubt, a nagging voice which refused to go away. Despite it being none of her business, I still wondered whether she was right. The prospect filled me with a feeling of self-loathing, a fear that I was failing as a husband, as a partner, as a man.

But was it all Kat's doing? Had she put her mother up to it, hoping to shake me out of my self-imposed isolation? The thought irritated me. A sense of betrayal.

I had once loved Kat more than anything in the world, but since what happened, our relationship had become strained, initially frayed at the edges by my feelings for Imogen. And although those sentiments refused to leave me, was there something else pushing me further away? It felt as though Kat had grown tired of waiting for me to come back to her, tired of playing second fiddle to the ghosts of my past.

Ever since she suggested it, the thought of seeking professional help had been lingering at the back of my mind. Perhaps I needed someone impartial to confide in, someone more than a shoulder to cry on, like Luke and his overly optimistic attitude towards everything he heard.

Despite my attempts to reconnect with him, I couldn't shake the feeling of being used, especially after catching him in conversation with William and exchanging knowing glances with Kevin behind my back.

But the idea of seeking expert advice filled me with anxiety, a fear of exposing my darkest secrets to a stranger. What if they judged me? What if they delved so deep into my past that I crumbled and confessed to all?

With Kat's parents' train departing from St Pancras at just after eleven, I wanted to avoid them until they left our house. The time spent in their company made me feel unsettled, much as it had a few weeks earlier.

After rambling without purpose for a good hour, I spotted the entrance to our local park, and a sudden surge of anticipation coursed through me. I needed answers. Time to think, and the solitude of the park seemed like the most logical place to start.

It was where so much had happened, most notably where Imogen confided in me she was leaving Liam. And as I stepped inside, our meeting felt like it had taken place the day before. She looked crestfallen, yet a ray of hope appeared in her eyes as she faced me, only a step between us. Briefly closing my eyelids, I tried to picture her perfect features. Her mouth, her shiny, immaculate hair, and those captivating eyes which were the most beautiful I'd ever seen.

Then, a side of her emerged I had never witnessed before. She suddenly looked beaten, and appeared on the verge of tears, her gaze fixed on the ground between us. Without thinking, I reached out and held her hands until she raised her head to meet my stare. She appeared utterly disheartened, and it required all my strength not to pull her close and embrace her.

"Adam. There's no easy way to say this."

"What is it? Please, just tell me."

"I'm leaving Liam," she replied, her eyes flickering between me and the ground below. "And I wanted you to be the first to know."

As I recollected the hug that followed, I felt tears prickle from somewhere deep inside my eyes. Why hadn't I fought for her? Why had I let her slip away so easily? And as I attempted to push back those hideous thoughts, a wave of anger surged within me. Couldn't Kat have just knocked the scissors from Imogen's hands rather than striking her so venomously on the head?

A child ran out from the bushes to my right, scaring the hell out of me. I cursed her before I noticed what I assumed was her mother, chasing her out of the under-growth, still laughing. Catching me swearing, she threw me a scathing look, her eyes narrowing with disapproval. As she reached her daughter, she scooped her up protec-tively, shooting me a final, condemning glare before hurriedly retreating. My anger knew no boundaries, and it frightened me I hadn't changed at all. I'd just become more paranoid, more afraid, and, as in my youth, more isolated.

As I approached the cluster of trees where William had supposedly found Tom's football, further confusion crept into my mind. It seemed too convenient, too perfect. Did William know who hid it, or was it simply lying there, waiting for him to stumble upon?

Could someone else have been there the morning before, someone who knew Tom and his grandad would be at the park, and had deliberately placed the ball exactly where William couldn't fail to find it? But who? And why?

With a sense of determination, I stepped into the copse, scanning the ground for any signs of disturbance.

But try as I might, I found nothing – no footprints, no traces of someone else's presence.

I pictured William's animated grin. *"Tom pointed to the spot where he thought you lost it, so I took a stroll into the trees. It wasn't that far inside…"*

Doubling back on myself, I left the copse, and re-entered a little further along. Again, nothing. I repeated my actions another two or three times, beginning my search from a fresh entrance point each time, but my foraging was useless.

Frustration bubbled up inside me, my mind racing. Who was behind all of this? And what did they hope to achieve by tormenting me in this way?

Finally giving up, I begrudgingly left the park where, only minutes earlier, I'd entered with a little enthusiasm. How quickly such eagerness could dissipate from my thoughts. Instead, I trudged home. Even my pleasure at the prospect of seeing my son was waning.

32

———

The police called around later that afternoon, a few hours after Kat and Tom had escorted her parents to St Pancras station and set them on their way. Neither of us mentioned them when she returned.

The officers wanted to give an update on their investigations into the paint-throwing incident. However, the *update* soon transpired into a *"we've got fuck all to tell you session."* They had nothing. I doubted they even put much effort into their enquiries.

As they made it clear there was little else to discuss, Kat asked if that would be the end of the matter. Officer Anderson confirmed his doubt that any fresh evidence would come to light, and without it, he couldn't envision how to progress the investigation.

"Of course," he said, as they slowly stepped in tandem towards the front door. "If anything else happens, or you feel you are being targeted in any other way, then be sure to call us immediately."

I glanced at Kat, and as soon as I looked back at the officer, I knew he'd spotted me. My cheeks flushed.

"Do you have anything you wish to share, sir?" he asked in an authoritative voice that I always found people in power somehow acquired.

"No," I replied far too quickly. "Sorry, no. Nothing else has happened." I turned to Kat. "Has it, darling?"

She glared at me as if to tell me to calm the fuck down.

"No," she reiterated, fixing on a smile for the officers. "Nothing at all."

As soon as they left, Kat repeated Officer Anderson's question. "Has something else happened that you're not telling me about?"

Retreating to the kitchen, I shook my head. "Nothing has happened, Kat."

"So why did you look so bloody guilty in front of them?" she probed, quickly catching me up before retrieving two coffee capsules from the box. She lifted them in her hand to silently ask if I wanted one. I nodded.

"Well, what about the football?" I asked. "I looked every damn where for that."

Kat tutted exaggeratedly before placing a fresh mug underneath the machine and loading a capsule into the top.

"Not that again," she said. "Who the hell would wait in the trees, steal a football, and then put it back where they found it a few days later?"

I shook my head. "I don't know, Kat. I really don't know. But that's exactly what—"

She stopped what she was doing and turned to face me. Her expression was a mixture of concern and exasperation. "No, Adam. That's not *exactly* what happened. The ball went into the trees and you couldn't find it. Dad went in and by the time he got there, the leaves or something else had moved so he spotted it straight away. If you'd gone to the park with us, you would have found it." She jabbed her finger at me to ram home the fact that I chose not to be with them that day.

It was on the tip of my tongue to tell her what her mum said whilst they were at the park, or the feeling of being watched wherever I went. But it was useless. If I brought up the past, she would inevitably revert to me needing help. And then she would link it to my ongoing feelings for Imogen.

To be fair, on either count, she wouldn't be far wrong.

33

———

"COME IN," I said, taking a small step backwards to allow Luke to pass. He smiled his usual exuberant gratitude and stepped by me, carrying a bunch of fresh flowers in one hand while the other gripped the handle of a holdall flung across his back. Ignoring what could be inside, I moved to close the door, but as I did, I noticed a car pull away. Quickly, I strode outside and watched as it disappeared around the corner and continue its journey towards the city.

"That was my taxi," Luke said as I returned indoors. He hadn't budged, waiting patiently for me to direct him to wherever he needed to be.

It was a few days after the police had come round and the Friday evening when Luke had finally accepted our invitation for dinner to meet Kat. Although it gave me some respite from everything else, the prospect of spending time making small talk wore me down as the days ticked slowly by.

Like most subjects, neither me nor Kat mentioned the officers' update again, nor did we discuss anything else of

142

importance. I'd kept things to myself and tried to ride the storm and hopefully come out the other side unscathed. Who was I kidding?

"Ah," I replied, trying to determine his reasoning. "I thought you would have got the tube. A cab must have cost a fortune?"

"I was running late," he said. If he was lying, he was bloody good at it. "I should have travelled with you after work, as you suggested."

The sound of footsteps alerted us to Kat approaching from behind. After a quick smile at me, he turned to face her.

"You must be Luke," she said rather stupidly. Who the hell else were we expecting? "I'm so pleased to meet you at last."

"Likewise," he replied. "I've wanted to meet you for ages."

Why the fuck have you wanted to meet my wife for ages?

"These are for you, Mrs Chapman." He held out the flowers.

"Oh, my," Kat said, momentarily flummoxed. "Thank you." She admired the bouquet before sniffing the vibrant petals. "They're beautiful."

She moved away rather abruptly. It seemed a little too quick, rude even, and I realised she must be blushing. "Oh," she called over her shoulder as she hurriedly made her way back to the kitchen. "Call me Kat. I don't like that Mrs Chapman rubbish."

Luke turned to me again, lifted his eyebrows and shrugged his shoulders. It was as though the initial exchanges were going exactly to plan.

After meeting Tom, and asking all the right questions about school and football and his favourite games, we excused our son to watch some TV whilst "the adults had a meal at the table." Tom had already eaten, and despite taking an obvious liking to Luke, grown-ups could still be boring in his own little world.

Kat did most of the talking, and Luke remained polite and inquisitive throughout the evening. Initially, the conversation flowed around work, but Kat obviously wanted to get to know him better and enquired where he lived, where he grew up and what he'd been doing since we parted ways fifteen years previous. If anything, Luke was somewhat evasive, only volunteering the vaguest of details. He was similar when Kat probed him about his personal circumstances, but even I intervened at that stage and said not to embarrass him.

At close to midnight, I lay awake, waiting for Kat to join me. I was in our room, not the spare one, because Luke was going to be sleeping in there, wasn't he?

After dinner, and an hour after Tom had gone to bed, Kat asked if Luke would like to stay over. We'd had a few drinks, and he conveniently had some spare clothes in his holdall. I considered it was something he must have prepared for, in anticipation of an invitation, especially when he almost snapped her arm off and jumped at the opportunity. A while later, a combination of genuine tiredness and boredom threatened to overwhelm me, and I made my excuses to retire upstairs, hoping it would be the catalyst for us all to do the same. However, Kat suggested a nightcap, and again, Luke readily accepted. They barely glanced in my direction as I left them alone.

Eventually, after a lot of giggling and muffled voices from downstairs, I heard the distinct sound of footsteps on the stairs which proceeded quickly along the landing as they traipsed past my door.

"You're in here," Kat said, obviously tipsy and failing miserably to keep her voice low.

"Thank you," Luke replied, a definite sincerity in his tone.

Then everything fell quiet. For far too long. I shuffled uncomfortably, hunching myself up onto my elbows, straining my ears. Finally, our bedroom door opened, and I flopped down and closed my eyes tight. I didn't say a word to Kat, which appeared to suit her fine.

At three in the morning, I woke with a start, sitting bolt upright. I instantly looked to my left, and there was Kat, sound asleep, her breathing steady.

Another creaking floorboard outside on the landing alerted me to what must have stirred me. Believing it must be Luke on a toilet visit, I allowed myself to lie back down, listening, my eyes slowly becoming accustomed to the dark.

Patiently, I awaited his returning footsteps. But they didn't come. As earlier, I hunched myself onto my elbows, sensing something was awry. Where the hell was he? Even if he needed a number two, he shouldn't be taking that long. Perhaps he'd gone downstairs to get a glass of water? But again, how long would that take?

Finally, I lifted my side of the duvet and slowly slid out of bed. With another quick glance at Kat, I shuffled across the floor and opened the door with the faintest of clicks. Leaving it off its latch, I stepped onto the landing and noticed the spare room door was ajar.

Where the fuck is he?

Creeping along the landing, the first door I came to was Tom's. I peeked inside and aided by his nightlight could make out his untroubled face, fast asleep. After leaving him in peace, the last door was the bathroom. It was closed, but there was no light escaping from underneath. Either Luke was sitting in the pitch dark or he wasn't in there at all. A sound from downstairs alerted me to his whereabouts.

Slowly, I descended the steps, desperate not to alarm him, but equally intrigued by what the hell he was doing. And finally, I found him in the lounge.

But he didn't notice me. Instead, he stood at the curtains which were opened a few inches in the centre. Wearing only a pair of boxer shorts, his back to me, Luke stared intently through the gap. He was looking directly at the house opposite. Imogen and Liam's house.

34

———————

"Shh. Don't wake him," Kat whispered.

She tapped me on the shoulder, making me jump from my skin. How the hell had she reached me without creating a sound?

"What the—"

She immediately pushed her finger to my lips.

"Shh," she repeated. "He must be sleepwalking."

I looked from Kat to Luke and back again.

"Sleep—"

"Shh," she insisted. "Go back to bed. I'll see to him."

With a thousand questions on the tip of my tongue, I glanced over at Luke again. Was Kat right? I'd never seen anybody sleepwalking before, but he appeared to be in some kind of trance, totally oblivious to two people within such proximity. Reluctantly, I did as I was told and tiptoed back upstairs, leaving our bedroom door ajar. I remained at the opening, ready to pounce if something untoward unfolded. Goodness knows what I considered *untoward*.

Minutes later, I heard footsteps ascending the stairs. I stood frozen in our dimly lit bedroom, only the light from downstairs creeping up to illuminate the landing, casting elongated shadows from the balusters. A chill raced down my spine at the sight unfolding before me as Luke came into view, closely followed by Kat, her palm hovering over the centre of his bare back. His eyes were shut tight, his movement erratic, swaying from side to side as if being pulled by invisible strings.

But then something changed. I watched in fascination as he neared my bedroom, his hand brushing against the wall as if seeking guidance in the darkness. My heart hammered in my chest, the sound so loud I was convinced it would wake him. And then, as if sensing my presence, his eyes fluttered open.

For a moment, time seemed to stand still. His expression was vacant, yet there was something desperately unsettling about it, a knowingness that sent shivers down my spine. And then, to my horror, a twisted smile spread across his lips.

I recoiled instinctively, my breath catching in my throat as I scrambled backwards and fell onto the bed. The fear coursing through my veins was palpable as I watched him disappear towards his room, leaving me wondering if I'd just imagined the entire thing.

"What the fuck is wrong with him?" I asked Kat after she closed the door behind her. I spoke as quietly as I could, although I found controlling my emotions was getting harder by the day, by the hour. Nothing appeared normal, my resolve forever being stretched to its limits.

"There's nothing wrong with him," Kat said, as if discussing what we might have for breakfast. "He's just disorientated. It's pretty common, especially if you wake suddenly in a strange house."

"Kat," I said, pulling the duvet tight to my chest. "He just fucking smiled at me as he walked by."

Removing her dressing gown, she climbed in beside me, making herself comfortable. "That's either in your imagination, or he was dreaming as he passed you. As I say, it's all pretty normal."

Why was she dismissing everything I said as pure conjecture? Or was the issue with me? I considered that Luke could have been dreaming. When he first appeared, he had his eyes tightly shut. And when we found him downstairs, he just stared through the curtains, lost in his own world.

"Why did it take you so long to come to bed tonight?" I asked, changing the subject while staring at the ceiling in the dark.

"What?" she demanded, propping herself onto one elbow. I instantly felt vulnerable, her sudden advantage in height making me feel uncomfortable. "We were talking. Luke was telling me where he's planning to go on holiday next year."

"Not downstairs," I replied, maintaining my casual stare. "After you showed him to his room." I turned my head to face Kat, her silhouette visible against the backdrop of the dim light emanating from the moon. "I heard you speaking, telling him where he was sleeping. And then it went quiet. For ages."

Kat shifted herself further upright. I could only imagine the look of thunder on her face.

"You need to get a fucking grip," she scowled.

"Shh," I replied, already regretting asking. "I'm sorry, okay?"

She slid back under the duvet, turned her back to me, and lay perfectly still, making it quite clear the conversation was over. However, as I lay staring into the dark, I realised she had never answered my question.

.   .   .

Luke left first thing in the morning. There was no mention of peering across the road to our old neighbour's house. I witnessed no further hidden looks between the pair of them, suggesting nothing unusual could have happened the previous night. Instead, everything was normal. The four of us ate breakfast together, and chatted about inane subjects and our plans for the remainder of the weekend. Luke intended to spend time online looking for flights to Croatia, the place he allegedly told Kat he wished to visit as they conversed late into the night. As I say, all normal, so what was that itch that I couldn't reach to scratch?

I spent most of the morning in the garden. I managed to steer clear of Kat, her superficial conversations, and her indiscreet questions about how I was doing. It also excused me from hearing about the one subject that had ceased to be the centre of my attention: the business. Kat couldn't stop discussing it. It even overtook the daily chatter regarding Tom and his schooling. She was becoming obsessed with it. Crunching numbers, analysing customer statistics. Her determination to succeed was palpable. I'd overheard her talking to her parents on Face-Time the previous weekend, their replies full of admiration and pride at their daughter's continued good work. Of course, I didn't get a mention, not a single note of praise, despite us being a data software house where I was the senior developer. The guy who made all the fucking money.

However, I had noticed something else during those recent days. Kat's fixation on the future of the company seemed to intensify further, but she became more secretive, more distant. After Tom went to bed, she would take her seat at a newly acquired pine desk at the rear of the dining room. She had also purchased a high-backed office chair, a flexible table lamp, and an external monitor to save on eye strain. It was quite the setup, although I never asked how much it all cost. But, unlike Kat, money no longer bothered me. A few months earlier, it had been my driving force, almost my sole purpose in life. But we were pulling in different directions, and it felt as though we were living separate lives under the same roof, such was her quest for success. It's why I'd kept the phone call a secret. The call I received during William's impromptu visit to our office a week earlier. But I also knew I couldn't keep it a secret for much longer.

35

On Monday morning, as I stepped into the office, the familiar sights and sounds of the workplace greeted me, but, as always, my mind was elsewhere. Before I could even settle at my desk, Kevin's voice cut through the air, pulling me back to the present.

"Recovered from your night with Luke?" he asked casually, a hint of what sounded like sarcasm in his tone.

I froze. How did Kevin know Luke had been to our house? Fortunately, Luke hadn't yet arrived. But before I could formulate a response, Kevin continued. "I rang Kat on Saturday while you were in the garden. She mentioned Luke spent the night with you guys."

My mind raced. Would he be upset because we didn't invite him too? He certainly did not appear that way, quite the opposite. More pleased that he knew something I didn't expect him to. But why hadn't Kat mentioned it to me?

"What did you call Kat about?" I asked.

"About work, of course," he replied, as if he found the question utterly ridiculous. Kevin leant back in his chair

152

and folded his arms across his chest, tucking both hands inside. "What else would I be calling about?"

"Why didn't you contact me if it's concerning work? And what couldn't wait until Monday?"

I knew I had to calm down, but as I glanced around the office, the sense of unease that had plagued me returned with a vengeance. It felt as if there was something going on, something I couldn't quite put my finger on. And try as I might to ignore it, I couldn't shake the feeling that I was being scrutinised by unseen eyes. But who was watching me? The question swirled around in my mind.

"Hey, Adam," Kevin replied, his smile tight, lacking any warmth or sincerity. "Chill out, pal." He unfolded his arms and leant forward, propping his elbows on the desk. "I called to speak to you, but as I say, you weren't available. So I spoke to Kat instead. I need to leave work before lunch, and I didn't want to wait until this morning to spring it upon you."

A flush spread across my cheeks. "Oh, okay," I stammered. "I had no idea. Sorry."

Kevin clicked his mouse to bring his monitor back to life. He began tapping at a few keys as I unpacked my laptop. But still he wasn't quite finished, and he had one last twist of the knife up his sleeve.

"I'm surprised Kat didn't tell you." He looked up again, that familiar smirk on his face. "Don't you two talk to each other?"

Throughout the morning, I caught myself staring at him. My growing dislike towards Kevin simmered beneath the surface like a pot ready to boil over. There was something about him, something unsettling since the day he joined us. It wasn't just the way he always seemed to know more than he let on. It was something deeper, something darker, that unnerved me more.

Why did I agree to take him on in the first place? However, wasn't it Kat's recommendation, a suggestion that had appeared innocent enough at the time?

"So," she said, her back to me. "What do you think of my idea?"

"What idea?" I replied.

"Taking on Kevin Doyle, of course."

But now, as I recollected that decision, I couldn't help but wonder if there was more to it than meets the eye. Had Kat known something I didn't, something that made her so eager to bring Kevin into the business? And then there was his girlfriend, the girl I still hadn't met. Did she even exist?

However, whatever my opinions on Kevin Doyle, there was very little I could do about it. We had too much work to allow him to leave, and besides, he was good, a fast learner and he required a minimal amount of my time on a day-to-day basis. Replacing him with someone new might take weeks, months even, and then longer still to get them up to the same level. Not only that, how could I explain to Kat that I let him go? On what grounds? He could take me to a tribunal if I didn't have something significant on him.

You've been there before.

As I stared at him through the glass panel, the phone rang on my desk, a shrill sound that cut through me. Kevin looked up just in time to catch me watching him.

"Hello?" I said, nodding towards Kevin.

"Adam Chapman?"

I recognised the voice immediately. Priya Singh from the Equity Alliance Group. The call I'd been dreading.

"Hey, Priya." I leant forward on my desk, rearranging a stapler, attempting to mask my anxiety. "How are you?"

Priya's tone was far from friendly. Her tone was grave, confirming my worst fears. "There's been a development," she began. I glanced at Kevin again, irritated that he was still staring at me, as if trying to eavesdrop.

"What development?" I asked, stepping over to the door and closing it softly. I avoided Kevin's gaze entirely.

"It's about what we discussed before," Priya replied. "When I called you a week or so ago."

"Go on."

She reiterated what I already knew. Her company had been made aware of my background and recent issues. When I pressed for specifics, she said her board of directors was concerned about my role in the business. The more I questioned, the more Priya clammed up. She repeated it wasn't anything unethical with our organisation, but purely personal.

"What exactly have you found out?" I asked, frustration mounting. "Purely personal? That's unfair—"

"Adam," she interrupted, her tone firm but measured. "Someone contacted me. They said you may have issues—"

"That's not true," I shouted, pacing to the window. "Who told you that?"

Priya remained calm, waiting for me to finish. "Let's wait and see. If it's nothing, then we can reconvene. However, my board has decided that if you weren't part of the company, the deal would still be on."

"What do you mean?" I demanded, my voice cracking. "Are you saying the deal is off?"

"For now, Adam," she replied firmly. "Yes, it is."

36

———

As soon as Priya hung up, I called Kat. Her reaction only made things worse.

"Have you lost the bloody contract?" she asked after I recounted the conversation, omitting the most damning parts about me. I explained it was more about our background. Despite guessing what her response would be, I still couldn't believe Kat wasn't more supportive.

"No, I haven't lost the bloody contract. How can you think this is all my fault?"

"Personal, Adam. Personal. The clue is in the word."

Kat rarely swore, but I could imagine her at home, pacing as she spoke.

"It could be you," I replied defensively. "She said they've done further due diligence into our background. Someone might know about you, too."

"Me?" she laughed sarcastically. "It's you, Adam. You're paranoid, thinking people are setting you up, watching you. You've been a nervous wreck for months. Priya must have noticed. Your unstable behaviour. She said it's personal." She paused. "Is this about Imogen?"

I stood abruptly and paced my small office. "Imogen? What are you talking about?" But my voice wavered.

"Can you fix this?" Kat asked, ignoring the previous topic. "Or should I call Priya myself to reassure her?"

Although I suggested she could try, I knew it was futile. Priya had decided, or at least her board had. They wouldn't proceed with us unless I left the company. But if it was really about me, when had I given Priya the impression that I was unstable? And if I hadn't, then somebody else must have contacted her, casting doubt on my mental health and advising against trusting us with the contract as long as I was involved.

The sound of knocking on the office door startled me. Kevin poked his head around without invitation.

"Yes?" I asked abruptly. He looked slightly taken aback.

"Sorry to interrupt, but I need to get off now."

I'd already forgotten he was taking time off.

"Okay," I said with a flick of my wrist. "You go. Have a nice day."

Kevin smiled amicably before looking at the phone on my desk. "Everything okay?" he asked. It appeared genuine, and I recalled all those times with Liam when we were on the verge of losing the Wheelwright Solutions contract. Maybe Kevin was as worried as I'd been about the future.

"Yeah," I replied, again with no conviction. "Just a blip. Nothing we can't handle." I tried to remain upbeat. "Are you doing anything nice this afternoon?"

He glanced at the phone once more, as if it held all the information he required, something I obviously wasn't willing to share. "I'm meeting Victoria. We're going to look at a flat together."

"That's great," I replied. "Exciting. Where is it?"

A glimmer of enthusiasm flashed across his face. "Not too far from where she works now, actually. Near Liverpool Street. She's found an apartment."

"Nice area," Luke called from behind him. The sound of him intervening, physically obscured by Kevin, caught me unawares.

"Thanks, mate," Kevin replied, spinning around and adding a little more inflection to his voice. "Aren't you house hunting, too?"

Luke stood so I could see him, or more likely, so he could see me. "Yeah, I am actually. A place near you, Adam, as it happens."

Something stirred inside. Again, with no evidence to back up my theory, I couldn't help but wonder why he would choose anywhere close to me. "I didn't realise. You didn't say."

"I've been looking around for a while, and when you said you lived somewhere convenient for work, I thought I'd have a look."

Did I say that?

"So," he proceeded, paying no attention to my confused stare. "I had a look at a flat after I left you guys on Saturday morning. Didn't Kat tell you?"

Luke's face held an expression of one-upmanship and I'm sure Kevin smiled smugly, too.

"Kat? Why would she tell me?"

He glanced at Kevin. "Because I left my electric toothbrush at yours," he continued, a bemused tone to his voice. "I called in on my way back to the station. She said you were out."

"Right," I replied, my mind slipping into overdrive. Not only did Kat not inform me about Kevin phoning, but now Luke had called round too. Why hadn't she mentioned it? But was it so inconsequential it wasn't worth alluding to? If he had just knocked on the door and she'd passed him a bloody toothbrush, maybe she'd forgotten. But hold on. *"She said you were out."* I wasn't out. I was in the garden.

"Yeah," he said, dripping in that unmistakable air of superiority once more. "She makes the most wonderful coffee, your wife."

He sat back down and returned to his work, leaving me to only envisage his look of gratification in getting one over on me again. What had Kevin said to me earlier that very morning?

"I'm surprised Kat didn't tell you. Don't you two talk to each other?"

Was he right? Did we not talk enough? Was it normal not to discuss visitors or phone calls, especially if they held little significance? However, putting it another way, why would you withhold such information from your partner? One reason. Because you didn't want them to know. But again, why? Why not tell me that Luke dropped by to pick up his toothbrush, or more importantly, that he'd been to look at a flat near our house? And he stayed for coffee, too. How long is that, twenty, thirty minutes? So why not beckon me in from the garden, inform me he was there?

My mind drifted back to the phone call with Priya.

"Someone contacted me. They said you may have issues…"

37

AFTER KEVIN LEFT, I paced the tiny office, my thoughts fixated on the contract with the Equity Alliance Group. What would we do now it was lost? I needed to speak to Kat to check if there was enough work to justify keeping on both Kevin and Luke. And now they were both bloody house hunting, no doubt buoyed because we had just landed a massive deal, it made everything even more fraught.

Kat was angry with me, but I was equally angry with her. And then another thought hit me. Did she suggest Luke look for a place to buy near us because that's where *she* would like him to live?

Quickly, I donned my jacket, pushed down my laptop lid, and left my office. One or two of the staff looked up and nodded in my direction. After all, it was lunchtime, and they would only presume I was popping out to grab something to eat. I smiled back, but inside my stomach was doing somersaults.

Once outside on the streets, the first thing that hit me was the cold, late November chill. The wind had picked up since morning, and I guessed the breeze was from a northerly direction, given the biting edge it carried. I almost laughed at my reference to meteorological terminology. What the hell did I know about wind and how fucking cold each direction conveyed?

After strolling into Regent's Park, I called Kat and asked whether she had contacted Priya yet. She had tried, but to no avail. Priya obviously didn't want to discuss the matter any further with anybody from our company. She'd made it clear. The board had decided. Kat was still angry with me and I therefore concluded it probably wasn't the best time to quiz her about Luke calling round. But thinking straight was something I no longer did.

"He called for his bloody toothbrush, Adam. Why the hell are you asking me about that?"

Before I even finished my question, I knew I'd made a mistake. But there was no backing down. "I'm just surprised you didn't tell me, that's all."

Kat sighed heavily down the phone with an exaggerated humph.

"Kevin also said he phoned on Saturday," I continued, pushing my luck as far as it could go. "Told me he had asked for this afternoon off. It made me look stupid, Kat. He even questioned if we talk to each other, and to be frank, he has a point."

"Well, whose bloody fault is that?" she replied.

The silence soon became overbearing. I suddenly felt eyes on me and smiled at a couple of passers-by, convinced they knew what my call was about. I considered asking whether they would take my side, surely having sympathy with the guy whose wife no longer conversed with him. Ignoring them, I walked back out of the park only minutes after strolling in. Kat speaking snapped me from my reverie.

"So," she began, her voice even and in control. "You honestly think me not telling you about Luke dropping by for a coffee, or Kevin phoning to take an afternoon off…" she paused. "And I have every right to sanction his time off, by the way." She got back on track. "You genuinely believe all of that much more important than losing a client the size of the one you have lost all by yourself?"

"Come on, Kat. That's not…"

I fell silent, my attention drawn away by the sight of the car turning the corner and slowly approaching, completely interrupting my train of thought.

"Adam?" Kat called down the line.

My eyes followed the vehicle. It didn't increase its speed, instead crawling by me at no more than a snail's pace.

"Adam? Are you there? We need to talk…"

"I'll see you later," I said, absentmindedly pulling the phone from my ear. It wasn't until the white BMW disappeared from view altogether that I remembered I was still connected to Kat. I pressed the *call end* button without even checking whether she was still on the end of the line.

38

____

Now and then, I found myself drawn to the office window, peering outside in search of any sign of the elusive white car. Frustration gnawed at me, a relentless itch that refused to be scratched. I cursed myself for not jotting down the registration number, but even if I had, the chances of tracing the owner seemed slim at best. After searching online, I discovered no easy way to track down a keeper of any vehicle: data protection made it nigh on impossible. The idea of hiring a private investigator briefly crossed my mind, but what would I be paying for? There was no concrete evidence to suggest that the car had anything to do with me, only my usual overly suspicious thoughts.

By three o'clock, I'd had my fill of futile speculation, though the prospect of returning home filled me with a sense of dread, too. Facing Kat and the possibility of interrogation about the Brighton contract, or my irrationally anxious state, was the last thing I needed.

Stepping outside, I scanned the bustling streets, my eyes darting nervously from side to side in search of the ambiguous BMW. But despite my vigilance, there was no sign of it anywhere. Moments later, the Sunset Wine Bar beckoned me invitingly inside as I walked past, the bitter-sweet memories of happier times ricocheting around my thoughts.

I recalled the Friday nights spent there with Liam, our continual laughter as we shared a few drinks and swapped stories. In those early days, it had been just the two of us, lost in conversation about work, sport, and everything in between. Liam was fun to be with and had a knack of drawing people in with his easy-going manner.

But beneath his jovial exterior lay a side I despised, forever chasing girls hoping to prove his ongoing masculinity. He loved to flirt and would chat with any woman who crossed our paths. And yet, for all his boasts and bluster, I could never understand why he wasn't content with Imogen. In my eyes, she was perfect, yet Liam seemed determined to test the limits of her patience at every turn.

A good hour later, after endlessly strolling around the streets surrounding our office block, I boarded the tube and began the familiar route home. But once I rounded the final corner, a wave of foreboding settled over me, as I immediately sensed something was amiss. It wouldn't be until I reached the front door that my heart skipped a beat, and I detected that Kat and Tom were not alone inside.

Sure enough, as soon as I turned the handle and pushed the door open, I heard the familiar laughter of my wife, quickly followed by Luke's dulcet tones. What the fuck was he doing there again?

"You're home early," Kat announced, looking a little flustered as I stepped into the kitchen to join them.

"Where's Tom?" I asked, ignoring her remark. I

glanced at Luke. He appeared somewhat sheepish as I caught him taking a step back from Kat. They were hovering at the worktop, two empty bottles of beer before them.

"He's at Max's house, remember?"

I didn't recall any such arrangement, and I shook my head slowly. However, the very mention of Max's name made me think of his mother. I still had her number.

"Call round anytime. It can be lonely on your own."

"At a sleepover. I told you last night," she added, a hint of annoyance in her voice. But I genuinely couldn't recall her saying anything. I would have remembered if Tom wasn't coming home. I would have enquired what his plans were.

"I don't think you told me. I would remember something like that."

Luke's eyes drifted to Kat as if he doubted me, as though he was searching for some kind of confirmation that I was again confused.

"Well," Kat continued, collecting the two empty bottles before dropping them into the recycling bin. It also allowed her to put further distance between herself and Luke. But why were they standing so close when I arrived? "I one hundred percent let you know last night. You specifically asked what time we need to collect him tomorrow." She let the bin lid drop with a bang, making me flinch as my nerves jarred further. "You even said you wouldn't mind going."

Unsure why I couldn't remember any of what Kat was saying – I certainly would have volunteered to go – I instead turned my attention to Luke.

"And what brings you here?" I asked, trying to remain neutral, although realising my tone was far from it.

"I called round after viewing the flat. I arranged

another appointment after our chat with Kevin in the office. He made me realise I need to act quickly when it comes to buying property in London."

"Right," I replied, not really knowing what else to say. It didn't help that Kat stared at me scornfully, as if I was making it quite clear that he wasn't welcome in my home.

"You should perhaps think before you speak," she eventually said before turning to Luke and smiling warmly, apologising on my behalf. "Would you like another beer?"

"I'm good, thanks," he replied rather nervously. He glanced at me before addressing Kat once more. "Listen, it's probably best if I get off." His eyes flickered between us. "I don't want to cause any trouble here."

But Kat was having none of it. "Nonsense," she said, straightening her back and standing tall as if to show her authority. "I've said you're welcome to stay the night, and you will."

Stay the night? Again?

"Do you mind, Adam?" he asked innocently, like the perfect child who would never hurt a fly. What the hell was his game?

"No…" I paused. "No. It's not a problem at all."

"That's sorted then," Kat said, collecting two fresh bottles of beer from the fridge before passing one to Luke and clinking his with her own. She didn't even offer me one.

"I'm going to grab a shower," I called out as they recommenced their conversation and laughter. Although I didn't hang around to see, I'm sure neither of them acknowledged my disappearance. Instead, I wearily made my way upstairs, contemplating why on earth he would be stopping over again, and wondered if he had deliberately set up the flat viewing so he could visit our house without my presence. Could he have followed me when I left the office and knew I would be a while wandering aimlessly around?

As I trudged along the landing, I noticed the spare bedroom door was ajar, and sat on the floor was Luke's rucksack. Again, it made me wonder if he'd set the entire thing up. Who takes a bag with them everywhere they go, especially with overnight gear inside?

While standing still, I arched my body sideways to listen for sounds from below, and I was soon reassured that they were still engaged in deep conversation in the kitchen. His laughter made me cringe. The same infectious laugh that I once found reassuring, knowing how relaxed he was in my company and how at ease he felt. But now the tables were turned, and he seemed to love being in the presence of my wife instead, and in turn, she adored his company too.

Unsure why, I quickly dashed into the spare room, picked up his holdall and placed it on the bed, my hand gripping the handle, holding it upright. Carefully, I slid the zip apart in both directions until the front flap dropped forward, exposing the contents at the top. With a quick glance over my shoulder, I pulled it further open, trying to see within, and yet having no idea what I expected to find.

Lifting out a jumper, I saw a shirt plus one or two other items of clothing, neatly folded. Realising I couldn't start taking stuff out without making it obvious someone had been delving around inside, I instead slid my hand down the back of the clothes. Rummaging about, I felt something small and square. Tracing it with my fingers, I discovered three prongs sticking out, soon realising it was a charger, most probably for his phone. I searched again and gripped the spine of what was obviously a book. A hardback book. Slowly, I dragged it along the rear of the rucksack, careful not to spill any contents from the top. It was a novel by a well-known author. I quickly thumbed the pages, unsure what I was actually looking for, but my heart still raced with anticipation. But I found nothing, despite hanging it upside down and shaking it vigorously.

Reluctantly, I returned the book to the back of his holdall, dejected yet determined to find out what Luke Wilson's real motive was.

39

"FEEL BETTER AFTER A SHOWER?" Kat asked, her voice infused with what sounded like genuine concern, her eyes softening as she waited for the response. I wondered if she felt guilty about how she'd greeted me earlier, or whether the beer had made her mellow. Glancing at Luke who was sat at the table, tapping the keys on his phone, I forced a smile in her direction.

"Yeah, good thanks," I replied, although my voice didn't match the intended enthusiasm. Luke looked up, no doubt detecting my apprehensiveness. Kat stopped preparing whatever she was cooking, hopefully not a plate full of vegetables, especially as we had a guest.

"You sure? You sound worried," Kat probed.

"I'm good," I reiterated more firmly and stepped over to the fridge. Grabbing a beer, I lifted the bottle to Luke to ask if he wanted one, too. He shook his head, saying something about having to compose a message to the estate agents about the flat, although I wasn't really listening. "Kat?" I asked, repeating the gesture with the bottle.

"No thanks. I've had two and they've gone straight to my head."

She giggled and looked over at Luke. His eyes momentarily left his phone, and he smiled before returning to his all-important text.

After popping the top off my beer, I took a long swig and strolled over to the table.

"So, where is this flat exactly?"

My sudden cordial demeanour caught him off guard, and he anxiously glanced past me at Kat. Why did he need her bloody approval to answer my question?

"Er, it's about four blocks from here," he stammered. "It's really nice." His eyes flickered around the room as I stood over him. "In fact, I made an offer when I was there." He lifted his phone and turned it to me. "The owner accepted while you were taking a shower."

"Isn't that wonderful?" Kat interlocked her arm into mine. I hadn't even heard her approach, although I realised she was trying to help Luke out as his words tripped over one another. "We'll virtually be neighbours."

"That's great," I continued in an upbeat tone. "Have you got the address?"

For just a moment, the room fell silent, a brief pause that made me believe he was reluctant to share it with me.

"Yeah, sure." He recomposed himself. "Hang on."

Kat let go of my arm with a tug. She glared at me, her eyes narrow and her forehead scrunched, as if to say, 'What's your game?' and I shrugged my shoulders in return. "Just interested, that's all."

Luke passed me his phone, a photograph of the exterior of the block of flats occupying the screen. I quickly swiped through the other pictures and read a little of the description. I knew where it was, only a five-minute walk from our house.

"Looks nice," I said, returning his mobile. "And you'll be living there alone?"

His eyes widened, and a fleeting moment of astonishment flickered across his face. "Of course I will." His tone matched his look of surprise. He glanced at Kat again. "Who else would be there?"

Kat stared at me once more, obviously as keen on my reply as Luke.

"Just wondered, that's all. I just didn't know if you had a partner. It's no big deal."

I heard Kat sigh as she returned to the worktop and began chopping an onion. I watched the knife as she effortlessly chopped it into symmetrical pieces. Luke's eagerness resurfaced, and he cleared his throat to regain my attention. He informed me that because the flat was vacant, and he was effectively a first-time buyer, he could complete in as little as six weeks. He already had a mortgage agreed in principle, and the price he'd negotiated on the flat meant he needed less than he'd anticipated. It was all simply a formality. Luke would live along the road in just over a month's time.

"That's wonderful," I said, now bored by his news. "We'll be able to travel into work together."

"Yeah," he replied, his mood swings changing like the British weather. He glanced over my shoulder to Kat. "I'll definitely be seeing more of you guys once I move in."

40

Unlike the previous occasion when Luke stayed over, we all headed to bed simultaneously. Kat's cooking provided a welcome departure from our customary vegetable-heavy fare, and Luke seemed to enjoy the homemade chicken curry too. Later, we settled down to watch a new movie on Netflix, providing a much-needed break from the usual work-related chatter or inevitable discussions about Luke's flat.

His presence had at least diverted Kat's attention from grilling me about the Equity Alliance deal, a subject that I realised would be discussed as soon as we were alone. With both Luke and Kevin in the process of buying property, if we had to let either of them go, it would only be fair to tell them before they signed on the dotted line. However, instead of having a negative effect on me, the prospect of informing both of them they were no longer required kept my spirits intact.

During the film, I caught Kat looking at Luke a couple of times, although he didn't appear to notice. Once the movie finished, she stood abruptly and announced she was going to bed. I looked at her, surprised by her sudden movement.

"Thanks for having me," Luke said, standing too. "Think I'll retire too. I'm knackered."

"Anytime," Kat uttered, a smile returning to her face. Was she craving his attention? "We'll be able to stay at your place soon," she added with a playful grin.

At least Luke had the decency to blush slightly, glancing at me awkwardly before nodding to Kat.

A few moments later, I heard them in the kitchen, grabbing a glass of water whilst discussing the movie we'd just watched.

"Good night, buddy," Luke said, peering around the edge of the open door before following Kat upstairs. They were like a fucking couple and I was in the way.

"Yeah, good night," I called after him, attempting to listen in to whatever they were giggling about as they climbed the stairs.

Within minutes of lying down, I fell into a deep, dream-filled sleep. Kat had already drifted off by the time I emerged from the bathroom. However, like the last time Luke stayed over, I jolted upright about three hours later, my heart pounding.

"What the fuck?" I muttered, my breathing erratic.

Instinctively, I looked at Kat's side, but she wasn't there. Just an unoccupied space and the duvet pulled back. A distant voice snapped my attention away from the empty spot and towards the sliver of light seeping from beneath our bedroom door. My heart quickened as I strained to hear more, the faint sound of talking unsettling me.

I eased myself out of bed, a knot of dread forming in

my stomach at the thought of Luke sleepwalking again. The memory of that eerie smile spread over his face flickered through my mind. But where was Kat?

With painstaking slowness, I opened the bedroom door, peering cautiously through the gap until the landing came into view, illuminated by a light from downstairs. Steadying my nerves, I tiptoed across the carpeted floor which fortunately muffled any noise.

As I descended the steps, the definite sounds of Luke reached my ears. My heart pounded in my chest as I approached the kitchen. With trembling hands, I pushed it open, expecting the eerie outline of Luke, walking slowly, arms outstretched like a mummified creature from an old horror movie. But instead, probably more to my dismay, he sat at the table, a glass of water in his hand. And sitting beside him was Kat.

At first, a sense of relief washed over me as he appeared calm and in control, yet the sight of them together, barely dressed, made the hairs prickle on the back of my neck. "Kat?" I whispered, my voice hardly audible in the stillness of the room.

She turned towards me, her expression weary, mixed with a hint of disappointment. "Couldn't sleep," she muttered. She was wearing a flimsy negligee revealing an awful lot of cleavage, leaving very little to the imagination. Luke sat beside her, uncomfortably close, and just as the time we caught him staring across the street, he was nearly naked, wearing only a pair of boxer shorts.

I nodded towards Kat's chest, attempting to make her realise exactly how much flesh she had on display. She glanced down momentarily before looking back up and smiling directly at me.

"What, neither of you could sleep?" I said, stepping into the kitchen. I flipped the light switch, causing all three of us to close our eyes instantaneously with the sudden burst of brightness. "That's a bit convenient, isn't it?"

Kat stood, finally lifting her top a little higher. Luke didn't move from his seat, again forcing my mind into overdrive.

"Don't be childish, Adam," she said, collecting her glass from the table and taking it over to the sink before refilling it. "I heard Luke wake, and I thought he might be disorientated, that's all."

I looked from Kat to Luke. He remained speechless, his expression lacking any emotion. I couldn't gauge what was going through his head at all. "I thought you might be sleepwalking again," I eventually said.

Luke looked at me, as if stunned by my remark. "Again?" he asked. "What do you mean, sleepwalking *again?*"

Quickly, I tried to recover. "Oh, it's just the last time you stayed, we caught you walking around the house in the middle of the night."

Kat shuffled uncomfortably next to me.

"I didn't sleepwalk the last time I was here," Luke insisted. He looked at Kat for reassurance.

"You did," I said, although losing conviction by the second. "Kat helped you back to bed." I turned to her. "Didn't you?"

Unbelievably, she shook her head. "You must have dreamt it, darling," she replied. "Luke didn't sleepwalk."

My eyes continued to flicker between them. Were they playing a joke? Trying to wind me up? But they both looked deadly serious.

Finally, Luke stood. I noticed Kat watching his near naked body. My hands clenched in and out of fists.

"Thanks for the water, Kat," he said nonchalantly.

She nodded and smiled.

Then he looked at me. "I'm still wide awake. I think I'll go and read my book."

Did he know I'd been in his bag? He had stared directly at me as he declared his intention. Coincidence? But more importantly, what about the sleepwalking? How on earth could I have imagined that? Kat had instructed me to leave him alone.

"Shh," she whispered again. "He must be sleepwalking."

I looked from Kat to Luke and back again.

"Sleep—"

"Shh," she insisted. "Go to bed. I'll see to him."

Had he been sleepwalking at all, or had she told me that to get me out of the way? My mind was doing cartwheels, my palms felt as though I could wring out the sweat.

"Kat," I said as she eventually climbed into bed next to me. She had been in the en suite a long time. Doing what?

"Uh-huh," she replied, rolling to face me.

"Did you just try to protect him, you know, when you said he hadn't sleepwalked last time he was here?"

She tutted aloud. "Not that again. Just let it go, Adam. I honestly don't know what's wrong with you."

Again, I cursed under my breath. *What's wrong with me?* It's what was wrong with everybody else that was causing me so much bloody concern. Why was everyone in denial, counter arguing everything I said?

"And why were you sitting downstairs with him? It's the middle of the bloody night." She remained silent in the dark. "And what were you wearing? Nearly naked next to him."

Finally, she moved, inching nearer until her hands met mine.

"Turn you on, did it?" she asked seductively. "I noticed you looking."

"What?" I replied, astounded by her reply.

She lifted my hand and pushed it down her top.

"And does this turn you on?" she said, moving her face closer to me until I could feel the warmth of her breath on my cheek. Reluctantly, I admitted defeat as she won me over. It was as though she was draining any last fight I had left inside me. She kissed me deeply before sitting up and lifting her negligee over her head and dropping it to the floor. Then she slowly pulled down my boxer shorts before inching herself on top of me, groaning as I slid inside her. We hadn't been intimate for months and at that moment I realised how much I'd missed her; or was it someone else? Closing my eyes, my mind drifted. That time with Imogen in her spare room…

It wasn't until Kat lay back by my side, her arm straddling my chest, that I considered she too had not been thinking of me.

Then I heard what distinctively sounded like a floorboard creaking outside on the landing.

41

―――――――

BREAKFAST WAS DIFFICULT, the conversation stilted and the atmosphere thick. I noticed Kat and Luke exchange the occasional look but couldn't determine whether it was anything to do with their middle of the night rendezvous or just trying to think of something to say. Whenever I spoke, they would immediately stare at me, as if afraid of what I might utter next. Perhaps they harboured doubts about why I'd suggested Luke had been sleepwalking and their concern for me was genuine? But I somehow doubted that. Luke didn't care about me, of that I was now certain, but what were his true intentions? Was there something sinister at play? The uncertainty gnawed at me, my trust in him evaporating by the day. That chance encounter in the bookstore.

As we exchanged pleasantries, I couldn't shake the feeling that something was off. Was the meeting more than just an accident – that perhaps Luke's presence was intentional?

I turned my focus to Kat. Was she in cahoots with him? But why? Purely sexual attraction? A retaliation for what happened between me and Imogen? And now he was moving in only a few blocks away; had it been Kat who found the flat and suggested it to him? But she wouldn't play with fire like that, would she? It could have such a detrimental effect on the business to begin with, and that was her sole concern. Then again, the prospect of me not being around to screw up future contracts could easily have the opposite effect. But would Luke be interested in raising Tom? He'd gone through life living alone and such upheaval surely wasn't on his agenda. Again, I considered Kat too shrewd to risk everything for a fling. And then I pictured them sitting together, near naked, downstairs in the middle of the night. Also, that prolonged silence when she showed him to his bedroom the first time he stayed. And why was he staying over so damn much?

Scraping my chair back, I noticed them both flinch. I poured the near full contents of my cold coffee down the sink and placed the mug into the dishwasher. It sparked Kat into life too, and she cleared the table. I took it as my opportunity to go upstairs and brush my teeth. But as soon as I closed the bathroom door, I heard the distinct sound of conversation flowing again, quickly followed by laughter. It felt as though my presence was making them awkward and they were much more relaxed without me around.

Attempting to ignore it, I instead looked in the mirror and saw the reflection of a man who appeared to have aged considerably during the past nine months. Lines were etched deep into my face, dark shadows lingered beneath my tired eyes, and the weight of unspoken worries seemed to stoop my shoulders. It felt as though my world was collapsing around me and there was nothing I could do to stop it.

I told myself I wasn't going mad. If anybody was crazy, it was them, not me.

I knew what I'd heard, what I'd seen. Kat had definitely told me Luke was sleepwalking. They'd also had a secret meet up in the dark of the night. And what about the other occasions where my sanity could be questioned? Somebody had certainly been roaming around the rear of Imogen's house carrying a flashlight. Kat's parents were undoubtedly interfering and showing far too much interest in both my professional and personal life. The sudden appearance of Luke Wilson after years of non-communication. A bloody white BMW sat outside my office block. Tom's reappearing football. And the one thing nobody could deny, a tin of red paint daubed over our front door. To top it all, someone had tipped off Priya Singh that I wasn't of sound mind.

Who could I turn to? Kat dismissed everything I said as pure conjecture. She even told me to get professional help, and she appeared to be moving on without me. There was nobody else. I was in this alone.

As I stood before the mirror, confronting the worn and sad individual staring back at me, I knew something had always been eating away at me deep inside. I had history. A blemished upbringing spending far too many hours and days wallowing in self-pity in the bedroom at Aunt Cynthia's house. Far too many thoughts can linger deep in your psyche when you spend so much time alone.

My troubles began long before I met Kat, and years before I set eyes upon Liam and Imogen Daley. Maybe the demons needed taming once and for all.

You've got history, Adam. It's why you found it so easy to kill again.

42

The bitter wind sliced through my coat as I trudged along the icy pavement towards Aunt Cynthia's house. The thick clouds overhead threatened to release a fresh blanket of snow at any moment. Even the weather appeared to mirror the desolation I felt inside.

Clutching the crumpled Christmas card in my hand, the cheap paper crinkling between my fingers, my anger seemed to build with every step I took. The card was the annual reminder of Aunt Cynthia's distant acknowledgement, a stark contrast to the warm memories of growing up with my mum and dad. The recollection of running downstairs on Christmas morning, my squeals of excitement that Santa Claus had carried out his duties and dumped a pillowcase full of presents down our non-existent chimney. Mum and Dad would saunter through, their eyes barely open, cursing that it wasn't even six in the morning. Mum would rub my hair and tell me it was because I'd been a good boy whilst Dad lit up a cigarette and inevitably began coughing his guts up. Those endless times I searched for reassurance from Mum, and she would simply smile, nod, and then light one up herself.

So, as I warily made my way towards my aunt's house, the crumpled card in my hand only added insult to injury, arriving just *days after yet another redundancy notice from a dead-end job I'd been clinging onto for far too long.*

It was a record year for me. Three jobs, three redundancies, or three sackings, if the truth be told. I'd had no interest in any of them. 'Office Junior', 'Assistant Van Delivery Man', and finally, 'Door-to-Door Insurance Salesman'. Salesman! Me! Jeez, I couldn't drum up the enthusiasm to sell ice cream to kids on a scorching hot day. No, my heart lay in computers and I needed the cash to buy one and teach myself how to use it. Then I could find a job in IT, a job with prospects, a job that paid serious money.

As I approached Aunt Cynthia's house, the memories of my time living with her came flooding back, each step echoing with the weight of years of resentment. She had raised me with an iron fist, her strict rules and harsh discipline shaping me into the withdrawn, lonely man I had become. It was the first time I had visited since I left home four years before.

With my heart pounding, I knocked on the door, the sound echoing through the silent street. The door creaked open, revealing Aunt Cynthia's stern face, her disapproving gaze piercing through me like a knife. She resembled someone who had seen a ghost. A ghost from the past that she had never wanted to set eyes upon again.

"What do you want?" she snapped, her tone as icy as the winter air.

I swallowed hard, steeling myself for the confrontation I had been putting off for far too long. "I need to talk to you," I said, my voice even, desperate to keep it under control.

Aunt Cynthia's eyebrows shot up in surprise, but she stepped aside to let me in. Expecting a roaring fire, or radiators turned to the max, an icy chill greeted me instead, barely any different from the streets I left outside. I breathed hard, watching a cloud of vapour escape like the smoke from my dad's cigarettes.

We sat in a dimly lit living room, the only sound the ticking of a clock on the wall. As it always did, it told the wrong time, a point-

less accompaniment to the otherwise empty space. I took a deep breath, gathering my thoughts before speaking.

"I need to know why," I began, my voice trembling with suppressed emotion. "Why did you raise me the way you did? Why were you so strict, so unforgiving?"

Aunt Cynthia's expression softened slightly, but there was still a steely resolve in her eyes. "I did what I thought was best for you," she replied, her voice displaying no regret. "You needed discipline, to prepare you for the harsh realities of the world."

"But you've made my life miserable. A hell," I protested, the years of pent-up anger bubbling to the surface. "I have no friends, no existence outside of my four walls. You took away my childhood, and for what?"

Aunt Cynthia's lips tightened into a thin line, her silence speaking volumes. It was a silence I had grown accustomed to over time, a refusal to acknowledge the pain she had caused.

Tears stung my eyes as I realised the futility of our conversation. Aunt Cynthia would never accept responsibility, would never recognise the damage she had done.

But as I stood to leave, the weight of years of resentment still heavy on my shoulders, I knew that closure would remain elusive. Some wounds ran too deep to ever fully heal.

"I need some money," I disclosed. "I need to buy a computer. To invest in a future for myself."

"Ha!" she snapped. "I never thought I would see you again, and yet here you are, pleading for money." She stepped towards the living room door and opened it for me to leave. "Look after yourself, Adam," she said, her eyes avoiding mine as I walked past. "Just like your mum," she continued. "Always begging me, she was. And always for another packet of cigarettes. Oh, the irony."

I snapped. Bringing my mum into it was not on the agenda. She had no right to use her name against me. Years and years of grieving, only topped by the strict and lonely upbringing of my aunt, crashed down on me with the force of a tidal wave, overwhelming me. I screamed, the sound echoing off the walls, reverberating throughout the entire house like a thunderclap.

Frantically looking around, I grabbed the poker from the fireplace and recall it being freezing cold to the touch. My aunt gripped the doorknob as though her life depended upon it, her eyes mesmerised by the long, black steel object I held above my head.

The last thing I remember was her imploring gaze as I brought the instrument down with such force I momentarily congratulated myself for the strength I held. Once on the floor, I hit her several more times, only forcing myself to stop once her yells of anguish halted completely. The blood was already seeping into the threadbare carpet around her skull.

Quickly, I ran upstairs to her bedroom, suddenly fearful that what I just did might have been in vain. There! Her jewellery box, with chipped white paint and glass top, cracked down the middle. Lifting the lid, the ballerina popped up, already in a pose, yet she didn't spin. No music played. The fucking thing was broken when I lived there, so I knew she wouldn't have repaired it since.

My hand shook as I lifted out the red felt top layer containing cheap earrings and a couple of worthless necklaces. They weren't what I was after, but underneath was the treasure I sought.

I quickly counted the notes. Over five hundred pounds in hard cash. More than enough to get a decent computer.

With one last glance at the lifeless body on the living room floor, I left via the back door and the alleyway that ran along the rear of the row of terraced houses. Nobody was about. The neighbourhood was full of old folk and it was bloody freezing outside. After discarding the poker in the local canal, I went to a nearby computer store, one of those that fix them and sell spare parts, and did a deal for a near new PC he had just taken collection of.

43

ONCE I DROPPED Tom and Max off, I resisted the urge to call Lauren to enquire if her offer was still on. She asked if I would like to go back to her house after seeing the boys safely to school. There was something about her that put me at ease, a sensation I hadn't felt for a long time, and I craved more. Yet I hesitated, wary of crossing boundaries and falling into old patterns. Was I truly ready for that? Resisting the temptation to grab my phone, I instead headed to the tube station, determined to keep the promise I had made to myself earlier that morning.

After changing lines at Notting Hill Gate, the underground train soon emerged from the tunnels of the city and out into the suburbs of West London. The carriage was almost deserted by the time I disembarked at West Acton station. Once outside, a light drizzle greeted me, and as the cemetery was a good thirty-minute walk away, I grabbed a coffee at the station kiosk and ordered an Uber.

As I finally approached the graveyard, a sense of

melancholy enveloped me, matching the dreariness of the November day. But despite the chill, I felt a bead of sweat trickle down my back, my heart beating faster as I reached my destination. The dampness seeped into my bones as I made my way through the cemetery entrance, a stone archway, which gave the impression of something much grander on the other side.

The air was thick with the aroma of wet earth and decaying leaves mingling with the distant sound of traffic from the nearby streets. The gravestones rose at all angles, jutting forwards and backwards. I tried to read some inscriptions, but apart from the occasional year of passing, I found it impossible to distinguish who lay below from the majority.

I pulled my coat tight around me, desperate for its warmth as I trudged along the moss-ridden footpaths, but as I turned the final corner, I was certainly not ready for what greeted me.

My steps slowed as I reached the path leading to Imogen's grave. The sight before me left me dumbfounded. Fresh flowers adorned the otherwise barren ground, their bright yellow petals stark against the browns of the soil below.

As far as I knew, I was the only one who ever visited Imogen and Liam's grave. They had no relatives, and from the extremely sparse attendance at their funeral, no friends made the effort, either. But it was the realisation that *somebody* had been there, someone probably unbeknownst to them, which disturbed me the most. Questions raced through my mind, although none had an obvious answer. Who could have left the bouquet? And why then, after all that time?

With hesitant steps, I approached the grave, the fresh

scent of the flowers mingling with the damp earth. As I knelt beside the headstone, I couldn't shake the feeling that somebody might be watching me, hidden behind a gravestone or one of the dismal-looking leafless trees.

Glancing around, I picked up the fresh bunch of yellow roses and searched for a card tucked away inside the cellophane wrapping. But there was nothing. No clue as to who left them. I'd certainly told no one I ever visited, but did somebody know I'd left flowers on three previous occasions? And where were those flowers? I realised they would be dead, wilted and brown, but it definitely hadn't been so long that they would have rotted altogether. And then I remembered.

All three bunches contained a personal note from me. A handwritten message to Imogen as I struggled to put into words how much I missed her and how sorry I was for everything that happened.

Fuck.

Had Kat visited? That may explain her sudden obsession with Luke, as well as her disregarding all that was happening to me. Her sudden interest in him living close by. Was she seeking revenge? Then again, could somebody act so childishly just to get even?

Reluctantly, I trudged back along the cracked pavements, my head bowed as the rain fell harder. But as I approached the stone archway and the cemetery exit, something stopped me in my tracks for a second time within minutes. There, in the waste bin, were several discarded bunches of flowers, and lying on top were mine. I quickly retrieved the first one, spinning it around, desperately searching for the small square card tucked inside a plastic pouch to save it from the elements. But it wasn't there. The next bunch, too.

So, the person who laid the beautiful yellow roses took time to clean the grave and dispose of the dead plants. But it didn't feel like a good deed, a genuine attempt to keep things tidy. Instead, whoever it was, knew I had visited and would undoubtedly visit again soon, and they ensured I realised they had read my messages to Imogen.

44

———

MY PHONE VIBRATING STARTLED ME. I dashed for cover underneath the stone archway and my heart sank as I retrieved my mobile and saw the caller ID. I also noticed seven missed calls from the same person.

"Kat!" I exclaimed, far too theatrically. "What's wrong?"

"You can start by telling me where the hell you are."

She was deadly serious, and I instantly knew something was awry.

"Er…" I looked around me, suddenly fearful she might spring from behind a gravestone. "I came for a walk. I couldn't face work."

Kat's sigh rang heavily down the line. I heard a stifled voice and soon recognised who it was once he spoke again, this time much clearer.

"Are you with Luke?" I asked, stepping back out into the rain, yet somehow oblivious to the downpour.

"Yes. I asked him to come round. I've tried calling you over and over, but you never picked up. I was really worried, Adam."

"So worried you called Luke? Not Lauren, not—"

"Lauren? Who the fuck is Lauren?"

I rapidly scurried under cover; the rain running down my back and sending my entire body into shivers.

"You know, Max's mum. Surely she would have been the person to call to check if I was okay?"

"Oh yeah," Kat replied sarcastically. "I noticed how much you stared at her when she collected Max from Tom's birthday party. Did you know her husband left her recently?"

Shit. Surely she can't know? There is nothing to know. Yet.

"Call round anytime. It can be lonely on your own."

"Are you there?" Kat called down the line.

"Yeah, yeah. No, sorry. I did not know about her marital situation. Why would I?"

It was Kat's turn to fall momentarily silent. I heard something bang and Kat whisper, "Thank you.".

"Kat?"

"Yes, anyway," she recovered. "I got Luke to come round. We need to discuss the business. Now you've..." she stalled. "I mean, now we've lost the Brighton contract, I've been crunching the figures again."

"Wait," I interrupted. "Is Luke within earshot?"

"Yes, why?" she asked like there was no other possible answer.

"Because it's our bloody business, Kat. It's none of his concern." I knew I was raising my voice, and if they were sitting at the table together, there was every chance he was overhearing everything I said. But what right did he have to be involved in the finances of the company?

"Luke is very experienced, actually," Kat replied with a hint of a smile in her voice. I could just imagine them sitting there, looking into each other's eyes as she dished out compliments. I visualised them holding hands across the table, him giving hers a gentle squeeze as she bestowed her commendation upon him. Maybe he was in his bloody boxer shorts again; so what was Kat wearing? "He's run businesses before," she interrupted my overactive imagination. "Similar to ours. I thought he was the ideal person to ask."

My mind raced with intrusive thoughts. Every detail seemed to fuel my unfounded fear. I tried to focus on her words, but the image of them together was too overpowering. My stomach churned as jealousy and hatred gnawed at me.

"And what does Lord Luke suggest we do? Make himself a director and take the shares off my hands?"

"Don't be so bloody facetious," Kat replied, the irritation returning to her voice. "It's a damn good job I called him. He has a contact in the City and thinks he can persuade them to give us their business. It's not as big as the job you lost, but it will certainly allow us to maintain our current staffing levels."

I heard Luke say something before the connection appeared muffled.

"Kat? You still there?" I called down the line.

"Adam? It's me. Luke."

"Oh. Hi," I replied. The rain was coming down even harder, and I had to stand with my back pinned against the cold stone of the arch to stop it from soaking me. It was almost as if Luke himself were pinning me to the wall.

"Listen, mate," he continued in that self-assured tone, which was infuriating me more than ever before. "If you think I'm prying or treading on anybody's toes, then I'll back away immediately. Just give me the nod, buddy."

"No," I heard Kat plead in the background. "There's

no need for that." She raised her voice. "Tell him, Adam."

"No, she's right," I reluctantly agreed. "If you can help, it's all good."

"Great," he replied, that instant bounce back in his tone. He was like the perfect fucking human being that every single parent in the world would be proud of. I imagined William and Edwina approving as they tossed me out with the garbage. "What about we meet in the Sunset in about an hour to discuss it?"

"Yeah, that sounds like a plan," I replied, glancing at my watch.

"Okay," he said. "See you there." He passed the phone back to Kat, and she said her goodbyes, a little too swiftly. Did she have other plans to fill the hour before our hastily arranged meeting?

After ordering another Uber, I soon found myself heading for the tube and travelling back into London. The carriage rattled and squeaked before finally returning to the darkness of the underground tunnels, the contrast barely noticeable after the leaden skies. My mind drifted to the grave and who could have left the fresh flowers. They could only have been a day old. If it hadn't been for the stupid meeting with Luke, I would have hung around to see if anybody showed up. Maybe that was something I could do the next day, but how would I get away from the office again?

And then it struck me. Kat only asked where I was the one time. Why hadn't she pushed me for an answer? Did she even care, or did she already know?

45

My mind was awash as I stepped inside the Sunset. It was as if I was in a trance, going through the motions on autopilot, yet barely remembering the short walk from the tube station to the wine bar.

"Hey, buddy," Luke said, slapping me on the back. It made me recoil and my irritation towards him instantly resurfaced.

"Luke," I replied noncommittally, my eyes looking straight through him. "Good to see you." I recalled him sitting downstairs with Kat in the early hours, near naked. The creaking of a floorboard outside our bedroom door. "Sorry if I was a bit off on the phone earlier," I lied.

"Think nothing of it," he countered. "I'm only trying to help."

"Yeah," I nodded slowly, glancing around the bar and thinking that I might have been followed. "Yeah, I know."

It wasn't until he returned a few minutes later with two ice-cold beers that I realised Luke didn't even enquire where I was when Kat called me. Did they both know, and was Luke the mystery flower deliverer?

"Thanks," I said as we found a table towards the rear. Thankfully, it was Tuesday lunchtime, and with the weather showing no respite, the Sunset was quieter than usual.

Luke clinked my glass with his before clearing his throat. "First things first, buddy," he said, his voice dropping to something near normal, so much so, I had to strain to hear. "I like you." I looked up from my bottle to see Luke beaming with that incandescent smile. His perfect white teeth and strong jawline were prominent. "And I like Kat."

I shuffled uncomfortably. What was his point?

"Yeah," I replied weakly. "We like you too."

Luke sat back and took a swig of his beer as if taking in what I'd said and trying to interpret its true meaning.

"Thanks," he continued, leaning forward once more. "And we go back a long way. That junior software role seems a long time ago." Luke looked me directly in the eyes and I shuffled in my seat once more. Did he know what happened? If he did, he wasn't letting on. "And I genuinely want to help. You've got a good little business there, and I think it can thrive, given time and the right amount of energy."

Energy? Who the fuck was he kidding? I had about as much enthusiasm for the job as a turkey on Christmas morning. "That's great to hear. Thanks, Luke." Saying thank you became harder with each passing moment.

The door swung open, allowing the sounds of London to seep inside. A young couple stepped in, maybe in their mid to late twenties, their sodden hair glued to their heads and their coats drenched from the rain. I watched as they peeled off the garments and shook them over the doormat. They both looked familiar, but me attempting to put names to faces was something from the past. I studied them as they hung their coats on individual pegs before heading to the bar.

"Someone you know?" Luke enquired. I turned to him and noticed he, too, was watching as the couple made their way across the floor.

I shook my head. "I don't think so. The guy looks like someone I've met before, but not somebody I could put a name to." I stopped staring after them and turned back to Luke instead. "So, this company in the City. Do you think they'll come on board?"

Luke spoke inanely for several minutes about some firm south of the river who he used to do business with. He'd never mentioned much about his past work experience, and if I had an inkling of interest, then maybe I would have pushed him. Instead, I allowed him to waffle, content with the sound of his own voice. As soon as he finished, I smiled broadly and said it sounded great. He nodded knowingly.

In the meantime, the couple who had entered before Luke's elongated spiel sat opposite, both drinking what looked like Coca-Cola. They positioned themselves on the far side at a table facing ours, and because of my damn paranoia, I could have sworn they'd done it on purpose.

Luke noticed me glaring at them. "Are you okay, mate?"

My attention snapped back to him. His face was full of concern. Mr Perfect to the rescue once more.

"Yeah, yeah," I stammered. "Yeah. I'm fine. It's just everything. Well, you know how it is?"

Luke looked at me incredulously, his eyes widening as he spoke. "Me? What do you mean, I know how it is?"

I took a swig of my beer. It was going flat and was no longer refreshing.

"You know? When we talked before, and you

mentioned that you were depressed? Around the time you left the company we both worked for."

He took a long drink before meticulously placing the glass in the centre of his beer mat. He shook his head slowly from side to side. "Not me, mate. Do I look like the kind of guy who gets depressed?"

Just as with the sleepwalking, Luke denied it all. I tried to recall exactly what he'd said, but the more thought I put into it, the hazier his actual words became. Had I imagined it? Had I imagined the sleepwalking too? If not, then what was his game? Trying to send me bloody crazy? Like the football, the plant pot. I was in danger of losing my fucking mind.

The couple stood and made their way to the doorway. The girl stared in my direction as they donned their still sodden jackets, before the guy said something in her ear and they both laughed. Finally, they opened the door and disappeared into the rain.

I turned back to face Luke, but he was already looking at me. He appeared to be trying to read my thoughts, his eyes boring into my forehead as if having the ability to see inside my head. It unnerved me considerably. I'd had enough. All those games and tricks, desperately striving to unhinge me further.

As Luke began talking about himself yet again, I vowed that if I ever intended to get my life back on track I needed to find out what the hell was happening. Luke fascinated me. His reappearance after all those years.

Waiting patiently until he finished his drink and returned to the bar, I quickly composed a text, unsure whether I was doing the right thing.

46

———

Tom squealed with delight as the cork rebounded off the kitchen ceiling. Kat yelped too, hugging our son as I half-filled two champagne flutes and waited patiently for the bubbles to subside before filling them to the brim. I splashed a little into Tom's orange juice to make him feel part of the celebration, too.

"Cheers," Kat said, clicking both my and Tom's glasses.

"Cheers!" Tom shouted back, taking a sip of his drink. His nose scrunched up and his eyes closed tight as the disgusting taste hit the roof of his mouth. Kat giggled and I couldn't help but smile, despite wanting to celebrate Luke's good work like I wanted a hole in the head.

"Didn't he do great?" Kat proclaimed after drinking half her glass in one. She held out her glass for a refill, a huge grin spread across her face.

"Really good," I replied, placing the bottle on the worktop. If she wanted any more, she could bloody well refill it herself. Or better still, get darling Luke to come round and have her drink out of a glass slipper.

"Well," she said, obviously picking up on my lack of enthusiasm. "It won't cover half of the Brighton deal, but it's a start, and it means both Luke and Kevin can go ahead with their flat purchases, with no worry about their financial futures."

Another little dig at my ineptitude. Why couldn't she accept some of the blame for the Equity contract, too? It was because of *our* past and what happened was why we lost that deal, and Kat had played an integral part in it.

My phone beeped.

"Not going to take that?" Kat asked, looking at my jeans pocket.

Reluctantly, I retrieved my mobile and saw I had a new message. Noticing me pause, Kat took a step closer, craning her neck to see the screen. Quickly, I put it back in my pocket.

"Junk," I said. "Yet another finance company asking if we want a loan or something."

Kat grinned and had another long drink. Even my lying would not spoil her moment.

"What a good job we took Luke on," she continued, retrieving the glass from Tom before pouring the contents down the sink. She refilled it from a carton in the fridge and placed it on the table in front of him, an action she had done so many times in the past, it was as if she was on autopilot. "And it's allowing you to take your time, Adam. Luke and Kevin are so reliable, we can trust them to keep producing the goods while you get over all that's happened."

I glanced at Tom to confirm that he was still engrossed in his game on the iPad.

"What's that supposed to mean?" I asked. "You think they are capable of coping without me? That I'm somehow replaceable in the business?"

Kat rolled her eyes before downing the rest of her champagne. She stepped to the worktop, collected the bottle, and refilled her glass.

"I'm not even going to talk to you when you're like this," she declared. "I'm off to watch a movie on Netflix and enjoy my champers." She raised her glass with a wry smile. "Now, could you run Tom a bath and make sure he's ready for bed in an hour, please?"

She kissed Tom on the top of his head and disappeared into the lounge. Tom looked at me as if wondering what my next move might be.

"Oh," Kat called from the adjacent room. "I forgot to tell you."

Glancing at Tom, I dreaded what might follow.

"Mum and Dad are arriving on Friday to stay for a few days." A moment's silence ensued as she awaited a response. My heart sank and my body slumped. Tom smiled. Pleased his grandparents were coming or happy because I looked so pissed off at the prospect?

"I said me and Tom would take them to the London Eye on Saturday afternoon." Another pause. "You don't fancy coming, do you?"

"Er, no thanks," I answered. "It's really expensive and I've been on it twice already."

"Thought as much," Kat shouted back. "Can you bring that bottle in here, please?"

I necked my drink and told Tom to be upstairs in five minutes.

Whilst the bathtub filled, I sat on the edge and read the text I'd received earlier. I was still unsure whether I was doing the right thing, despite my surprise that she got back to me so quickly. After adding a capful of luminous red bubble bath directly underneath the torrent of water,

I composed a reply and hit 'Send' before I could change my mind.

"Come on, champ," I shouted downstairs. "Your bath's ready."

"Okay," he called back, a hint of annoyance in his voice that he had to put down the iPad.

My phone pinged again as Tom entered the bathroom.

See you then. Look forward to it.

47

———

FRIDAY AFTERNOON CAME AROUND ALL TOO SOON. I was never one of those people who lived for the weekend, mostly because I had no friends to celebrate it with. What was the saying? *Work to live or live to work?* For me, it was definitely the latter. A loner, who, after leaving the confines of Aunt Cynthia's prison, spent far too many weekends sat alone in a bedsit watching the world go by from a tiny window. I had grown accustomed to the tedium of my existence, the relentless cycle of work and solitude. There were no plans to look forward to, no social engagements to break up the monotony. It was just me, alone with my thoughts, trapped in the constricting borders of my mind.

I often pondered the age-old question: what was the purpose of it all? Was there more to life than this endless cycle of work and isolation? I envied those who seemed to find meaning and fulfilment in their relationships and social interactions, while I remained adrift in a sea of loneliness.

There were times when the weight of my unpopularity felt like a physical burden pressing down on me. I always longed for a reprieve, a fleeting moment of connection with another human being that would offer some respite from the suffocating solitude.

But those moments were few and far between. As Friday afternoon faded into evening, I resigned myself to another weekend spent alone, with nothing but my own thoughts for company. And as the darkness closed in around me, I couldn't help but wonder if that was all there was to life.

Thank goodness I finally met Sandra Law. She was like a ray of light cutting through the gloom. Sandra differed from anyone I had encountered before – kind and always ready with a friendly smile or a sympathetic ear.

For a while, her presence brought a new meaning to my otherwise sterile existence. Whenever I interacted with her, even if only for a brief exchange, it was as if a weight was lifting from my shoulders.

In Sandra, I found a rare connection. She offered me a glimpse of hope and an understanding that I had been yearning for. We dated for almost two years, much to Luke's disdain. It was obvious he harboured feelings for her too, perhaps the reason why he kept in touch with her long after we went our separate ways after those days as junior developers.

But, as time passed, and the novelty of our interactions wore off, I grew bored with Sandra's company. The conversations became repetitive, mostly around moving in together, or even longer-term plans. What once seemed like fun and a break from the monotony was quickly becoming burdensome.

Meeting Sandra had been important to me when I needed it most, but as I continued to grow and change and finally develop some social skills of my own, I realised that our connection was not as deep or meaningful as I had initially thought. Despite her kindness and warmth, Sandra could not fill the void that existed within me, and eventually, I drifted away.

To begin with, I made subtle hints, cancelling trips to the pub or cinema at the last minute, but still she clung on, accepting my lamest of excuses. One day, I caught her crying in the office, Luke consoling her, his arm around her shoulders as she silently wept into his chest. He told me later that I should treat her with more respect and be grateful that such a fine woman would want to spend as much time with me as she did. I replied by informing him to mind his own fucking business.

Eventually, we separated. But like with everything in my life, I couldn't even do that properly.

"Any plans for the weekend, Kevin?" I asked as he and Luke packed away their laptops. I'd been isolated in my cubicle most of the day, desperately trying to write some meaningful code and get my mind back into what I was good at. But it was hopeless. I either couldn't concentrate, or more worryingly, couldn't remember the syntax of enhanced programming. It was as though I'd written nothing other than basic statements before. By mid-afternoon, I recalled my brief conversation with Kat from a few days earlier.

"You think they can cope without me? That I'm somehow replaceable in the business?"

And I knew it. I was dispensable. And watching Luke and Kevin tapping away on their keyboards all day only rammed it down my throat further. Had Luke spoken to Kat about me and my growing incompetence?

"Vic is dragging me to Ikea," Kevin replied, although he looked at Luke as he answered, as though he was the one who asked the damn question. I wanted to wave my arms and shout, I'm over here, but knew even that would be futile and the pair of them would glance at one another before breaking out into raptures of laughter at my expense.

"Ooh," Luke chuckled. "Tough luck, mate. Shall we send a search party if you're not out by midnight?"

I laughed, but it came out forcibly, as if even being happy was a step too far. They both looked at me, but neither joined in with my joviality. My cheeks flushed, and I wanted to help pack their bags so they could hurry away and leave me alone. Alone in my cubicle with the door closed to the outside world, the window nailed down to stop me from jumping.

"When are we going to meet this infamous girlfriend, then?" I asked, desperate to regain some credibility despite wishing they would fuck off.

"What?" Luke's eyes opened wide. "You haven't met her?"

I noticed Kevin look at the floor.

"No. Why? Have you?"

Luke glanced at Kevin and realised he'd put his foot in it. "Oh, sorry. I thought you'd met before I joined?"

I looked at Kevin again. In turn, he was looking at Luke.

"No," I replied. "We've never met. When did you get to meet her, Luke?"

"In the Sunset," Kevin interjected, his confidence returning, albeit slowly. "You weren't around those times," he addressed me.

"Those times? As in plural? Wow, how often have you guys got together?"

The revelation hit me like a hammer blow. It wasn't as though I particularly felt left out. Jeez, the prospect of making strained conversation with Kevin, Luke and the infamous Victoria was my idea of hell. But it was the fact they'd done it behind my back. Had they deliberately arranged the meetups when they knew I wasn't available or had they just organised them anyway and not invited me?

"It's like Kevin said, buddy," Luke took over. "You weren't around. I think it was when you were having all those discussions with the Brighton mob, or you had to pick Tom up from school. Anyway," he added flippantly, "it isn't a big deal." He glanced at Kevin. "I'm sure you'll get to meet her one day."

48

———

IT FELT like another arrow through my heart. A reminder of my latter childhood when everybody in the classroom invited each other to their birthday party, or the chatter on a Monday morning about the football match the boys had played in over the weekend, or the girls discussing what they'd bought during their Saturday afternoon pilgrimage to the shops. Everybody did something. Nobody stayed in their room from Friday night until the start of the new week. Everybody had a life. Except me. And now, over two decades later, the boys were still meeting behind my back. Sniggering about the way I acted. Laughing at the weirdo with no friends. But these two were supposed to be my buddies. I employed them. I paid their wages. I personally asked them to join us. And this was how they paid me back.

My rage was incandescent. I waited until Luke and Kevin left and slammed the door to my office. Storming over to the window, I watched as they strolled down the street, Luke patting Kevin on the back, the pair of them laughing.

What were they laughing at?

You, you stupid twat. Everybody laughs at you, don't you know?

My fist banged against the glass. Once, twice. Three times. But nobody looked up from the crowded street below. Why should they? They were on their way home to their loved ones or to a bar for an end-of-week drink with their pals. Who gave a shit about Adam bloody Chapman, locked in his office, all by himself?

My mind flashed back to striking Mark Harris on the back of his head with a heavy rock before dragging him into the river. That feeling of power. The sensation that I could knock the very last breath out of a human being.

I caught myself smiling.

And then I recalled dropping the pills into Bob's and Pauline's tea. Watching their eyes dilate, listening to their speech slur, their fingers twitch, the saliva foaming at the corners of their mouths.

Oh, it felt good.

But don't forget Liam. Imogen's favourite pair of dressmaker scissors penetrated his chest with a lovely popping sound, like puncturing the tyre of a vehicle until the air – or in his case, the life – hissed out of his system.

That's better.

And never forget where this all started, Adam. Those strikes on Aunt Cynthia's skull. How many? Six? Seven? Eight? Wow, a multitude, each connecting perfectly. Blood splattering the threadbare carpet and the hideous faded wallpaper beyond.

Any more?

That will do for now.

Collecting my laptop, I ensured everybody had left before setting the alarm. I craved a drink. Alcohol to calm me down. However, Kat's bloody parents would be at the house when I arrived home, so I needed to keep my wits about me. That familiar feeling was rising again, deep down inside the pit of my stomach, like a volcano ready to burst its molten rock, spewing lava across anybody who dared get in its way.

The sensation of Lauren's lips lingering on mine evoked renewed feelings within me, igniting a firestorm of conflicting desires. As I walked home, dazed and reeling from the intensity of the moment, I tried desperately to control my emotions and not give anything away once I stepped inside my front door.

After I settled in the Sunset and began my second glass of red, I summoned up the courage and messaged Lauren, asking if she would like to join me. She said she would love to, sending an initial surge of energy through me, but she needed to collect Max from football practice in just over an hour. However, it was her follow-up message that sent my heart fluttering as she confirmed she was alone until seven o'clock. Quickly, before I had time to think, I gulped down my wine and went to the bar, ordered a double whisky, necked that, and made my way to the tube station.

Lauren surveyed the street from left to right before pulling me inside. She pinned me against the wall and kissed me deeply, my emotions doing somersaults, my heart racing out of control. We barely spoke as she led me upstairs, she as desperate as me for what was about to happen.

Twenty minutes later, we lay on our backs, staring at the ceiling. The only thing missing was a cigarette to complete the quintessential scene. And neither of us wanted to talk, both caught up in the moment and not daring to ruin the unspoken joy and relief of what we'd done.

Although wanting the night to last forever, Lauren snapped me from my trance and confirmed she had to collect Max. I nodded, leant over, and kissed her again. We watched each other as we climbed out of bed and found our abandoned clothes mixed in a pile on the floor. We giggled as we untangled underwear. I eventually located my second sock, discarded so far under the bed I had to get down on all fours to retrieve it.

I departed via the back door, along the garden and through a gate which led onto a road running parallel to the one where her front door lay. I'm not sure the smile left my lips until somebody glared at me as I re-entered the underground system, as if they thought there was something inanely wrong with me. I nodded at their well-formed opinion.

"William, Edwina," I proclaimed as I stepped into the kitchen. I could taste the alcohol on my breath as I spoke. Stale wine and sour whisky, and an altogether distinct taste of sweetness and saliva.

"Hmm," William replied, looking me up and down. "Have you been drinking, Adam?"

Purposefully keeping my distance, I leant against the wall to keep myself steady. I'd only drunk two glasses of wine followed by a double whisky, but I was drunk on emotion, giddy with the unexpected rush of adrenaline that surged through my veins.

"Just a couple, William," I replied. "I wanted to cele-brate the news of our new contract." I looked at Kat, who just glared at me in return, her cheeks flushed and her neck coming out in blotches. "Did you tell them the news, darling?" She didn't reply, and I took it as my cue to carry on, regardless. "Oh, yes," I said. "Luke Wilson is our knight in shining armour, isn't he, sweetheart?"

"I think you need to go and sleep it off," Kat eventually replied.

Nodding my head like a demented dog, I said I would take a shower instead. Despite my drunken state, I still realised I might smell of something more than alcohol. As I climbed the stairs, clinging onto the handrail, I heard footsteps from behind. Kat looked up at me as I half turned.

"I picked Tom up from football practice earlier," she declared.

"Oh, right," I replied, my heartbeat turning up a notch.

"Yeah. Max's mum was there too."

49

———————

Contemplating staying in bed on Saturday morning until they all went to the bloody London Eye, Tom came in to tell me he'd scored two goals at football practice and his coach said he was in the starting line-up for the game the following weekend.

"That's great, champ," I said, a genuine rush of pride momentarily overwhelming me. Knowing I was depriving my son with so little of my attention, I asked him to describe his goals, before getting the full build-up and who passed to whom and exactly what part of the net the ball eventually hit. But the distraction was just what I wanted. I needed time to recover myself and think what the hell I'd done the night before.

Kat had brought me some pizza at around nine o'clock after ordering Tom his favourite as a special treat for how well he'd done at football. Although it made for a pleasant change from the plate of shit we'd normally eat, I barely touched it, nibbling at a couple of slices before discarding the crusts back into the box. I watched a little

TV in our bedroom, Kat's parents not once asking my whereabouts. It suited me fine.

But Kat was still livid with me. Fortunately, after showering, I'd had the foresight to stick my dirty clothes at the bottom of the laundry basket hoping any lingering scent of Lauren would be long gone by the time Kat got round to washing. She didn't mention my drunken behaviour, although I was more concerned about her declaration of whom she bumped into at the football. However, her silence regarding Lauren actually troubled me more than if she had mentioned her. Why tell me she had seen her at all?

"Are you coming on the London Eye, Daddy?" Tom asked. Kat had joined us in the bedroom, a towel wrapped around her and her hair wet from the shower. She looked at me, waiting for an answer.

"Er, not today, champ," I said. His mouth quivered and his enthusiasm waned before my very eyes. "You see," I continued, "it's very expensive and I've already been on it twice. I just wouldn't get much out of it."

"Apart from being with your wife and your son, of course," Kat said, returning to the en suite.

Turning my attention back to Tom, I ruffled his hair and told him to have a great time with his grandparents. He nodded unenthusiastically and slowly mooched out of the room, his head bowed and his shoulders slumped.

"Happy?" Kat said, joining me once more. It felt as if the en suite had a revolving door and she would keep reappearing, only to twist the knife a little deeper.

"Leave it out, Kat," I replied, climbing out of bed. "I'd only ruin your day. Don't forget you're forever reminding me how bloody miserable I am." I pecked her on the cheek as I stepped by. "I'm surprised you haven't asked Luke to go with you."

"Maybe I should," she said, but by the time I'd turned around, she was pacing to the door. She offered me a knowing glance before slamming it shut.

Regent's Park was quiet for a Saturday, hardly surprising given the weather. The wind was bitter and the leafless trees did nothing to halt it. Again, rain looked ominous, the thick clouds gathering over the usually busy park. The only sounds were the distant rumble of traffic and the occasional squawk of a lonely bird seeking shelter. It was a desolate scene, one that mirrored my own thoughts as I had serious reservations I was doing the right thing at all. How would she react to seeing me, and what would we find to talk about if she didn't open up on the subject I had on my mind? I was also extremely anxious about how I would behave when I saw her again after all those years, especially given that I'd not seen her since unceremoniously ending our relationship whilst sat in my car.

Grabbing a coffee at one of the kiosks dotted around the myriad of footpaths, I found a bench underneath a row of conifers offering some respite against the dark browns of other trees looking on in envy at their evergreen foliage. It was a secluded spot, and despite the park being quiet, it was still Central London, and there were a few people milling around. Finally, the sight of someone crossing a small bridge caught my eye, and I recognised Sandra Law for the first time in almost fifteen years.

Unsure whether to stand or remain seated, I eventually stood as she reached me at the bench. I struggled to read her expression as her features gave nothing away, like a blank canvas to draw on a smiley or downturned mouth: take your pick, Adam.

"Sandra," I said, my voice high-pitched and unnatural. "It's great to see you."

"You too, Adam," she replied. My heart skipped to hear her speak again in person. All the memories came flooding back in a heartbeat. The times I sat on her desk in reception and we laughed and talked, often planning where we would go that evening. Cinema, pub, maybe a trip to the theatre, although I always hated that particular choice. And as time drifted by, her probing me for commitment, asking where our relationship was heading. She was forever demanding whether it was just fun I was after or whether I could ever see us settling down and getting a flat together? Why did she have to push me into a bloody corner? I'd only just dug my way out of the biggest hole I could ever imagine falling into. Depression and a never-ending footpath that always went full circle and finished up where I bloody well started. "Just chill," I would say to her, even though my patronising tone grated on me after a while.

"You're looking tired," she continued, again expressionless, so I was unable to determine if she was being sarcastic or concerned. "But still handsome," she added, the familiar dimples in her cheeks showing for the first time.

"I doubt that," I replied, feeling my face flush. And then I stalled. I couldn't think of a single thing to say.

"Don't worry," she helped me out. "I didn't expect you to find me attractive."

50

THE MEET-UP HAD GOT off to the worse possible start. I wanted Sandra's help, not to be plagued by guilt coursing through my veins like a river.

"Coffee?" I asked, again my tone totally alien as it escaped my mouth.

"No, thanks."

Her abruptness was making me uneasy. "Where do you live now?" I enquired, not really caring but desperate to keep the conversation light and Sandra on my side.

"Out Ealing way."

Don't you want to know where I live?

"Okay. It's nice out there."

She smiled.

"Did you ever get married? Have kids?"

"Can I ask why you wanted to meet me after all this time, Adam?" Sandra's bluntness made it quite clear she had no desire to be there.

"It's about Luke. Luke Wilson."

"Uh-huh," she replied, filling the void until I spoke again.

"Do you mind if I ask how much you two have been in touch?"

Sandra fidgeted uncomfortably from foot to foot. Not knowing where to look, I clung desperately to my cardboard cup, the contents now lukewarm.

"What… lately? Or since me and you last saw each other? When was that? Fifteen years ago?"

Why did every single person in the world have the upper hand over me? Everyone I encountered left me having to grovel for their approval, to eat out of their hands as if I should be grateful they'd even taken the time out to talk. I shrugged my shoulders, not knowing which option was more relevant. "Either," I eventually replied.

She laughed, although I didn't understand what she found so funny.

"We've kept in touch over the years," Sandra said. Was that a hint of one-upmanship in her eyes? I recalled when Luke gave me her number.

"That's Sandra's number. You know, if you ever want to reach out. We still send each other the occasional message."

I'd texted her four days earlier, the night I was in the Sunset with Luke and he denied ever saying he'd suffered with depression, despite it being ingrained in my memory that he had admitted the exact opposite. I wanted to know more about him, to find out what his intentions were. Sandra replied to my message an hour later, accepting my offer to meet in the park. I thought she sounded keen, but it just proved how you can interpret the tone of a text completely wrong.

"Listen, Sandra," I said, standing and tossing my half-empty cup into a waste bin. I felt awkward face to face, so I sat back down, and looking up sycophantically, our eyes locked. "I'm sure you know what happened to me a few months ago." I waited until she inevitably nodded. "And I feel kind of strange about Luke turning up out of the blue. It all feels…" I paused. "Feels too much of a coincidence."

Sandra's dimples became more pronounced as she grinned broadly, a familiar glint of mischief twinkling in her brown eyes. Her chestnut hair framed her face like curtains, and though her features were unremarkable at first glance, there was a certain kindness in her expression that always drew people to her. She carried herself with a quiet confidence. Her voice was gentle but held a distinct authority.

"What do you think he's after then?" she asked.

Had she answered one of my bloody questions yet?

"That's what I was hoping you would tell me. You're the only person I know he's kept in contact with. He won't share anything about the time between us all going our separate ways and the day he turned up in a bookstore and tapped me on the shoulder." I sighed heavily. "I don't know anything about him, Sandra, but he's messing with my mind."

I told her about the depression, about the supposed sleepwalking, and finally about buying a flat only blocks from our house. Sandra appeared to listen intently, but I couldn't be sure if she was just pacifying me with her subtle nods and the occasional tilting of her head to one side, as if taking it all in. But once I finished, she hit me with yet another question disguised as an answer, and this one felt a lot more personal.

"Well, have you got anything to hide? You seem angry that he's tuned up, prying, as you call it."

I stood again, paced to the rear of the bench, and gripped the top rail, allowing me to lean forward.

"What kind of question is that?" I asked. She was

pissing me off, and instead of offering any form of assistance, the meeting was having the opposite effect.

"You remember the day you finished with me?" she replied casually, as if discussing whether the clouds would break and the rain would fall again. I nodded, my hands becoming clammy against the already damp wood of the bench. "That day when you told me it was all over, and I cried?" All I could do was stare at her, wondering where she was going. And then it hit me. The car. That's where I ended our relationship.

"You sent the toy to Tom, didn't you?"

A blue Ford Escort. My first ever car.

"Yes. I'm sorry," she admitted. "But when Luke told me he had seen you again, he knew your address and you told him your son had a birthday the following day."

"He called you that night?"

"Yes," she replied without elaborating, as if my question wasn't worthy. "So, the next day, I waited along the street from your house and had one of the parents take the gift for me." She paused and appeared momentarily lost, embarrassed even. "Hmm, I guess it was quite childish, but I've never really forgiven you, Adam." Her face softened. "I'm sorry. Maybe that was a bit silly." I remembered hiding the car in my sock drawer.

What if it wasn't from one of his mates, but from an adult instead? But that still made no sense. Apart from his friends, who would even know it was his birthday? And not only that, who could possibly be aware what my first car was?

I couldn't find any words, so Sandra filled the awkward silence.

"The thing is, Luke never thought much of you about the way you dumped me, either."

"What?" I exclaimed, pacing back to the front of the bench, realising I didn't want to sit down, so paced behind it again. "It was nothing to do with him. Why the hell did he get involved with—"

"And a couple of months later, he reached out to me. Once you two had left the company."

Where was this going? I'd got Sandra there on my terms, yet not one second had passed by where I was in control. As with everybody else in my life, she was taking the side of Luke. "And?" I asked impatiently.

"And he knew how upset I was. He said how out of order you were." Sandra smiled again.

Of course he did. Luke always had feelings for her.

My burgeoning friendship with Sandra was not without its complications. It soon became apparent that Luke harboured a similar interest in her, his outward confidence masking a hint of possessiveness whenever she was around.

"Did you tell him anything else?" I asked, knowing she would understand what I was alluding to. But Sandra just continued to smirk, an expression which gave nothing away, yet infuriated me further.

"Why? What else was there to tell?"

I opened my mouth to reply, but Sandra halted me, her confessions complete, the conversation over.

"I think we should leave it there, Adam. Don't you?"

51

SANDRA'S QUESTION didn't anticipate a reply and marked the end of our short time together. She turned to leave without a goodbye, her departure towards the lake signalling our final encounter. As she strolled away, I watched as she faded into the distance, soon becoming a mere memory. I knew I would never see her again.

My mind swiftly returned to Luke. So, was revenge his intention all along? Was he attempting to take me down, finish me, and take my wife and business with him? All because of the way I finished with Sandra?

Not only that, Adam.

Yes, I could have handled the situation better, but how was I to know she would react so badly? The memory of her tearful pleas and desperate threats resurfaced as if it had only happened the day before. I recalled a month or so after we separated when I discovered she had even contemplated taking her life, feeling inadequate to continue. Luke had obviously held me responsible.

But there was more. Sandra must have known of my

involvement in his downfall at the software house. Had she told him?

"That's Sandra's number. You know, if you ever want to reach out. We're still in regular contact."

Could that be the reason for his sudden reappearance in my life after all these years? Out of the blue, my name featured prominently in the news. Luke had an opportunity to track me down, find out where I lived. He even gave my address to Sandra to send a bloody toy car as some kind of sick reminder she had never forgiven me for ending our relationship.

"Fuck," I shouted aloud, slamming my hand against the back of the bench. Luke Wilson hadn't accidentally bumped into me at that bookstore. He'd been hunting me down. Tracking my every move ever since the recent stories came to light. My mind raced with a torrent of thoughts, each one more sinister than the last. His sudden appearance in my life, his effortless charm, his uncanny ability to worm his way into Kat's good books – it all seemed too calculated, too perfect to be mere coincidence. He wasn't just a friendly acquaintance, he was a predator, stalking his prey with cold, premeditated precision. And, after all those years, I was his victim of choice.

I cursed myself for ever letting my guard down, for allowing Luke to insinuate his way back into my life. How could I have been so blind, so stupid to trust him? But what did he want from me? Money? Power? Retribution?

My heart pounded inside my chest, a steady drumbeat of fear and delusions. I couldn't shake the feeling that Luke was watching me, lurking in the shadows, knowing about my meeting with Sandra. They were *in regular contact,* after all.

But I couldn't go down without a fight. I would keep my eyes peeled and my defences up. Luke Wilson may think he had me cornered, but he had underestimated the depths of my resolve. Did he really know who he was dealing with?

Luke Wilson was good at his job. Too good. Within weeks of us starting, I couldn't shake the feeling of being overshadowed. His skills were unmatched, his work ethic unparalleled. Everybody liked him too, a concept totally alien to me. If I didn't speak to Luke or Sandra Law, I didn't speak to anyone. But Luke had an affinity for all those he came into contact with, either the joker of the office or the shoulder to cry on. He soon struck a chord with our line manager too, often seen joking or backslapping one another as they discussed the weekend's football – even though he didn't like the sport – or fixing complex code for a problematic customer.

And as time passed by, it seemed he was assigned more challenging tasks, more responsibilities, while I remained stuck in the same junior position. It grated on me, this constant reminder of my own limitations compared to his seemingly limitless potential. It wasn't as though I was useless. Far from it, but Luke was on a different level. He also questioned everything I did, not just professionally, but personally too.

But somehow, our relationship survived. We were good friends, in his eyes at least. He would still do anything for me, help with complicated tasks, go to the pub after work to chat about mundane things. Apart from Sandra, Luke was my first real acquaintance whom I could genuinely call a pal, and despite his obvious feelings towards Sandra, he didn't relinquish his friendship towards me once I started dating her.

However, as weeks turned into months, my resentment grew. It wasn't fair that Luke received all the praise and opportunities while I languished behind. So, when Sandra mentioned Luke's rumoured promotion to me towards the end of our third year with the company,

I saw my chance to get even. I began to subtly raise fears about his integrity, suggesting to our line manager that Luke wasn't as honest as he seemed. I hinted he had a habit of taking credit for others' work, hoping to sow seeds of doubts in his mind. One day, I was called into our senior manager's office to confirm what he'd heard on the grapevine. Of course, I was careful, telling him I didn't want to get Luke into any trouble, or I felt bad for going behind his back. But our boss was grateful and thanked me for making him aware before it was too late.

The fallout was swift and devastating. As rumours spread, tension gripped the office, and Luke found himself under scrutiny like never before. Unable to bear the pressure, he decided to leave the company, citing a lack of future prospects. As I watched him pack up his desk, a mix of guilt and satisfaction churned in my stomach. Luke may have been gone, but his departure was a bittersweet victory. He never knew the role I played in his downfall, and for that, I was grateful.

No, only I was aware of what really happened to Luke at that software house.

Wasn't I?

52

———————

IN A WORLD of my own as I drifted around the park, the clouds became heavier and finally admitted defeat as the rain came tumbling down. Running for the tube, I considered texting Lauren to see if she was available. But she would have Max to attend to – Sean only had him Tuesdays and Fridays – and besides, I needed to keep my distance. I was screwing up enough lives already. So instead, I reluctantly headed home, to the cauldron of tension that would inevitably await me in the form of Kat and her parents.

Along the journey, I considered whether Sandra would have already contacted Luke about our meeting. I was now convinced they were in cahoots, planning my demise as an act of revenge, although I doubted Sandra had as much reason as Luke – or inclination. She appeared sheepish and embarrassed for sending the toy car and it wasn't the Sandra Law I remembered at all. Therefore, she *must* have told Luke of my part in him never gaining that promotion and he'd convinced her to send the gift.

That was it! That's why he gave me her number, knowing I would eventually crack and wonder what she was doing, or more importantly, why she had kept in contact with Luke. He realised I wouldn't be able to resist, and he was right.

The day I ended things with Sandra Law was following a trip to the cinema. I hadn't concentrated on the movie at all, so much so, I can't even recall what we went to see. As soon as it finished, we walked to the car park, and that's when I ended my relationship with her. In my blue Ford Escort. My initial concerns when I discovered the toy amongst Tom's new pile were based around somebody knowing I once owned such a vehicle, but it's what happened inside it that was the real reason for the *gift*. Sandra's tear-streaked face, her anguished cries echoing in the confined space of the car, haunted me long after I left her that evening. I never expected her reaction to be so intense, so devastating. She pleaded with me, her voice raw with emotion, her desperation palpable.

And she had just admitted that Luke called her the time he bumped into me at the bookstore. He told her it was Tom's birthday the following day and knew the memories the car would stir inside me; a deliberate ploy to unnerve me, to make me realise somebody was onto something, and only Sandra and Luke would know what car I drove that day.

Breaking into a trot, I ran from the tube station to home, and inserted my key into the door before bursting indoors.

"In here," Kat called from the kitchen. "We didn't go on the London Eye, the weather was too..."

Her words trailed off as I took the stairs two steps at a time. Running into our bedroom, I dropped to my knees, opened the bottom drawer, and discarded socks, underwear, and old T-shirts onto the floor behind me. I must have looked deranged, but I didn't care.

The toy wasn't there. Frantically, I searched through the pile of clothes, but nothing. Pulling open the second drawer, I rummaged my hand to the bottom and swept it along from side to side. Again, nothing. Standing, I paced to the window and back before searching once more. But there was no car, no box. Perhaps Kat had found it and given it back to Tom?

Leaving the pile of clothes where they were, I descended the stairs faster than I'd gone up.

"Where's that toy car?" I asked, leaning against the doorframe, my breaths coming in rapid bursts. Kat, her parents, and Tom all looked up at me. They were sitting around the kitchen table, fresh brews of tea before them and the familiar orange juice for Tom.

"Nice to see you, Adam," William joked, looking at the others for some kind of confirmation that they considered him as funny as he obviously did.

"I said, where's that toy car? Have you got it, Tom?"

Kat stood and stepped over to me, apprehension on her face. But I brushed her aside and moved to the window instead. And then I saw something else.

"What's that?" I asked nobody in particular. I heard Kat tell Tom to go and put the TV on, followed by a silence thick with concern and consternation. But I just continued to glare out of the kitchen window to the end of the garden.

"What's what, love?" Kat finally replied, momentarily snapping me from my trance. I turned and glanced towards her before returning my full focus to what I'd spotted.

"That," I heard myself reply, but more for my benefit than anybody else's.

Without waiting for anyone to say anything, I stumbled to the back door, opened it, and wandered into the garden. I caught the sound of chairs scraping and muffled voices behind me, but my mind was foggy and my attention was solely on the oblong terracotta pot sitting at the foot of the garden fence. I reached it, and bent down to pick it up, but it was stuck, held by the roots from the plants that had sprouted through the holes at the bottom, anchoring it in place.

I turned to Kat. She stood a few metres away, her parents behind her in the open doorway. Kat's face was full of fear, and she wrapped her arms tightly around her chest as if trying to hold herself together.

"What's wrong, Adam?" she asked, her voice trembling. She glanced back at her mum and dad, making sure they were still there, just in case.

"The terracotta pot," I mumbled, looking between Kat and the object at my feet. "It wasn't there before."

Slowly, she stepped over and linked her arm through mine, guiding me back towards the house. Her parents moved aside as we entered.

"Adam," she said gently after sitting me down at the far end of the table. "That terracotta pot has been there since the day we moved in."

"No," I complained. "It wasn't…" I stalled, searching her face for any kind of explanation.

Kat glanced at her parents once more.

"It was, Adam. Before, when you said it wasn't there, I didn't know what you meant. But now I do. You were looking in the wrong place."

53

THAT AFTERNOON, I slept for over four hours, although the dreams were vivid and unsettling. Familiar faces blurred and morphed into sinister shapes as I found myself trapped in an overgrown maze. It was Imogen's garden, the grass so long it dwarfed me by several feet on all sides, and every time I thought I'd stumbled upon an escape, I ended up at the summerhouse. But the door was locked, and inside Liam's bones lay intact, his skull twisted to one side so his eye sockets bored into mine. The hideous grin from his skeletal skull mocked me before he laughed, the cackle reverberating around the room.

When I finally awoke, drenched in sweat and breathing heavily, I realised that somebody had been in the room with me. A distinct smell lingered, but not one I recognised. Like antiseptic. Propping myself up on my elbows, I noticed the floor was clear of my clothes, discarded earlier in pursuit of the missing toy, no doubt put away by Kat. I collapsed back onto the pillow with an exasperated sigh. It was cold and damp against my neck, but I didn't move, couldn't move, and I suddenly felt over-whelmed with tiredness once more.

Closing my eyes, I stumbled through the dimly lit corridors of my consciousness, fragments of memories and half-formed thoughts colliding. The missing toy car, the mysterious reappearance of the terracotta pot, the torch behind Imogen's house, the white BMW lurking in the shadows – each one a piece of a puzzle I couldn't decipher.

Was I losing my mind? Or was there something more sinister at play? Luke's animosity towards me only added fuel to the fire of my paranoia. He seemed determined to destroy me, to tear down everything I had worked so hard to build. The evidence was undeniable, the tin of paint daubed over our door, the fresh flowers on Imogen's grave, each one a cruel reminder of the relentless efforts he was prepared to go to. And now he was moving in on my wife, too. He longed for everything I owned.

As I propped myself up once more, my head instantly complained, a deep throb originating from the rear, as if something blunt had struck me. My hand instinctively reached behind to feel for a lump and I pressed for the bruise, but there was nothing. Only a continual pulse like a beating heart inside my skull. The bedroom door opened, and I collapsed back onto the pillow once more.

"Feeling better?" Kat asked sympathetically. She carried a tray containing a hot drink and a plate of sand-wiches, the crusts removed. It was as if she were attending to a sick child, pampering them with a treat, thinking it might just perk them up a little. I studied her face closely as she approached, searching for any sign of genuine concern beneath the mask of maternal care. Her eyes, usually sharp and calculating, now seemed softened with worry, and her lips curved into a gentle smile.

"Thanks," I mumbled, forcing myself to sit whilst accepting the tray with a nod of gratitude. The warmth of the mug seeped through my fingers.

As I sipped the steaming, sweet tea, I couldn't help but notice the tension that lingered in the air, like a taut wire stretched to its breaking point. Kat's movements were careful as she busied herself throughout the room. She made the bed around me, pulling the covers back into shape and neatly overlapping all three sides. Next, she opened a drawer, retrieved two clean towels, and placed them at the foot of the bed, as if I was staying in a hotel.

"Kat…" I ventured, breaking the silence. She looked up and half-smiled.

"There's two paracetamol on the tray," she replied. "You should take them once you've eaten something."

"Kat," I repeated. "What's going on?"

She eventually came and sat beside me before placing her palm on my forehead, checking my temperature. "The doctor's been," she admitted, sighing heavily, as though it had taken all her effort to bring herself to say it. "He gave you something to help you sleep."

I tried to prop myself up further, but she moved her hand to my shoulder and held me down.

"A doctor? Why the hell did you get me a doctor? I don't need medical help, I need—"

"Shh," she replied, mopping my brow with the back of her hand. "You just need rest." She paused. "He said it might be an idea if you take a sabbatical. Maybe a few weeks at the holiday home at the sea?"

"Kat," I protested, pulling my arm away. "I don't need a bloody holiday. Can't you see? Luke is trying to send me crazy?" But my words faltered as her face changed from concern to annoyance, her lips pursed and her eyes narrowing. And that's when I realised. Was she in on it, too? Part of their little collaboration to tip me over the edge? It would fit the rhetoric fine. Her fondness for Luke, coupled with the distance forever stretching between us. Maybe he'd followed me to Lauren's too, relayed my visit to Kat. And he was more than capable of running the company. He'd already proven himself by landing new business, and everyone in the office had taken to him, unlike me. Kevin worshipped the ground he walked on. Luke had even met his girlfriend. For fuck's sake, he'd got his feet firmly planted under the table of every person connected to the firm.

And then there was Kat's attraction toward him. The long silence when she showed him to his room, the middle of the night rendezvous when they sat around the table scantily dressed, her obvious delight that he would move in just a few blocks away.

Fuck. Why hadn't I seen it before? There *was* a toy car and someone had moved the terracotta pot. I contemplated Luke might well own a BMW, too. Had he been to the park and replaced Tom's football, so William found it? And now I considered Kat's parents; were they in on it too?

It was obvious. Everybody was trying to send me crazy. Tip me over the edge into oblivion, and at the same time, set themselves up for life.

54

Doing as instructed, I ate three of the four sandwiches and then popped the two paracetamol. My head still hurt like crazy and although I doubted they would work, I soon drifted off into another comatose sleep. I didn't wake again until Sunday morning.

"Has your headache cleared?" Edwina asked as I followed the early morning chatter into the kitchen. Just like the day before, the four of them huddled around the table in the same seats, drinking the same drinks. I did a double-take, querying my mind whether time had somehow stood still and I hadn't slept at all.

"It's a bit better, thanks," I replied with no enthusiasm for starting a conversation whatsoever. "Morning, champ," I added, playfully patting Tom on the shoulder. He simply nodded, his eyes stuck on his mum rather than acknowledging me direct.

"Hey," I said until he finally looked up. "I said good morning."

"Leave him be," William said, his brow furrowed and his mouth straight.

"I'm sorry?" I said, straightening my back and glaring directly at him. "Did you just tell me not to talk to my own son?"

Kat stood and moved into the space between me and her dad. She stroked my arm, her eyes pleading for me to move away. "I bet you could murder a coffee," she said, her tone forced and struggling to be heard amid the tension smothering the room. Seconds later, she repeated herself, her voice more animated. "I said, would you like a coffee?"

"Huh? Oh, yeah. Yes, please."

I'm sure Edwina stifled a laugh, but when I looked up, she was staring at her husband. Reluctantly, I joined the others at the table, nudging Tom along with my backside. He groaned as my weight moved him, leaving him no choice, even if he didn't want to.

"So," William said, breaking the silence. Kat stopped preparing my drink.

"Dad," she snapped, tilting her head slightly to one side.

"What?" he replied with a chuckle and a shrug of his shoulders. "I was just going to ask Adam if he ever found the toy car he was looking for."

I took a slow, deliberate breath, keeping my composure intact despite the derision in William's words. The mention of the toy car sent a wave of anger through me, but I maintained a neutral expression.

"No, I didn't," I replied, meeting William's gaze head-on. "But I'm sure it will turn up, eventually. It's not a matter of great concern." I paused. "Well, not for you, anyway."

William's eyes narrowed slightly, as if trying to come up with a better quip himself. "Oh, shame. I thought it might have been some valuable collector's item or something. Must have been disappointing to lose it."

His words dripped with sarcasm, but I refused to rise to the bait. Instead, I kept my tone measured. "It was sentimental value more than anything else."

The air in the room was thick with unease, and I could sense Kat's frustration at her father's line of questioning. Why did she never stand up to him? She busied herself with pouring my drink, her movements tense, and she continually glanced over her shoulder. Tom shuffled in the seat next to me. He was playing on Kat's iPad. The sound was turned to silent, and I glimpsed the brightly coloured characters dodging around the screen.

Changing tack, I steered the conversation in a different direction. "Actually, William," I began, my tone casual. "Do you happen to remember what type of car I once owned?"

Kat stepped over with my coffee, her eyes narrow, questioning why I would ask him that.

The sudden change in topic clearly took William aback. He glanced at Edwina before addressing me once more. "Um, I'm not sure, to be honest," he replied, scratching his head. "I don't think it's something our Katrina has ever discussed with us?" But he was struggling, my choice of conversation catching him unawares.

I nodded, hiding my relief. "I thought Katrina shared everything with you?" It was my turn to drip my words in sarcasm. William stalled again, his eyes darting everywhere but at me. "And has she told you all about Liam and Imogen Daley?"

The very mention of their names seemed to leave William flabbergasted, and he exchanged a puzzled glance with Kat. She didn't appear to know what to say or do, apart from telling Tom to go and watch TV. I stood to allow him to shuffle by, but still he couldn't look at me.

"I'm not sure why that's relevant," Edwina said slowly, a definite nervousness in her voice. I had them on the ropes and I loved the control I exerted over them. It was a rare occurrence, and I could feel my chest puff out.

"It's just a curiosity of mine," I replied smoothly. "I was trying to understand how much you knew, that's all."

Before William could press further, I tested the waters with another question. "So, speaking of Liam and Imogen, do you know where they're buried?"

William and Edwina, obviously taken by surprise, exchanged a perplexed look. "Why do you ask that?" Edwina enquired, her tone full of concern. Kat glared at me.

"Why the hell are you asking these questions, Adam?" she said, folding her arms.

I shrugged nonchalantly. "Just curious, I suppose. I visited their grave a few days ago."

Kat's look dripped with a, *you did what?*

William shook his head, his voice shaky. "Sorry, Adam, I'm afraid I don't know. I'm not sure why you think we would be aware."

Edwina nodded in agreement. I noticed her hands trembling. They were both so far removed from their comfort zone.

I waved off their concerns with a dismissive gesture. "Oh, it doesn't matter. Ignore me."

As they seemed genuinely clueless about Liam, Imogen, and the car I once owned, I silently breathed a sigh of relief. However, William had turned up at work, and I'd caught him thoroughly engaged with Kevin and Luke while glancing at the computer screen. He'd obviously taken a shine to Luke, no doubt fuelled by Kat constantly singing his praises and relayed his feelings to Edwina. They wanted the best for their daughter, and I wasn't part of that plan, though maybe they were merely meddling in-laws after all.

With that realisation, I mentally dismissed them from my list of potential threats, attributing their behaviour to nothing more than their inherent dislike of me. Still, it didn't stop me from imagining the pair of them meeting an unpleasant demise.

55

Kat's parents left within an hour of our conversation coming to an abrupt end. I'm sure their train wasn't due to depart until mid-afternoon, but they made their excuses, disappeared upstairs for a while, and left before lunch. They called Kat to join them whilst they packed and I heard faint sounds and the occasional raised voice from William. Now and then, Edwina joined in too. They repeatedly mentioned my name, and I knew exactly what they were advising their daughter to do: leave me.

I said my goodbyes, struggling to contain the smile which threatened to break out across my face, but William still wasn't quite finished.

"Perhaps the doctor was right, Adam? Maybe you do need to take a sabbatical. Time to yourself, away from Katrina and Tom. Luke can look after the business in your absence."

He was standing on the doorstep. I half ignored him and instead concentrated on the spot where I'd scrubbed the red paint away. William noticed too, and offered me a wry smile.

"I'll think about it, William," I replied sarcastically. "You have a safe journey now."

"Smarmy little shit," he said under his breath as he turned to leave. "Come on, Edwina," he shouted over my shoulder. "Let's get out of here." He gave me one last stare and stomped heavily to the end of the footpath, where he paused and looked across the road to Imogen's old house. After what felt like an eternity, he gradually shifted his gaze towards me and nodded his head modestly. "Perhaps you asked us so many questions because you're scared we know the truth, Adam," he called down the pathway. It was like his confidence had returned once he found himself on neutral ground.

"Let it go, William," Edwina shouted from over my shoulder. She approached me, her limping exaggerated and her face wincing in pain. "Let's hope our Katrina sees sense."

I smiled at her, grabbing her arm as she tried to get past. "Maybe I don't need your Katrina either," I whispered in her ear. "Maybe I can be intimate elsewhere."

She pulled herself free and took two or three steps along the pathway. "You're not right in the head," she said, tapping her temple with her forefinger. "You need help."

"Perhaps I'll be visiting your grave soon, Edwina," I replied, grinning. "That's all the help I'll need."

Kat was sheepish all afternoon, forever glancing at me as we both pretended to watch TV. She assembled Tom's train set, which he played with for an hour before resorting to the iPad once more. He was spending far too much time on it, but I had no energy to entertain him, and Kat's enthusiasm to keep his eyes away from a screen appeared to be waning too. Perhaps she considered it wasn't her solitary role, and if I couldn't be bothered, then why should she? Or did she have other things on her mind, such as Luke and their scheming to send me over the edge? But Kat was the least of my worries that afternoon.

"So," she said, breaking the deafening silence and catching me off guard. "How often do you visit Imogen's grave?"

I'd been expecting the question ever since I broached the subject with her parents. I always assumed I could read Kat like an open book, and until a few months prior, I still thought I could. But she had changed. At first, I believed it was all because of the company and owning a business with the potential to turn it into something quite substantial, but then, as I thought back, there had been other subtle changes too.

It wasn't just her preoccupation with the business; it was a shift in her demeanour, her priorities, and her interactions with me. Small signs surfaced, barely noticeable at the outset, but gradually accumulating into a troubling pattern.

One of the first changes I noticed was her increasing distance. Kat had always been affectionate, but since what happened, physical intimacy had waned. Our once passionate moments dwindled, replaced by brief kisses and perfunctory gestures. It was as if she were pulling away, erecting invisible barriers between us.

Her focus on Tom also seemed to diminish. Kat had perpetually been a devoted mother, doting on his every whim. But as the months drifted by, her attention towards him appeared more fleeting, her interactions with him less engaged. It was subtle, like allowing all the screen time and playing by himself. The old Kat would never have allowed such things.

Moreover, she talked less about the company with me and became more distant in our conversations about our future plans. It was as if her mind was elsewhere, preoccupied with thoughts she wasn't sharing with me, or the fact that she didn't see me as part of those aspirations anymore.

"Don't you know?" I replied, focusing on her for any sign of guilt. "I thought you knew everything, Kat?"

"Well," she said, standing. Kat could never sit still when she was agitated. "I can't say I'm surprised."

"You've not answered my question," I called after her as she left the living room. "You tell me how often I visit the grave."

Moments later, she reappeared in the doorway, an exasperated expression on her face. "As I said, I'm not surprised. Do you take her fresh flowers too?"

She disappeared again, a broad smile across her face, leaving me with another hundred questions on the tip of my tongue. Was that a vague hint? *Fresh flowers.* Like yellow roses?

Yet again, she'd had the last word. Just enough to leave a nagging doubt that she might well be involved, or at least know who had left them. And if she did, it was obvious who that somebody was.

I knew I had to put a stop to it all before I reached a point where I could no longer think straight at all. I was on the brink. Imagining things, doctor's visits, pills to help me sleep.

"You're not right in the head," Edwina said, tapping her temple with her forefinger. "You need help."

56

Monday marked the first day of December, and the first
time I saw Luke since my meet-up with Sandra.
Convinced he would know all about it, I still kept things
quiet and didn't give him the satisfaction of knowing that
their not-so-secret little tête-à-têtes bothered me in the
slightest.

"Morning, Adam," Kevin said cheerily. His insignifi-
cant grin shouldn't have irritated me as much as it did. I
was aware of the minimal attention I'd given him
recently, leaving him in Luke's oh-so-capable hands. But
he was supposed to be my protégé, to develop under my
guidance and expertise. Who was I kidding? I couldn't
care less about Kevin Doyle and rued the day Kat ever
suggested we offered him employment. Besides, he was
lukewarm towards me, never mentioning his girlfriend,
yet Luke knew all about her. I contemplated whether they
had met for more drinks over the weekend, or maybe they
went for a nice meal together; Luke's treat, of course.
And no doubt, I would have been at the centre of their
discussions, as they laughed and ridiculed me from a

distance. Another thing entered my head as I unpacked my laptop, and glanced at Kevin. Did he know if anything was going on between Luke and Kat? Another little secret to belittle my fragile existence. And if Kevin knew, did Sandra know too? I cursed myself for not probing more when I met her in the park. However, I had no intention of calling her again.

"Morning, Kevin," came the distinctive cheery tone of Luke. "Oh, morning, Adam," he added, leaning forward to peer inside my door. "Didn't see you there."

"Morning," I called back, my voice offering the slightest of intonation of nervousness.

I noticed them glance at one another, Kevin's eyes opening wider and I could only imagine the smirk on Luke's hidden face.

"Good weekend, buddy?"

At first I thought Luke was talking to me, and foolishly opened my mouth to reply when Kevin answered.

"Yeah, great, thanks. Me and Vic went to Ikea again. She's spending a bloody fortune, mate."

Luke laughed naturally as I watched him set up his laptop for the day ahead. "Be careful," he replied, his effervescent enthusiasm for everything in life rising to the surface once more. How could he always be so fucking cheerful? "You'll have yourselves a little showroom there soon."

Kevin's laughter echoed through the office, mingling with the sound of animated conversation between him and Luke. Their discussion about flat buying and solicitor's fees seemed to consume them, while I sat in silence, feeling like a bystander in my own life.

I couldn't muster any enthusiasm to join their discussion or even begin my work. The login page on my screen remained untouched, a stark reminder of my growing apathy towards everything around me. As their voices grew louder, I retreated further into my own thoughts, detached from the world outside my office. And with each passing moment, the weight of my depression pressed down on me like a suffocating blanket. It was a familiar sensation, yet somehow deeper and more asphyxiating than ever before.

As Kevin and Luke's conversation continued, I felt a sudden surge of frustration and anger rising within me. I pulled at the collar on my shirt, desperate to circulate some air inside, before standing and pacing to the window and back again. How could they be so carefree, so oblivious to my concerns? Did they ever take a moment to consider who their boss was, who paid their wages? It was as though they simply didn't give a shit about me, about the turmoil wreaking havoc with my thoughts.

But they are aware, Adam. They know. Everybody knows.

"You're not right in the head… You need help…"

In that moment, a sense of desperation washed over me, pushing me to the brink of action. I couldn't continue living like this, suffocating under the weight of my own despair. I needed to do something, anything, to break free from the chains.

Making my excuses, I left the office, and soon found myself across the road at the entrance to the park. I could feel Luke's and Kevin's eyes boring into the back of my skull as I quickly departed and realised I would have become the sole focus of their conversation once again. Even the girls in accounts stared at me as I stormed past, beads of sweat clinging to my forehead, my face pasty white, like I was carrying some kind of tropical disease.

With trembling hands, I reached for my phone, my heart pounding in my chest as I dialled the number. As the phone rang, my mind raced with a million thoughts and fears, but beneath it all, there was a glimmer of hope. Perhaps reaching out for help was the first step towards finding my way back from the darkness.

As the call connected, I took a deep breath, steeling myself for whatever lay ahead. With one quick glance upstairs to my office window, I braced myself, determined to rediscover my path to the light, no matter how dark the trail may be.

"Hello?" came the voice down the line.

Should I reply? This is it, Adam. A point of no return.

"Hello? Who is this?" Their tone was expectedly annoyed. After all, I wasn't really sure who I was dealing with. "I said, who is this?"

I cleared my throat.

"It's me," I replied, barely above a whisper despite the sounds of London surrounding me. "It's Adam Chapman."

My mind was so focused, I didn't even notice the white BMW until it pulled away.

57

THE WEEK DRAGGED by painfully slowly. I worked from home a couple of days, anything to avoid saying something I shouldn't. But when Friday eventually came around, I suggested the three of us go for a drink. Maybe it was to make the entire situation appear more normal, to give me an alibi, witnesses to exonerate me of any involvement. I'd even given them both ample warning earlier in the week, knowing I couldn't take the chance of either of them finding an excuse not to attend, especially Luke.

"Looking forward to a few beers tonight, guys?" I asked, so artificially I instantly felt my cheeks burn.

Kevin and Luke looked at one another.

"Yeah, sounds good," Kevin replied on their behalf, sounding as though he'd sooner insert knitting needles into his eyes. *A night out with the depressed and deranged boss, whilst I've got a beautiful girlfriend at home. What more could I want?*

"Yep, I'm up for it," Luke added, although I admit he sounded a little more genuine at the prospect. After all, he was the twat who found a positive in everything he did. I couldn't help but suppress a smile.

As expected, the Sunset was packed. It was less than three weeks until Christmas, and office parties were out in force, girls scantily clad and boys planning on finally landing their catch after eyeing up their counterparts throughout the year.

"There's a table free near the back," I said, my voice raised above the din. I felt awkward. So far removed from my comfort zone, I could actually feel my body shaking. I noticed another exchange of looks between the pair of them and I knew I needed to keep the surreal arrangement as ordinary as possible. "What are you guys drinking?"

Standing at the bar, I could only imagine the conversation taking place back at the table, but I hoped Luke's ability to see the positives in everything would persuade Kevin I was just trying to be nice. They both stopped talking as soon as I joined them, glancing at one another as I placed three beers on the small round table.

"Cheers," I said, raising one of the glasses. They both collected a drink and raised theirs in return. "Ahh, that's good," I genuinely commented as the ice-cold liquid reached the pit of my stomach.

"So," Luke said, thankfully not allowing a silence to descend between us. With nothing to say, I prayed he would be the one to keep the conversation flowing for at least an hour. Otherwise, it could become fraught and extremely awkward before the night had even begun. "What's all this in aid of?"

Following another nerve-calming drink, I admitted I'd been a pretty awful boss since they both joined the company and I wanted to make some amends by taking them out for a Christmas drink. "I know what you both must think of me," I concluded, a line I had been rehearsing all week. It had the desired and anticipated effect, as they fell into silence, looking at one another as if pleading for the other to say something.

"I'm guessing it's been a tough year for you," Luke eventually replied. Kevin nodded, although I knew he was struggling with the situation. But like the instance I planted the USB stick on him, a part of me felt sorry for Kevin, caught up in the middle of another one of my schemes to get even and attempt to set my life on the correct course for the umpteenth time. He fidgeted with his cufflinks and spun his glass on the table. Kevin Doyle was making it quite clear he didn't want to be there.

The conversation stuttered and stalled before the inevitable work talk took over. It then moved on to flat buying and I soon switched off, nodding at the right times and asking the occasional question about moving dates and removal companies. After an hour or so, as we began our third beer, the door opened, allowing a cool gush of air inside. With the discussion stifled, we looked up in unison, as if expecting a fourth guest, somebody who could make us feel at ease and finally enable the evening to be marginally enjoyable. However, the sight of the young couple entering unnerved me, the same two people who had come into the Sunset a few weeks prior, the day I'd been there with Luke. I effortlessly recalled the occasion, torrential rain, them both soaked to the skin, hair clinging to their scalps before peeling off sodden coats. And just as that day, once they settled, their eyes scanned the bar, searching for someone, before they eventually stopped looking when their gaze met mine.

Luke had asked me on that day whether they were

people I knew, and I'd told him they looked familiar, although I couldn't put a name to either of them. The guy appeared the older of the two, late twenties or creeping into his thirties. He had short brown hair, not set in any particular style, and was of stocky build, albeit more overweight than any kind of gym freak. The girl was maybe a year or two younger, and again, had no redeeming features. Somebody you wouldn't look at twice if you passed them in the street. Her hair was similarly brown, wavy, and reached the middle of her back. And like her partner, if they were indeed an item, her complexion lacked colour, although she certainly didn't carry the excess weight of her boyfriend.

"Do you know them?" Luke asked again, looking from me to the couple.

Finally, I averted my gaze, and they too stopped staring before fighting their way through the crowds to the bar.

"No," I replied, although I somehow knew I did, but could not put a name to either of them. "They just look familiar, that's all."

Kevin left around nine o'clock. I'd been expecting it all evening, and it suited my plans fine. I never saw the young couple again, which only made me realise I had given them far too much thought. They were merely locals, likely regulars at the bar, whose comings and goings were of no consequence.

With Kevin out of the way, it also allowed the deed to be finally put into motion.

58

THE SIGHT of the two senior police officers standing on our doorstep filled me with alarm. I had to do a double-take, instantly recognising them, yet never seeing them before in uniform. What the hell were they doing at my house?

Glancing over my shoulder, I wondered if Kat was there, watching; everybody in it together. My heart raced with fear, knowing that their presence could only bring bad news. I had spent the entire night tossing and turning, consumed by the fear of what might have happened, or more to the point, if it *had* happened. But now faced with those two, I couldn't decipher whether I'd been set up once more, another part of an elaborate scheme to tip me over the edge.

As they addressed me, their solemn expressions confirmed my worst fears.

"Mr Chapman..." The officer's voice cut through the silence, snapping me from my trance as I just stared at them outside on the freezing cold December morning.

"I'm Officer Davies and this is Officer Clarke." They looked intently at me. "Can we come in, please?"

I ushered them indoors, the knot in my stomach tightening with each passing moment. Tom's innocent voice rang out from the living room as we stepped past, a stark contrast to the tension that filled the air.

"Who is it, Daddy?"

"It's nothing to concern you, champ," I called back. I tried to fix on a grin for the officers, but instead, I felt my lip quiver and my legs go weak. "You just watch the TV. I'll be in soon."

Kat's gasp seemed to echo through the kitchen as we entered, her eyes wide with fear. "What on earth's wrong?" she asked, her voice trembling. She held a tea towel in her hands, clenching it so tight the whites of her knuckles were prominent. "Is it Mum? Dad?"

I moved to her side, the weight of the situation threatening to overwhelm me. Officer Davies's sympathetic tone did little to ease the growing dread that gnawed at my insides.

"Mrs Chapman, please," he began, his speech filled with sadness. "It's nothing concerning your parents. But we do have some bad news, I'm afraid."

My heart sank as Kat turned to me, desperation in her eyes. I knew she was searching for answers, but all I could offer was a feeble attempt at reassurance.

"Oh, no," I murmured, the words seeming hollow, my acting pathetic. But in that moment, I realised I had to keep up the pretence. "What the hell has happened?"

Officer Davies nodded to his partner. She stepped forward with authority and asked us to sit. Contemplating whether to say something, I looked from one to the other, still not believing that those two people were actually in my home. But what could I say? Ask if they had been following me, staring at me in the Sunset? Had the police really been keeping a check on me?

The officer ignored my pathetic looks and explained something terrible had happened to Luke Wilson as he walked back to his place the previous night. A dog walker had discovered him at five thirty that morning, lying submerged from the waist down in a canal on his route home. He'd been beaten badly and rushed to hospital where he remained in intensive care with severe bruising to his brain. They couldn't be sure if he would wake at all.

He's not supposed to wake at all. He's not even supposed to be alive.

I heard Kat whimper beside me, but her hands did not reach out for mine. Instead, she held one to her mouth while the other stayed below the table on her lap.

"You okay, ma'am?" the officer asked. He looked at me as if wondering the same thing: why wasn't she seeking comfort from her husband, who sat less than a foot away? I moved to take her hand, but she withdrew it before I could make contact. Not once did she meet my gaze.

"I was out with Luke last night," I admitted, wanting it out in the open as soon as possible.

The atmosphere in the room took another downturn as I made my admission, and I grew more uncomfortable as all eyes focused on me. Officer Davies's brow furrowed in response, exchanging a meaningful glance with his partner before turning his attention back to me.

"I see," he replied evenly, his tone laced with suspicion, like he'd watched too many cops shows on TV. "And how long were you with Mr Wilson?"

You fucking know. You were watching me in the bar.

His question hung in the air, the implication clear.

The timing of Luke's attack, just hours after our planned rendezvous, was undeniably suspicious, even though I'd obviously expected it. The repercussions were always going to be inevitable. Kat tensed beside me, her silence speaking volumes. Reaching out to her again, I hoped to offer some semblance of comfort, a show of solidarity for the officers, but she recoiled, pulling away as if my touch burned her skin.

"Adam?" She nodded at the officers as everybody awaited my response. "They just asked you a question."

"A couple of hours at most," I stumbled. "You can ask Kevin. He was there too."

They made a note of Kevin's name and address, which at least offered me some respite that they would take my claims seriously. But my mind was all over the place, not knowing who or what to believe anymore. But despite the suspicion, I knew they had nothing on me. I'd planned it well. The three of us went our separate ways and I'd purposely sent Kat a text as I left the Sunset, informing her I was on my way home, and I duly arrived in adequate time to exonerate me from having any opportunity to follow Luke. She nodded to the officers when I confirmed what time I'd arrived.

"What hospital is he in?" Kat asked, my interrogation seemingly complete. I breathed an inward sigh of relief. Even Kevin would have to collaborate with the truth. "Do you think he will pull through?" she added as she noted down the name of the hospital, followed by a barrage of questions regarding Luke's wellbeing.

As I eventually saw them out, Officer Davies turned to face me.

"Your wife seems very interested in Mr Wilson's welfare?" He gave nothing away, although I could guess at the underlying reason.

"Yes," I replied, doing my utmost to remain calm despite inwardly fuming at her response in front of the police. "He's a valuable member of our team at work. I'm guessing she's worried about how we will replace him."

"And you?" he asked once I finished. "You don't seem to be anywhere near as bothered about what happened."

ONCE I SAW them off the premises, I leant against the cool interior wall of our hallway, my breathing shallow and rapid. After the officer accused me of not caring about Luke, I asked for more details. One, to cover my back, and two, to decipher if the attacker had done a thorough enough job. The response was inconclusive.

Again, I contemplated telling Kat that the same two officers were in the Sunset the night before, and it wasn't the first time I'd seen them either. Were they following me? But if so, why? The only plausible reason was to keep their eye on me, observe my actions, follow me, and wait for a mistake. Even so, the more I thought about it, the more incredulous I considered the entire situation. If the police had anything on me, they would have acted. It was months since the deaths of Imogen and Liam, and the others, and the chances of uncovering any fresh evidence were extremely remote. I'd have to kill someone with my bare hands in broad daylight with a myriad of witnesses to bring me down after all that time. Did they know I might be capable of such a thing?

"Adam?" Kat gained my attention as soon as I rejoined her.

"Uh-huh?"

"Did Luke say where he was going after he left you?"

I shook my head. She was still white as a sheet. Her hands trembled as she retrieved and clutched the same kitchen towel, her knuckles again prominent from the force of her grip. I could see tears welling in her eyes and her voice wavered as she spoke. It was clear that the news of Luke's assault had shaken her to the core. In spite of her efforts to maintain composed, the strain was evident in each line of her face.

"Only that he was going straight home," I replied, removing two coffee capsules from the container to make us both a fresh drink. Despite Kat watching my every move, I knew I was covered by my impeccable timings from the night before, even if she suspected something.

"One of us should visit him," she added, taking a seat at the table, her fingers now interlocking and pinging open like they were on springs. The prospect of seeing Luke Wilson in intensive care made my knees go weak, especially as I was the person who arranged the bloody attack.

"Yeah, I guess so," I reluctantly replied, doing my utmost to concentrate with my task at hand. "Do you want to go?"

"No," Kat responded immediately, taking me by surprise. "Er, no," she repeated. "I don't think I could face it. I've never been good at that kind of thing."

"And you think I have?" I forced a laugh, which immediately felt inappropriate given the situation.

"You're his boss. You were out with him last night. Don't you think it would look better if you went?"

She had a point. The officer had just implied I didn't

appear concerned about Luke's welfare and at least it might help to keep the police off my back. "Okay," I said, picking up the Post-it note with the hospital name scribbled across it in Kat's handwriting. "I'll go once I've had this. I need caffeine."

Kat nodded her approval, half smiling. She obviously didn't want to see him like that, beaten and bruised, his breathing regulated by apparatus. I turned my back to her and placed a capsule in the machine before pressing the start button until it whirred into action. A smile threatened to break out across my face as I realised she would hopefully never encounter him again. I knew it wasn't just work with Kat; they were undoubtedly having an affair, but the job was the only thing I could concentrate on. We would find a suitable replacement. He or she may not be as good, but I didn't need anybody better than me anyway, and it might help rejuvenate my passion for the job.

Biting my bottom lip, I turned and passed a coffee to Kat. She was in a world of her own, but at least she suppressed her tears and I suspected she was trying just as hard as me to hide her emotions, albeit for totally different reasons.

Visiting a hospital on a Saturday afternoon wasn't my idea of fun, even if it was to confirm the irrecoverable injuries of the guy who threatened my marriage and my business. They were such sorrowful places, stinking of cleanliness and full of sick people.

University College Hospital was just a stone's throw away from Regent's Park, the inevitable place Luke would be taken after I arranged the attack to happen so close by.

As I approached the enormous glass-fronted building, I felt a renewed energy, like one life ending might mean another reviving. But as soon as I stepped inside, my vitality waned as I realised what I was about to face. Was I ready for it?

"Er, I'm here to see Mr Wilson. A Luke Wilson," I stammered to the receptionist.

"Certainly," she replied, and I immediately wondered how she could be so bloody cheerful, meeting and greeting people all day long who were only there to visit patients knocking on death's door. "Do you know what ward he's on?"

"Oh, no. It's not like that. You see, someone attacked him last night..." I paused as the lady's face became much more serious. Gone was the smile and the sparkle in her eyes, as if I'd just switched them off at the plug. "He's in intensive care, according to the police."

"ICU?" she replied quizzically. "We have strict rules about visitors to ICU." She rambled on about the patient's stability, infection and controlled environments.

"I was out with him last night," I interrupted as my patience wore thin. She looked a little taken aback but soon recovered, and I again questioned how she could deal with the public in such emotional states. "The police just called round to tell me. They said he was here. Is there any way I can see him, even if from a distance?"

"Hold on a sec," she replied, dragging a keyboard towards her. She continued without looking up at me. "What did you say his name was?"

"Wilson. Luke Wilson," I said, thinking I may have to fucking spell it out.

A queue was forming behind me. Glancing over my shoulder, I saw a woman around my age with a young girl, and following them an older man carrying a fresh bunch of flowers. It only cemented my original thoughts of what depressing places hospitals were. I returned my gaze to the receptionist.

"Luke Wilson?" she asked herself aloud, tapping on the keyboard several times, clicking the mouse, exhaling an exaggerated sigh and restarting once more.

"Yes, Luke Wilson. L. U…"

"Yes, I know how to spell it."

She glanced at the queue behind me, and a guy in a hi-vis jacket carrying a huge cardboard box had now joined it. After some more frantic tapping and clicking, she finally looked up at me again.

"You sure the police said University College Hospital?"

"What? Yes, sure." I retrieved the scrunched-up Post-it note from my pocket and placed it on the counter. "There. My wife wrote it down when they told us."

After glancing at it, she once more looked at the queue behind me. "Well," she said, slowly shaking her head from side to side. "We definitely have had nobody under that name admitted to this hospital."

60

———————

"Can you look again, please?" I demanded, leaning on the counter, trying to peer at her screen.

"I've typed his name in several times, sir." She added *sir* rather condescendingly. "I would know if someone named Luke Wilson was admitted here last night, last week, or last year."

"Shit," I said, my anxiety levels growing by the second. If he wasn't there, where else could he be? But I'd heard Officer Davies say the name loud and clear. Kat had written it down too. Could they have made a mistake? "Can you check the other hospitals, please? It's really urgent I see him."

She shook her head. "It's patient confidentiality, I'm afraid. If he had been transferred from here to another hospital, then I would have the information at hand. However, as I mentioned, we did not admit anyone under that name to this hospital last night." She smiled apologetically. "Now, sir. If you don't mind, there's quite a queue of people behind you."

Following her lead, I glanced over my shoulder. The

lady with the child stared impatiently at me, and the guy in the hi-vis jacket tapped his foot. I felt like telling him to put the bloody box down.

"Listen," I said, my voice rising and full of panic. "He *has* to be here. Can you check again, please?"

"No, sir," she repeated. "The person you are looking for is not here. If I may make a suggestion, you should try the police and get hold of whoever told you of his whereabouts."

When I didn't move, she looked over to her right, and a huge security guard strolled over.

"Okay, okay," I said. I could feel the dampness of sweat forming between my shoulder blades. Why did they have to make hospitals so damn hot? "Thanks. Yeah. I'll call the police."

If I went home, I knew as soon as Kat saw the state I was in, I would receive a barrage of questions from her. However, she'd heard the same as me, so I needed confirmation we hadn't mixed up the hospitals. I quickly composed a text, asking the name and telling her that Luke wasn't at University College. My phone beeped within seconds and I imagined her pacing the kitchen and checking her mobile every time she returned to the table.

> What do you mean, he isn't there?

Ignoring her question, I asked for her to confirm the officer's names.

> Davies and Clarke, I think they said.

After thanking her, I left the hospital and was hit immediately by the biting wind outside, but it still felt good to be out of the confines of the sterile environment. With my phone in my hand, I noticed a bus shelter just along the road and ran to take cover underneath. As I brought up the keypad, I realised I did not know who to call. How do you determine which particular police station officers are based in, and how do you get hold of that number, anyway? I briefly considered dialling 999, but what would I ask for? It wasn't an emergency, well, not for them, and they would rightly cut me off when they figured out I was a fucking idiot.

I banged my fist against the Perspex wall of the bus shelter. My other hand shook as I held the phone in my palm, desperate for some inspiration about who on earth to call. I'd arranged for Luke Wilson to be beaten the night before. The police had found him lying half-in, half-out of a canal. They said he was in intensive care and it didn't look good. Everything had gone to plan, so where the hell was he?

Quickly, I launched Google Maps and typed in 'police station'. There, Holborn Police Station, not too far from where I stood. I tapped 'Directions' but soon discovered it was a twenty-five-minute walk away. However, upon opening the tube app, I realised it would be faster on foot than changing two or three times just to travel a mile. Hunching my collar up, I left the relative sanctuary of the bus shelter and followed the A501 eastwards. What choice did I have?

A taxi sounded its horn as I gave up waiting for the lights to change to cross the busy road at Russell Square. Raising my hand in apology, I sprinted across the street, towards people standing patiently on the other side, shaking their heads at my idiocy. I silently wished they'd get knocked down by a London bus or a speeding ambulance.

Following the arrow on my map, I continued to run and walk, gasping for air, yet determined to reach my destination as quickly as I could. Passing Great Ormond Street Hospital, I soon turned right onto Guilford Place, the road where the station was located. Pushing my phone into my pocket, I ran as hard as I could until I found myself outside.

Taking the steps one at a time, I tried to get some air into my lungs, realising I couldn't go inside as if a set of muggers had chased me. I almost laughed at the irony of the situation. Here I was, only at the police station because I'd orchestrated a group of muggers to target Luke. The lines between truth and deception were blurring by the minute.

"Yes, sir?" An officer greeted me, looking me up and down. I knew my overall demeanour reeked of suspicion. It was freezing outdoors, yet I was sweating profusely and my entire body trembled. I hadn't thought it through, didn't know what to say or how to act.

Less than five minutes later, I stood outside, people stepping past me in haste to get out of the wind and the cold. But I no longer felt it. I was numb from the head down, oblivious to anything and anybody.

Not only was Luke Wilson not admitted to University College Hospital overnight, but the policeman had also just informed me they had no record of either Officer Davies or Clarke on their system.

They didn't exist.

61

As EXPECTED, Kat greeted me at the door as soon as I pushed it open. Her concern was for Luke, not once stopping to enquire about my welfare. She hit me with a myriad of questions, each one tripping off her tongue and blending into the other. Eventually, I raised both arms and stormed past her into the kitchen.

"Enough, Kat," I shouted. "I can't find him." I turned to face her. She looked momentarily crestfallen.

"What do you mean, you can't find him? He can't have vanished into thin air."

"Don't you think I fucking know that?" I yelled.

"Mummy!"

Tom came bounding in to join us and rushed to his mum before burying his face into her stomach. She cradled him, rubbing his back whilst glaring at me, waiting for an apology.

"Sorry, champ," I said. I felt dizzy and claustrophobic, as if the walls were creeping in on me. "I'm sorry. We've just had some bad news, that's all."

Slowly, Tom lifted his head from the safety of Kat's

embrace. He glared at me like I'd never witnessed before, his innocent features contorted with anger and hurt. Disappointment clouded his usually bright eyes as he pierced me with a raw intense look that shook me to my core. His small fists clenched at his sides, his entire body trembling with fury. In that moment, I saw a glimpse of the pain I knew I had caused him. His erratic behaviour at school. The day I was called in by his teacher. But before I could utter a single word to explain, he turned on his heel and ran off, his voice echoing through the room.

"I never want to see you again," he cried, his words laced with venom. "I hope you die in hell."

I stared at Kat, waiting, no hoping, for some kind of solidarity, yet she offered none.

"You need to find Luke," she said, her lips trembling and her eyes full of tears. "And once you have, you finally need to get some help."

I opened my mouth to respond, but she held her hand aloft to cut me off. "Because if you don't, I'm leaving you. And I'm taking Tom with me."

The rest of the day was a blur. I left the house without attempting to find Tom and try to win him round. His words were brutal, causing me to reel like a boxer on the ropes, knowing one more blow and I'd be down and out for the count. My only option was to sort out the mess I was in and attempt to deal with my son later. And Kat meant what she said too, but was that more down to the fact that she and Luke had already made plans?

I spent the afternoon returning to the same hospital before visiting two more, yet getting the inevitable same response wherever I went. Following that futile experiment, I tried another police station and received the same replies. By the time darkness fell, it was obvious. Luke Wilson wasn't in hospital and two bogus police officers had visited me. But more importantly, I'd paid a lot of money to an individual to put all my problems behind me, and somebody knew.

After drinking two bottles of wine in the Sunset, I slept on the office floor, waking the following morning knowing I had no choice but to call on Lauren.

"Adam?" Lauren said, her front door only a couple of inches ajar, hiding everything, or everyone, behind her. "What do you want? It's Sunday."

I tried to peer over her shoulder, but she closed the door tighter still, only one eye and the side of her face visible. Was her husband there, or somebody else?

"Where's Sean?" I asked, again straining my neck. She opened the door quickly before stepping outside to join me, shutting it just as rapidly behind her.

"Sean? Why the hell would he be here? And what the hell are you turning up at my house for without invitation? You know the arrangement."

"So you've not seen him? Or Luke?"

"Luke?" Lauren looked at me as if I were a total stranger, a door-to-door salesman who refused to go away. "I haven't seen Sean for over a week and do you mean Luke from your work?"

"Yes. Yes," I replied rapidly. My anger was rising faster than my frustration. Whatever I tried, it was falling on deaf ears. Nobody was helping me, and worse still, nobody was showing me any compassion. Was I not conveying the right signals, a desperate man needing answers? Or was that the problem? I was coming across so bloody wretched that I was actually scaring people away. "Sorry, Lauren. Let me start again."

"No, Adam," she retorted, her brow creased, her eyes stern. "I can't believe you've just showed up unannounced. What if Max sees you? Tells his dad that Tom's father has turned up in the middle of the day? Sunday of all days. Jesus, I can't cope with this…" Her words trailed off, and she looked to the heavens in despair.

"Can I just ask you one thing?" I pleaded, hoping the desperation in my voice would at least ensure she heard me out. She nodded.

"Be quick."

"Has Sean spoken to you about me at all?"

She looked at me incredulously. "About you? Why the—"

"Okay," I interrupted. "And you have had no dealings with Luke?"

Lauren turned to go back inside. I realised she did not know what I was talking about. That was one good thing, at least. However, I couldn't leave without yet another twist of a knife in my already peppered stomach.

"Adam," she said, her voice gentle for the first time since I arrived. Even amid my life going to hell, I still couldn't help but admire her beauty once she softened and her magnanimous side resurfaced.

"Yes?"

"I think it's best if we don't see each other again."

"No," I pleaded like a desperate dog. "No. I'm sorry. I shouldn't have come round. I'll make it up to—"

"Adam." She cut me off once more. "We made a mistake. Don't ever call around here again."

62

––––––

RELUCTANTLY, I left Lauren and trudged disconsolately to
the tube station. She had stepped back inside and closed
the door with a bang, the unmistakable sound of the
Chubb lock clicking into place seconds later. It would be
futile and make the situation irreversible if I knocked and
tried to speak to her again. She was adamant. Like everybody else in my life, she'd had enough of me. Sick of the
sight of me, the sound of my voice, my moods, my
temperament. Our relationship barely had a chance to
begin before she ended it so unceremoniously.

The wind had picked up further since morning and
the leaves blew wildly through the air, dancing a frenzied
waltz, settling briefly before being whipped up once more.
The sky above churned with ominous clouds, full of the
promise of an impending storm. Bitterly cold gusts swept
through the streets of London, causing an icy chill to run
over those unfortunate enough to be caught out in the
open.

I trudged along the pavement, my coat pulled tight
around me in a feeble attempt to ward off the biting air.

The sound of my footsteps echoed hollowly among the deserted Sunday morning streets. Above, the branches of the bare trees rattled ominously, their skeletal fingers reaching out to the heavens in a desperate plea for mercy.

As the first fat raindrops fell from the sky, I hastened my pace, my heartbeat thumping in my chest as I sought refuge from the impending deluge. Spotting a covered alleyway, I ducked inside, grateful for the temporary respite from the elements. The sound of rain drumming against the polycarbonate roof echoed loudly in the enclosed space, a steady rhythm that matched the frantic beating of my heart.

Pulling out my phone, I hesitated for a moment, my thumb hovering over the screen as I debated whether to make the call. But as the storm raged on, I knew I had to confront the truth directly, to face the consequences of my actions, no matter how dire they may be. He'd said no more contact, but he hadn't carried out his side of the bargain, leaving me no choice.

Taking a deep breath, I found the number in my contacts, despite being instructed to erase it, and pressed 'Call'. My heart pounded louder in my chest as the line tried to connect to the other end.

The number you have dialled has not been recognised. Please try again.

Fuck. Frantically, I hit 'Call' for a second time, only to be greeted by the same message. He'd changed his phone, disconnected the number. Where the hell was he?

The journey into work on Monday morning felt like a march towards the gallows. Dread weighed heavy on my shoulders, each step a struggle against the inevitable. What could I possibly tell everyone? How could I explain Luke's sudden absence?

However, as I entered the office, the girls in accounts greeted me with overly cheerful smiles, their unfamiliar chipper demeanour setting off alarm bells in my mind. I exchanged curt nods with them, avoiding their curious glances in return as I made my way to my cubicle.

But my heart nearly stopped dead when I saw Luke sitting at his desk, seemingly oblivious to the storm raging inside my head. Confusion mingled with disbelief as I struggled to comprehend his presence.

"Morning, boss," he said, that all-too-familiar bounce in his voice. "How was the hangover on Saturday morning?"

What the hell?

"Er, not great," I stumbled, looking around the open-plan office as if it might hold all my answers. My palms felt instantly sticky. I thought I would pass out. Blood wasn't circulating through my body as it should. "Did you get home, okay?"

Why did I ask that? Of course he got home safely, you idiot.

"Yeah. Why wouldn't I?"

"Yes. Why wouldn't he?" Kevin interjected. I hadn't even seen him or paid any attention to his whereabouts. He sat at his desk, his eyes fixed on me.

"Because we had a lot to drink, Kevin," I replied facetiously.

"Well," he said, a grin appearing on his face. "You didn't ask if I got home, okay."

What did he know? Anything? But how could he? Kevin had played no part in this. He left the bar early. It was strictly between me and Sean. The same Sean who hadn't been seen for days and whose phone no longer worked. But that smirk across Kevin's face; it took all my efforts not to step over and punch his fucking lights out.

Get a bloody grip.

Doing my utmost to ignore him, I stepped into my cubicle; the attention bestowed upon me playing havoc with my thoughts. Still, Kevin stared at me. Closing the door with a thud, I unpacked my laptop, going through the familiar routine on autopilot, my mind swirling.

Could I get away with it? If only Sean knew he wouldn't go blurting it to anybody else, he would be just as incriminated as me. *Well, not quite, Adam.* He hadn't actually done anything, apart from accepting money from somebody which he could easily dismiss as a payment for work he'd carried out on the side. It's what builders always did, cash in hand, rather than putting it through the books. Shit, shit, shit. I was in it up to my neck unless I could track Sean down and find out what the hell went wrong.

I remained at my desk for most of the day, refusing coffees from the café and skipping lunch altogether. At three o'clock, Kevin poked his head around my door.

"I need to get off, Adam. I'm meeting my girlfriend at work and we've got a solicitor's appointment at half past." He glanced at his watch as if to remind me what time it was. I nodded without saying a word. But there was still something strange about his behaviour, something I couldn't quite put my finger on. He'd been cocky all day as I listened to his banter with Luke from the safety of my cubicle.

Once he packed away and left, I stood at the window, watching him leave the office. He was on his phone, chatting to someone, his mannerisms animated. And then he stopped, turned, and glanced up in my direction. Immediately, he recoiled. He'd made a mistake, and he quickly ended his call and put his phone away.

Collecting my coat, I nodded toward a bemused-looking Luke and swiftly departed the building, my head down as I followed Kevin to the tube station.

63

———

IT WAS ONLY a five-minute walk to Baker Street Underground Station, and we cut a good minute off as Kevin dashed along Park Road before reaching Baker Street itself. The rain had turned to sleet, coming down sideways, leaving the pavement close to the protection of the buildings dry if you could fight your way through everybody else with the same idea. The weather was helping me. There was no possibility Kevin could hear me and the chances of him frequently stopping and checking on anybody following were next to zero. However, once inside the shelter of the tube station, he unbelievably paused and looked behind him. Flinging myself against a shop window, passers-by glared at me in astonishment. Seconds later, I straightened out my coat, brushed down the sleeves, and continued my pursuit.

I'd overheard Kevin tell Luke that he preferred to take the Circle Line to Liverpool Street. That's where his girl-friend worked, somewhere close to the station, and I'm sure he said he was meeting there before some solicitor's appointment. After placing my bank card on the tube station keypad, I made my way through the barrier and followed the signs for the westbound trains. And there was Kevin, standing at the far end of the platform. The station was busy, no doubt the weather playing a contributory factor, so I ducked behind a group of people, leaving just enough space to keep him in sight.

Once we boarded the train, I reflected on Luke's recent behaviour and my suspicions about his involvement in the unfolding events. The image of him from that morning lingered in my mind – confident, cheerful, and as exuberant as ever. Doubts began to creep in. Perhaps I had misinterpreted everything? Maybe there was no affair with Kat, and I had simply imagined it all. Was it possible that I had mistaken his actions and words, especially regarding his supposed depression and sleepwalking? Even the encounter at the London bookstore seemed less suspicious upon further consideration. After all, he had every right to be there as much as I did. What the hell had I done?

The train stopped at Euston, Kings Cross, and Farringdon. I checked the map on the wall of the carriage. Three more stops. I had no way of knowing whether Kevin was still on board, but if he'd been telling the truth, then he'd have to disembark at Liverpool Street, too. Left with no other option, I got off with a few others, suddenly very aware that he could easily spot me. Fortunately, the exit was at the far end, near the front of the train, the carriages where Kevin had boarded. He had done the trip a thousand times before and would know every shortcut to save himself a few extra minutes.

He stepped off the escalator when I was halfway up, hunching his bag up onto his shoulders. I watched until he navigated the barriers and then I quickly jumped the queue, apologising, saying I had a doctor's appointment and was already late. One couple took a step back whilst a gentleman in an expensive-looking suit tutted his disapproval. With one last nod of gratitude, I exited the underground and stood outside on the pavement looking right, then left.

There he was, head bowed against the rain, sticking close to the wall once more, which at least offered some protection from the elements. I noticed a pub opposite and the thought of going inside and drinking myself into oblivion almost overpowered me, but Kevin's behaviour all day compelled me to stick to the task at hand. Besides, I had nowhere else to go. I couldn't get hold of Sean. I now had my doubts about Luke's true intentions and Lauren had made it clear that whatever we had was well and truly over. And to top it all, Tom wished for me to rot in hell. I was on the brink, and I knew it. Without any type of closure, I knew I couldn't go on. Kevin was my last hope, my final desperate act to put some semblance of normality back into my life. I cursed Aunt Cynthia and promised myself that if I ever found some solace, I would visit her grave and dance upon it in the pouring rain.

You're fucking insane.

Joining the line of people making their way along the street, all sticking as close to the wall as possible, I considered we must look like ants from above. All following the leader. Wherever they went, we went. Zigzagging down the road like a group of pre-programmed robots operated by someone tucked away in the warmth of their home with a giant joystick.

I laughed to myself, huge chuckles of merriment escaping my mouth as passers-by glared at me, nudging one another whilst hurrying their step.

Ahead, Kevin turned right, snapping me from my

reverie. And then something struck me. I'd made this trip before. I looked back to where we'd come from. Yes.

"Leave the station and turn left onto Old Broad Street. Walk to the traffic lights, turn right onto London Wall and immediately opposite you'll find the office."

Sure enough, by the time I reached the traffic lights, Kevin had turned right and crossed the busy road. I quickly darted behind an old newspaper kiosk on the corner while he waited underneath the archway to the office block. My heart pounded. What the hell was going on? Kevin was standing at the entrance to Wheelwright Solutions – the same company that had fired him after he lost a USB stick containing thousands of rows of confidential data. The same USB stick I had planted on him after getting him ridiculously drunk on a cocktail of beer and sleep-inducing drugs. All so Liam's company could land the promised Eve Finance contract if Wheelwright Solutions mishandled their data again. I had set the entire thing up. Kevin had been acrimoniously sacked on the spot. So why was he there now?

A glass door swung open, and Kevin came to life, standing upright and immediately attempting to rearrange his damp hair. My view was partially obscured, and I couldn't quite see who he was meeting. But then I saw him lean forward and kiss someone before taking their hand as they turned to brave the weather together. And that's when I caught a glimpse of her face: Victoria. Vic. *Vicky*. The girl who had sat a few desks away from me and Kevin when we worked at Wheelwright Solutions. The girl who had called me a bastard under her breath on the day Kevin was fired.

Utterly astonished, I glared wide-eyed at the happy couple, completely forgetting why I was there. That's when Kevin looked up, nudged Vicky, and pointed directly at me.

64

BOB LANE PASSED me a cold beer. Although I had no time for him, it somehow felt good to be back in the wine bar.

"What's this all about, Bob? I haven't got time for it. I need to get home to my wife and son."

"Don't be like that," he replied casually. "We left as friends. Remember?"

He clinked my bottle with his own. Maybe he was right, and I at least owed it to him to be polite. But being courteous was becoming a strain. Doing my utmost to fix on a smile, I nodded for him to say what he had come to say.

"So," he continued, after taking the smallest sip of beer and meticulously placing the bottle on a beer mat between us. "Did you put two and two together the night I was sitting on the train? You remember, waiting for Kevin?"

Bob went on to recount the day's events in excruciating detail; the timings, the meeting, and the handover of said goods to Liam. He sounded as though he'd been watching too many spy capers, making him come across as naïve and childlike. I grew increasingly bored and tried to think of ways to get out of our meeting. Did he really take me there to gloat about his part in a so-called top-secret heist?

Noticing me glancing at my watch for the umpteenth time, Bob took it as his cue to finally cut to the chase.

"I saw you plant the drugs in George's drawer, Adam."

A fleeting moment of panic washed over me.

"I'd forgotten my phone," he added. "Remember?"

Of course I remembered. Clearly. But it was still Bob's word against mine.

"Can't say I do," I replied impassively. "And I don't have the faintest idea what you're talking about." I stood to leave. "Now, I really must get going."

Bob grabbed my arm. I stared at his hand, my temper threatening to boil over.

"I think you need to sit down," he said. His face was red, but not through embarrassment, and I noticed a sheen of sweat across his top lip. "It's not that simple, you see." Reluctantly doing as he asked, Bob let go of my arm. "You're misunderstanding me, Adam. Now, please, hear me out."

With little choice, I took a swig of my beer, which suddenly tasted flat and rancid.

"Last week, I went for a walk in Regent's Park and I met Pauline. She has been looking into the disappearance of Mark Harris. I'm not a hundred percent sure, but I believe she is making good progress. However, she won't tell me any more…" He paused. "Yet."

"So, why are you telling me?" I asked when he finally stopped talking. The subject may have piqued my interest months earlier, but I felt as if Bob and Pauline were chasing shadows. George was doing time for manslaughter. Mark Harris was his victim. As far as I was concerned, that particular show was over and I had much bigger fish to fry.

"Because something isn't right about the way they run a business. But it's not the shady deals, or how they make their money that concerns me, it's what they do to people who get in their way."

My heartbeat racked up another notch.

"*What do you mean?*"

"*Pauline thinks they had something to do with Mark's death. She doesn't know how or where, but she believes he was onto something big, maybe getting close enough to take them to the authorities. Then he disappeared. Vanished*" – Bob clicked his fingers – "*into thin air.*"

For the first time since Bob dragged me into the Sunset, I questioned whether he, or more importantly, Pauline, may well have been onto something. Bob obviously loved a story, a conspiracy theory. He also had an axe to grind with the Daleys, and his money must have been running low too.

"*What is Pauline planning to do next, then? Or you, for that matter?*" I cursed myself for sounding facetious. Fortunately, Bob didn't appear to notice.

"*We're meeting next Monday, in here.*" He nodded at the near empty room as if to remind me where we were. "*Five thirty. It will allow you time to arrive after work.*"

"*Me?!*" I exclaimed, pissed off that I'd suddenly become part of their little clique.

"*We thought you might be interested. After all, as I said, I did see you plant the drugs, and I know what you did to get hold of that USB stick.*"

Something snapped inside. The mounting pressure from the past few months reaching its peak, and I leant forward, my words escaping through tightly clenched teeth.

"*I've already said I haven't got a clue what you're talking about, Bob. Now, I suggest you stop playing your little game of cops and robbers and leave well alone. Don't forget you've taken money for your part in all of this.*"

He held his ground, not once flinching. "*Do you think me taking property off a drunk person on a train, and then handing it over to Liam, makes me the mastermind behind all of this?*"

Shaking my head, I stood for a second time and began to put my coat on. But Bob had another ace up his sleeve. "*The thing is,*

Adam, my money is running out. I have nothing. The redundancy package is all used up, and I can't find a job anywhere. I have children to support."

Knowing I had to somehow placate him, I offered a glimpse of hope.

"There must be something you can do. You know—"

He talked over me, as if somebody had pressed the mute button so only my lips moved.

"But you have money, Adam. You live in a huge house, in a sought-after area of London. I'm sure you can spare a little to help. How shall I put it, to keep me quiet?"

Is he blackmailing me?

"What are you suggesting?"

His voice changed to a matter-of-fact tone. He looked as though he was actually enjoying how the meeting was going, his latest plan playing out exactly how he intended. "What I'm suggesting is that you give me a little payment each month, you know, to top up my funds. And in return, I won't tell Pauline of your part in all of this. As I say, she's very close to going to the authorities."

"And what about your part?" I shouted, disregarding whoever may hear. "You stole the USB stick and handed it over to Liam. You're in this as much as me."

Bob raised his arms to show the palms of his hands, his patronising manner winding me up even more.

"It's your word against mine. You see—"

"And it's your word against mine, too! Neither of us could convict the other on say-so alone."

He smiled. He really was enjoying himself. "Very true, Adam. Very true." He leant across the table, the smile never once leaving his face. He lowered his voice, whilst maintaining the same unemotional tone. "But that's where you and I differ. You see, we have a witness. Somebody who works for Wheelwright Solutions knows what you did on Kevin's computer. And the same person watched you get Kevin drunk, and then half carry him to the station."

Who the hell does he mean? Then I remembered Pauline knowing where I worked too.

"You're lying. Nobody saw me do any of—"

For a second time, Bob held up the palms of his hands. "Remember Vicky?"

Vicky! The girl a few desks down from Kevin and me. Bob filled in the blanks.

"Vicky is Pauline's niece. She saw your CV, Adam. Recognised the company you used to work for." He paused, either allowing his information to sink in or just to revel in his one-upmanship. "So, she contacted her aunt and asked a few questions about you."

Recalling Vicky calling me a bastard under her breath as I was called into Samuel's office, I knew Bob was telling the truth.

65

———

HOLY SHIT! Pauline's niece. The same Pauline I murdered alongside Bob. I knew they were getting close to uncovering something significant about Mark Harris's death; it's why I had to stop them. What was it? A new witness? But amidst all my detailed planning, I had completely forgotten about Vicky. How could I have been so stupid? I assumed all she knew was my role in getting Kevin drunk, dismissing the possibility that she might have any knowledge about the USB stick. Perhaps she didn't, but maybe she had continued her aunt's investigation, trying to pin something, anything, on me. And that's why I had never been introduced. Luke had met her, and he and Kevin openly discussed her at work, but Luke would not understand the connection. Again, it exonerated Luke from any wrongdoing. Had I targeted the wrong person all along? Shit. I'd tried to have him killed.

"You'd make a pathetic spy, mate," Kevin said cheerfully as he and Vicky approached me, still hand in hand. "I saw you at bloody Baker Street."

"You knew I would follow you, didn't you?" I asked,

stepping from behind my useless hiding place. I glanced at Vicky, struggling to look her in the eye.

"I thought I'd planted enough bloody seeds," Kevin replied, chuckling. "Oh," he continued. "This is Victoria. I think you've already met."

I wanted to punch his perfect set of teeth, which had been on permanent display since he pointed at me from across the street, straight down his throat.

A gust of wind whipped down the exposed road, causing it to buffet awnings that I momentarily considered had been stupidly left to the elements. A lamppost rattled and debris from a nearby doorway was lifted and unceremoniously dumped a few metres down the street.

"Come on," Vicky shouted, looking at the sky. "Let's get out of this storm."

Feeling as if I had no other option, I scampered after them. Fortunately, the rain had abated, but the wind was blowing at gale force and I feared roof tiles cascading down on us from above. Not once did the happy couple look behind to ensure I was in tow. They knew I would follow. I needed a conclusion, and I guessed they needed it too.

We walked briskly for about fifteen minutes before veering off the main road and entering a maze of confined streets, all lined with high-rise apartment blocks. I counted the buildings as we passed: six floors, ten floors, before we turned left again into an extremely narrow lane. A 'Dead End' sign stood prominently at the entrance, with a square 'No Turning' notice underneath it. Vicky finally let go of Kevin's hand, scooted in front, and stopped at an entrance, pressing several digits on a keypad. I caught up just in time to hear a buzzer sound and the door click open. Kevin looked at me, his smile now gone, and I suddenly doubted why I had followed them at all. As if noticing my hesitation, he grabbed my coat sleeve and half-pulled, half-pushed me inside.

"You need to get out of that weather, mate," he said, devoid of the cheery demeanour that had accompanied him all day in the office. "There's one hell of a storm brewing."

The first-floor flat was modest. A small, one-bedroom affair with an open-plan living room and kitchen. There wasn't space for a table, and I imagined them eating meals on trays whilst watching TV. The decor was nondescript, magnolia walls adorned with poster prints of the Golden Gate Bridge and similar famous sites from different parts of the world. I noticed one of those glass picture frames, full of multiple photographs of Vicky and Kevin, as well as other people around their age group. Photos on the beach, in bars, on top of tall buildings, mostly with drinks in their hands or selfies, complete with silly faces. Washing-up overflowed the sink and continued along the work-top. Stained coffee rings looked like an exaggerated Olympic flag, each overlapping the other, taking up almost every available free space across the surface.

"Tea? Coffee?" Vicky asked me. "Or something stronger?" Her matter-of-fact attitude was pissing me off.

"Where's Sean?" I urged, my eyes flicking from Kevin to Vicky and back again. They glanced at each other as if expecting the question.

"You need to sit down, mate," Kevin instructed, nodding at a chair in the corner. There was a matching two-seater sofa in the middle of the room. I complied, sitting down as directed, but neither of them joined me. Instead, they remained standing behind the sofa, holding power over me by their elevated position, an obvious show of strength in numbers.

"I asked, where is Sean?"

"I'm assuming you mean why wasn't Luke Wilson beaten to death on the way home last Friday night?" Vicky enquired, as if asking me who I thought might win the Premier League that season.

I felt myself colour and rubbed at my neck.

"It's why we had to finally intervene," Kevin took over. "We couldn't see anybody else get hurt. I think there's been quite enough of that..." He paused. "Don't you?"

Standing, I stepped to the window and looked down on the narrow street below. It was deserted. There wasn't even room to park your vehicle. It was as if I was in an area of the capital city that nobody else had yet discovered.

"How did you find out?" I asked, spinning back to them. I felt my jaw tighten and my nails digging into my palms.

"We've been tracking you, Adam," Vicky replied.

"Tracking? What the—"

"My aunt was onto something." She cut me off. "There was a witness. Unfortunately, Auntie Pauline couldn't follow it through to conclusion, could she?"

My heart beat faster still. How much did she know, and how much was she trying to fool me? Either way, I allowed her to continue.

"And we know all about your part in getting Kevin dismissed from Wheelwright."

"That's pure conjecture. There's no—"

"Remember Bob?" It was Kevin's turn to interrupt. I swung to face him, again not replying to his question.

"Well, Bob had two children from his marriage. The ones he gave his last pennies to every month."

I knew exactly who he was alluding to. Bob was a gentle giant when it came to his kids. The son and daughter who he barely saw yet contributed almost all he owned to set them up in life and continue their journey. He gave all his spare cash to his children.

"What about them?" I asked, a tremble in my voice and a cold sweat forming across my brow.

"Their names are Nathan and Belinda."

Is that supposed to mean something to me?

I must have looked perplexed.

"Or you might know them as Officer Davies and Officer Clarke."

66

STUMBLING AGAINST THE WALL, I barely kept myself from collapsing. Bob's children? The very same people who had come to my house disguised as police officers to inform me that Luke was in intensive care, all the while knowing that no such attack had occurred. Kevin continued, revealing that they had paid Sean off, offering him double what I had to ensure he wouldn't harm Luke. In return, Sean handed over his mobile and likely replaced it with a new one, leaving me with no way to track him. The sheer shock left me reeling.

"How did you know I contacted Sean?" I finally asked, my breaths shallow.

"We already told you," Kevin replied. "We watched you. There was always one of us available."

Between the four of them, they had observed my every move. Bob's kids had even had the audacity to follow me into the Sunset.

"We knew that eventually you would crack again. Belinda went as far as investigating the demise of your aunt all those years ago. Bludgeoned to death. But nobody was ever caught. Were they, Adam? Just like nobody was ever caught for Bob and Pauline, or Imogen and Liam."

I tried to regain some strength. "All of those cases were opened and closed. I wasn't involved."

Vicky couldn't help but laugh. A sarcastic 'Ha!' to inform me she knew better, even if she couldn't prove it. "You were good, Adam. I'll give you that. You covered your back wherever you went. It's why we had to keep an eye on you, waiting for just one more mistake. And you did. The day you met Sean."

Kevin took over again, explaining the time I called Sean out of the blue, asking whether he wanted a job was my first error.

"We knew you were screwing his wife," Kevin continued. "Or at least wished to. So we approached Sean outside Tom's school. Told him to let us know us if you ever contacted him, as we knew something about you. You're lucky we persuaded him to leave you alone, but I guess the right amount of cash can keep anybody quiet."

They knew about me and Lauren.

Kevin was far from finished and recalled from the very first day with our company. He had a feeling that something was wrong. "You were a mess," he said. "And then you took Luke on."

Luke. I'd forgotten about him again.

"I got to know him well. We went for beers after work, and when he enquired if you would join us, I told him I'd asked you, but you always refused. He didn't question it because he saw firsthand what you were like."

It was true then. Luke was an innocent bystander. Just a holier-than-thou meddler who had unwittingly stumbled into a web of deception far beyond his understanding.

"But I saw somebody walking around Imogen's house late at night," I intervened, studying the pair of them, looking for any telltale sign it might be them. Nothing. "Then, somebody put fresh flowers on Imogen's grave. Tom's football turned up…" I trailed off as Vicky and Kevin smirked at one another. "It was Bob's kids all along, wasn't it?"

"They didn't mention anything about flowers," Vicky took over, "but I guess it could have been them?" She glanced at Kevin who shrugged his shoulders. "But moving on, one evening in the pub with Luke, Sandra Law joined us." Vicky took over, having allowed me to answer my own riddles.

"Sandra? What the hell has she got to do with it?"

"And after a while, I got to know her well." Again, Vicky ignored my question. "She told me about the way you treated her." She air-quoted *treated* for effect. "You're just not an amiable person, are you, Adam?"

It was all conjecture, and they knew it, but I'd made mistakes. Why had I listened to Kat? I took Kevin on to ease my guilt. And then the chance meeting with Luke. Maybe it was a freak occurrence, maybe I would never know, but him coming back into my life only exacerbated my situation.

"I never meant to hurt Sandra," I said to nobody in particular.

"She told me something else," Vicky replied. I looked at her again. I'd gone cold, involuntarily shivering despite the heat of the small apartment. "She told me you stopped Luke getting promoted at the company you both worked for. Denied him the role he so deserved."

I'd regularly wondered whether that would come out. Sandra swore she would never disclose it to anybody, but as the years dragged on, and I had no further connections with either her or Luke, I always presumed I'd never hear any more of it. "Did you tell Luke?" I asked Vicky before turning to Kevin. He shook his head.

"No. The one thing we didn't want was for Luke to get caught up in all of this. But then your wife started inviting him round. I tried to warn him off. Tell him he didn't know who he was dealing with, but you know what he's like? He sees everything as a positive. Sees the good side in everybody."

"He was getting close to Kat." I struggled to fight back. "They were having an affair."

The pair of them fell into fits of laughter and it was difficult to tell whether they were being genuine or exaggerating for effect.

"Why the hell would he have an affair with Kat?" Vicky eventually asked once she'd contained herself. She dabbed at the corners of her eyes.

"I don't fucking know," I retorted, anger beginning to build back inside. They were mocking me, laughing directly at me. "He obviously knew we weren't getting on and moved in."

"You mean like you shagging Sean's wife? That kind of not getting on?" Kevin asked. It was evident that he read the anguish spreading across my face. "Don't worry. We haven't told him."

"Besides…" Vicky took over once more. My head spun from one to the other. They were playing me like a marionette. "Luke is already married. He would never jeopardise that. He loves her. They're buying a flat together."

"Who? What the fuck are you talking about?" I demanded.

"Luke married Sandra, Adam," Kevin replied, a grin stretching from ear to ear. He was loving the power he finally held over me. Revenge exuding in bucket loads for what I did to him that night. And Vicky was loving it even more. I'd killed her aunt, and although she couldn't prove it, she still knew. And if she knew, Bob's children would know about their father, too. I was fucked. "But he never told you," he continued. "He even removed his wedding ring whilst in your company." He paused. "I'm assuming Sandra removed hers too, the day you met her in the park?"

67

Suddenly, everything hit me like a sledgehammer. I felt my knees weaken, forcing me to sit down. My throat was parched, making it hard to swallow. No wonder I had been spiralling into paranoia. My instincts had been screaming at me for months, and I finally understood why. They had known everything from the start, playing me at my own game, and I had been their pawn all along.

"So now what?" I asked, looking at the stained carpet between my feet as I leant forward, desperately trying to get air into my lungs. The response took me completely by surprise.

"You can go," Kevin said nonchalantly, like a teacher dismissing a student after detention. I stared at him, searching for any hint of mockery or deceit, but his expression remained neutral, devoid of any malice. They even stepped back, leaving the path to the door unobstructed, solidifying their dominance over the situation.

"But," I looked around the room. "All this…" I struggled to find the words. "You've done all of this only to allow me to leave?""

"We've said all we have to say," Vicky replied. As with Kevin, her features gave nothing away. She was calm, in control. "We know you're guilty of everything we've spoken about, but just like the police, we have no way of proving it. My aunt was close, but she never had the chance to bring it to a conclusion." She looked at Kevin and then back at me. "We can't hold you hostage, can we?"

"We simply wanted to entice you here today to tell you what we know," Kevin added. "I'm sure we can trust you not to hurt Luke, or anybody else for that matter? Besides, I've got Sean's new number and I'm sure he'd be interested in your sordid, paltry affair with his wife."

"Does Kat know about me and Lauren?" I asked, a definite tremor in my voice. Kevin shook his head.

Without realising what I was doing, I stood, holding onto the arm of the chair for support. Were they really going to allow me to get up and walk out of the door? But they were right. They had nothing on me, well, nothing they could prove, and they knew I wouldn't go running to the authorities to say they had held me against my will. They also knew I would keep everything quiet.

But what about work? How could we continue to operate under the same roof, day after day? Me assigning Kevin tasks. Chatting to Luke about the bloody weather and football whilst I knew he was married to Sandra, my old girlfriend no less, and he'd kept everything from me. The guy I'd paid to have killed.

No, my days with the company were over. The smiles on their faces told me that. Kevin had probably already discussed the future of the business with Luke playing a more prominent part, knowing I could never intervene. Maybe that was Luke's true intentions with his over familiarity with Kat? To worm his way into the company, even if he presumed I would still be around. He was only looking after himself, no doubt prompted by Sandra, who still searched for retribution to our hostile separation. She knew one day I would be gone, and Luke needed to ensure he was more than ready to take over the reins.

Gradually, I crept towards the door, my eyes not once leaving them. But they stayed completely motionless, observing me as if a family member was departing after afternoon tea. My hand reached for the door handle, shaking as I attempted to turn it. Finally pulling it open, my eyes still fixed on theirs, Vicky smiled and Kevin spoke. "Be careful out there, Adam," he said as I left.

It was dark outside, the shortest day of the year nearly upon us, and the street lamps not venturing down the narrow lane by Vicky's block of flats. The wind howled like a banshee, as if the storm was directly overhead, threatening to lift me and hurl me several blocks away.

I glanced up at the first-floor window one more time. As expected, Kevin and Vicky stood still, their silhouettes dark and ominous, like two cardboard cutouts. Though I couldn't see their eyes, I felt their piercing gaze ensuring I left, knowing this would be the last time they'd ever see me.

Hunching my collar up against the biting wind, I stepped back from the pathway into the narrow road. But as soon as I looked up, I caught sight of the whites of the eyes of the couple in the car, illuminated by the flimsy glow of the moon. Belinda, Bob Lane's daughter, sat in the passenger seat, her face a mask of pure hatred, while her brother Nathan gripped the wheel. Their white BMW, lights off, roared down the tiny street at breakneck speed.

There was nowhere for me to go, even if I had time. Nathan's smile was the last thing I saw before the front bumper hit my legs with such force that it sent me flying. My head slammed against the windscreen as I somersaulted before landing with an almighty thud behind the car.

Pain exploded through my body, the worst in my back. I couldn't feel my legs, and when I looked at my right arm, it was twisted grotesquely at the elbow. Amidst the screams of agony reverberating inside my skull, I heard a door open. Gasping for air, I turned my head to see Kevin and Vicky standing in the entrance to their block of flats, hand in hand, staring at me with blank expressions.

I tried to speak, but only a gurgling cough emerged, a mouthful of blood and saliva splattering onto the tarmac. And in that chilling moment, I heard the BMW crunch into gear, the engine growling as it lurched into reverse. The tyres screeched as the car returned to finish the grim task it had begun.

'The Family' Psychological Thriller Trilogy

Have you read the series everybody is talking about?

Available in eBook, Print & Audio

*EACH BOOK AVAILABLE SEPARATELY OR AS A
BUNDLE - Just search for 'Jack Stainton Books'*

*'I was amazed at the twists and turns in these
books… brilliant… impossible to put down'*

*'Had to finish it quickly so I could get my heart
rate back to normal…'*

*'I love a good psychological thriller and I have
just found my new favourite author!!'*

*'I like to think I read enough thrillers to be able
to suss them out before finishing, but this one kept me
guessing until the very last sentence!'*

ACKNOWLEDGEMENTS

Thank you for reading 'Dead Ever After' — I sincerely hope you enjoyed it. It was fun to write as I explored all ways possible to exact revenge on Adam.

A huge thank you to my Advanced Reading Club. Yet again, they haven't failed to disappoint with their attention to detail. This book wouldn't be what it is without your help.

Talking of my Advanced Reading Club, a few of whom have asked if there will be a third book in the series — let me know if you would like to read one too!

As always, I'd also like to express my gratitude to my editor and my cover designer. And most importantly, I want to thank you, the readers. Without your continued support, I wouldn't find the energy to keep doing what I absolutely love. I'm not one of these writers who could carry on if nobody ever read a word I wrote.

Thank you once more, and keep an eye out for my next novel, scheduled for publication early 2025. In the meantime, if you haven't read all my books yet, head over to your favourite store and grab yourself a copy (or two).

Happy reading.

Jack

If you want to learn more about me and my books, please sign up to my FREE newsletter below…

www.jackstainton.com/newsletter

facebook.com/jackstaintonbooks
x.com/jack_stainton
instagram.com/jackstaintonbooks

REVIEWS

Enjoy this book? You can make a big difference

Honest reviews of my books help bring them to the attention of other readers.

If you've enjoyed this novel I would be very grateful if you could spend just a few minutes leaving a review (it can be as short as you like).

Thank you very much.

A GUEST TO DIE FOR

Jack Stainton's debut Psychological Thriller

Available online in both eBook and Print Versions

...I bought the book and read it in two sittings. Very good, lots of twists and red herrings.

This does exactly what a thriller should; it keeps you guessing until the end...

Excellent book full of twists and turns. The characters are brilliant... The ending was totally unexpected...

Sucking you in with a dreamy hope of a better start, the fear of what might happen next will keep you turning the pages!

A fantastic, gripping debut!